DARE TO BELIEVE
— BOOK ONE —

THE SILVER COMB

TRISH CARLOS

Typeset and design by Lucent Word, Co. Cork, Ireland
Cover photograph by Amy Frahill

ISBN: 978-0-9956464-0-7 (Paperback)
ISBN: 978-0-9956464-1-4 (Kindle)

For all those who dared to believe in me. . .

Thank You

We are the music makers,
And we are the dreamers of dreams,
Wandering by lone sea-breakers
And sitting by desolate streams;—
World-losers and world-forsakers,
On whom the pale moon gleams:
Yet we are the movers and shakers
Of the world for ever, it seems.

Arthur William Edgar O'Shaughnessy

GLOSSARY

Saoirse	*sear + sha*; meaning freedom or liberty
Sean	*shawn*; Irish form of John
Beibhinn	*be + veen*; bean meaning woman and finn meaning white or fair
Rua	*rue + a*; red as in fox red
Cobh	*cove*; harbour town on the Great Island in Cork
Dunluce	*done + loose*; ruined medieval castle on cliff edge in Co. Antrim

PROLOGUE

A lonely grey figure stood at the edge of the cliff. The wind was howling as though trying to sweep it into the tumbling waves below. The ferocious sea pounded the cliff, trying to capture the figure for itself. The sky was black. The storm clouds smothered the sliver of a new moon behind them. The rain had not yet started, but the air was heavy in anticipation.

She pulled the grey hood tightly around her face, took a deep breath and sighed: this was where she was meant to be, this was right. She had fought with the decision for weeks, but now that she was here she knew it was the right thing to do. It was for the best.

The wind caught her hood. Her long dark red hair escaped and danced freely in the gale. She made no attempt to readjust it, but delighted in the sensation. She stepped closer to the cliff edge, peering into the darkness below. She could feel the ocean calling her; she could feel the grip of its arms ready to welcome her. She took a deep breath and filled her lungs with heavy air.

It was time.

1

The heat was intense, like nothing she had ever experienced. It caught hold of her and robbed her of all her energy and strength and the smoke forced her to seek refuge on the floor in the small space under the bed, where she could actually breathe. This wasn't her bedroom, this wasn't her house, panic overcame her and she lost her breath, choking and spluttering until a little hand grabbed her ankle and she looked around. She recognised this soot-covered face, she'd seen him before and he smiled at her. His face was tear stained, but he wasn't crying, just crunched up under the bed, away from the flames and the smoke, but there was still the intense heat. Saoirse pulled at her clothes, sweating and uncomfortable. Fear and an aching grew in her lungs, she screamed but nothing seemed to come out. The little boy was calm, it unnerved her and the panic became overwhelming as the flames drew ever closer to the bed. She imagined being burnt alive, the excruciating pain, but as the smoke grew thicker she knew her lungs would give up before the flames ever got to her. What a way to die!

And then she appeared. Saoirse had only just begun to dream about her and here she was holding out her hand, Saoirse grabbed it and as she did, the flames melted away and she was back in the school library, her head tucked uncomfortably in her folded arms and her forehead slightly sweaty from the dream. She was a mess.

This time of year was always difficult for Saoirse. Returning to school after a full three months wrapped in the protection of her own private bubble at home was the toughest part. She knew in a week or two she would get into a routine and life would get easier, but these first few weeks in September she hated. These daydreams didn't help or the accompanying nightmares.

This year's return to school was not helped by an English assignment she was forced to do with another student. An assignment where she was afforded the opportunity to get to know herself, her background, her passions, her ambitions and all in the company of another human being. Saoirse shifted uncomfortably in her chair and looked around the freshly painted library. She knew everyone's face, one or two names, but no one past the odd hello in the corridor. To be honest, she didn't really know herself who she was, what she wanted and now she was being forced to open up her world to someone else, she sighed.

So who was she? She was Saoirse O'Donnell, a 'normal' almost-sixteen-year-old. Well, as normal as any teenager could be. She loved to read, listen to music and paint. These were her true passions. No friends were needed, no audience required. She lived her life in a haze of written words and lyrics that she recreated in her own unique way on canvas. She had never had the courage to show anyone these creations. The cocoon at home, surrounded by her mum, dad and grandmother, was all she knew and all she needed. She knew this was about to change, she knew she was being forced to allow someone else into her bubble. And whilst she wasn't okay with that; she knew it had to happen.

She was more concerned about what this other person would think of her. She was awkward, she knew that. Her tall, willowy figure stood over most of the boys in the year and that had always intimidated them. Her pale skin and long auburn hair weren't what was considered beautiful by social media standards. She saw them as a burden. Her skin burnt at the very hint of sunshine and her hair was a mass of untamed curls that took their toll on her long slender arms every evening as she waded through them with her hairbrush. And to finish, she was plain. Every girl dreams of being the ugly duckling that blossoms into the swan and Saoirse was still waiting for that moment, the day she would look in the mirror and not recoil at the pale, freckled face that stared hopefully back.

Her awkwardness did not end with her physical hardships, however. She was also painfully shy. School was a lonely place because she just couldn't find the courage or the words to speak to people. She wasn't into the things other teenagers were into. She didn't play sport, she didn't like fashion, she liked her own company. She feared she would be rejected instantly, and felt that she was regularly the butt of jokes and smart comments in the corridors. Boys frightened her the most. She had read about them, watched them in movies, but she had never actually had a conversation with one. She had never had a crush, never found one intriguing enough to step outside her bubble and speak to him. She lived in hope that someday she would experience that wonderful mystery that is love, but for now she prayed that it was a girl she was paired with and not a boy.

The teacher's voice drew her back into the library and Saoirse saw that a lot of the class had already been paired off. 'Saoirse O'Donnell, you're paired with Sean Fitzgerald.'

Her heart sank. He sat at the desk in front of her; she knew who he was: exactly what she didn't want. He was a budding young rugby player and had been hunted by several private schools and as far as she could remember he was seventeen. He should really be in the year ahead and she wondered why he was here when he could have been a year closer to college and in a private school without this stupid assignment to do.

He looked as unenthusiastic as she did, but he answered

the teacher in a smooth, flirty manner and this repulsed her. The idea of being paired with a flirt appalled her and the whole assignment looked as if it could ruin her year. She hoped he would be open to the idea of them doing it separately and saying they worked together and she held onto that.

'This assignment is due the 18th December. You are asked to work on it during study periods but you are also required to meet each other's families and visit each other's homes. You must get to know the person as well as they know themselves in order to be able to write about them.'

Saoirse sighed. She had deliberately gotten to school early to find a desk at the back of the library away from the gaze of the other students, but that had all been in vain. They would all be focused on her desk at the back of the class now. Sean was the most popular boy in school. He was like a god, a rugby god and all eyes were on them. She laid her head on the table and hoped she could wake up from this bad dream too.

'Say cheese!' Click. Sean held his phone up and Saoirse made an awful face, unsure of what he was doing. 'Just a quick snap for Kate, she'll want to know who is getting to know her boyfriend so intimately. She'll be checking you out on Facebook, see if there's any competition.'

He hadn't even sat down yet and Saoirse was intimidated. His size alone was menacing, let alone his popularity. He attempted to slide his 6'3" frame into the desk with the ease of an elephant and the noise rattled around the library and inevitably all eyes turned towards them once more. He took a playful bow, but Saoirse felt the heat rise from her neck and sizzle all the way to the top of her head. She didn't know where to look. This whole assignment irritated her and all she wanted to do was to stand up and walk out. Preoccupied with her desire to escape, she missed Sean empty the contents of his bag onto the table and it was only his deep inhaling breathe that brought her back. He had a new notepad held to his nose and looked a little embarrassed that she had caught him.

'I love the smell of new paper, text books in particular. September is my favourite time of year in school. I love all the new books, the new stationary. I'm a bit of a neat freak, but don't tell anyone, it doesn't really fit the profile.'

She wanted to answer him and tell him that she loved that smell too, but that the smell of an old novel, passed from hand to hand for years brought with it a smell that was so much better, so much deeper and so much more fulfilling: it had history, a story outside the one held between its spine. But she couldn't. All she could manage was an awkward snigger that sounded sarcastic. He looked offended and she wanted to die.

'So is sarcasm your thing?'

'I'm sorry,' Saoirse replied in a voice that was so low she wasn't sure he would even hear her. He looked blankly at her, he hadn't.

She coughed uncomfortably and raised her voice a little, 'I know it might sound ridiculous, but I smiled because as you were doing it I was thinking how much I love the smell of new notepads.' Her voice was pathetic and needy and her 5'11" frame crumpled towards the desk as she hung her head.

'You're a strange one, Saoirse. I like that. Shall we start again? My name is Sean Fitzgerald. Pleasure to meet you.' He held out his hand to shake hers.

'Hi, I'm Saoirse O'Donnell. Pleasure to meet you too.' She held her hand weakly and he took it firmly in his. She looked up and straight into his face. She was startled by the immediate eye contact and blushed as she looked away. Why was it so hard to just hold someone's look?

'You really are a strange one, Saoirse! I'm normally good at reading people, but you. . . you have me baffled, you're a mystery. So let's unravel that mystery. You don't seem like much of a talker, so let's just start with the basic questions that Ms Cremin gave us. Nothing too hard for the first day. Do you want to start by asking me those questions?'

Saoirse smiled; maybe he wasn't so bad after all. She took the questionnaire from her folder on the desk and cleared her throat.

'Date of birth?'

That was easy. Sean smiled and answered the question freely; he was seventeen since the 9th July. She was dying to ask him why he was a year behind in school, but thought better of it. She'd stick to the questions for now and hold that for when she was more comfortable.

'Siblings?'

Sean was the youngest of five, and the only boy. He giggled when he spoke of learning all about women from his four sisters and how he could charm any woman and French plait with the best of them. Saoirse marvelled at how comfortable he was talking about his life with someone he didn't even know.

'Question three: parents?'

Sean lived at home with his dad and one of his sisters. His mum, Mary, had passed away three years ago. She had fought long and hard against breast cancer, but it had won in the end and took her in the summer of his first year at secondary school. His dad had survived only because of his sisters and his love of rugby; he had immersed himself in helping Sean train and progress up the ranks of the Munster underage section and on to Irish glory. Saoirse saw the love and pain in his eyes when he spoke about his mother, but she detected a slight strain when he spoke of his father; nothing negative but not the same passion and love.

Again she was intrigued by his openness and his honesty, but now it was her turn. The questions were simple, the answers were obvious, but she still could not help but feel petrified. She had never shared anything about herself with anyone before.

'Right so, your turn. Date of birth?' He was smooth and encouraging and she smiled awkwardly, snorted almost and quickly cleared her throat.

'September 16th.'

'So your birthday is Friday week? The big sixteen! You planning anything? You having a party?'

Sweet sixteen, parties, planning. . . not really her thing at all. She liked birthdays for sure, but she liked them because of the beautiful old books she got from her grandmother. Books filled with the stories of Ireland's myths and legends, stories that in the past had been seen as something factual and true, taken very seriously, but now were fairy tales and folklore. Saoirse liked the intrigue and naivety of the past, the idea of believing without seeing. She always wondered where her grandmother produced these beautiful, hand-bound leather books from, but her grandmother was a stranger creature than she was and she hadn't ever found out.

'Saoirse, any plans?'

'Oh no, not my sort of thing.' He smiled, with a look that said he should have realised she wouldn't. 'So, siblings?'

'None,' this wasn't so bad after all. She was getting through the questions with some ease.

'Well, that explains a lot.'

'What's that supposed to mean?' She was cross.

'Just I should have known you were an only child: the shyness, not being a great communicator. All clear indicators of only child syndrome.'

She was furious, maybe there was truth in his comments

but how dare he judge her, when he had only just met her.

'Question three please.' She was short and a little put out.
'Parents?'

The bell shrilled, and she nearly sang out in relief.

'Saoirse, how about I call to your place on Saturday and we continue from here? You live in the Crescent right? They're fab houses, always wanted to see inside.'

Her mind wheeled, how did he know where she lived? The Crescent was a well-known, gently-curving terrace of thirteen houses, standing proud over the harbour and facing the beautiful gothic cathedral. It screamed money: old money. Something Saoirse's family didn't have. She often wondered how they had ever ended up living in their beautiful home, but it was a touchy subject with her mother and she loved it so much she was quite happy to just let it be. But how did he know where she lived?

'Everyone in town knows who lives in the Crescent. I'll be over about eleven on Saturday, if that's okay?' And with that he was gone. She had never had someone call to the house before, her heart raced a little, it was all organised. She had the rest of the week to prepare what she would say, but her stomach churned at the thought. She hated this assignment.

2

She bolted up in bed, sweat soaked her T-shirt and her head pounded. The same dream again. The same girl, but things were changing. She grabbed the notebook next to her bed and scribbled down the details of her dream. She read somewhere this was a good way to work through and understand your dreams, but she had found no understanding or resolution in the process, only more confusion and despair.

This one had started three weeks ago. It was the blonde girl from her daydream, she was about her own age, and appeared in this dream, walking the promenade in the sunlight. She was happy, carefree and beautiful, very beautiful. Saoirse wondered why she would be dreaming about a beautiful girl and had even questioned her sexuality. But over the course of the past two weeks the dreams had begun to change, and become more sinister and dark. At first it was a change in the girl's mood, from carefree to visibly preoccupied and then to troubled. Physically too she began to change. Saoirse had noticed bruises, which became open wounds and in this last dream the colour and life had drained from the girl. She stared blankly at her, a longing and despairing look in her eyes, begging Saoirse for help.

Saoirse began to shiver, still unsettled, she threw her legs out over her large double bed and walked to one of her windows. She pulled on her soft oversized fleece dressing gown and hugged it tightly around her. She didn't have curtains in her bedroom, she couldn't bear to block out the view. The sea calmed her and outside the window was one of the world's largest natural harbours; beyond its mouth were the ocean and a world of possibility.

The water was quiet tonight, and the lighthouse blinked hypnotically in the distance. It was calming, but not enough to erase what she had just dreamt. Why were her dreams so graphic and disturbing at the moment? What was wrong with her? Why didn't she dream about boys, about her ambitions, even her family? No, instead she was dreaming about a random girl she had never met slowly transforming into a living corpse. She shivered again at the memory.

She pulled at the cord on the bedside lamp and her room was filled with soft light. Oh, how she loved her bedroom: it was like her own studio apartment here on the top floor. Her parents had given her the floor her bedroom occupied, so she had her own bathroom and behind that she had her library and study area. But even though they had given her that dedicated space she had still ended up with a desk and easel in her bedroom. The view was too inspiring not to take advantage of.

Her dreams, while they had never been as vivid and real as the current recurring one, had always been dark. As a child she had been plagued with nightmares. She could never quite remember when she woke what they had entailed until now, but she had always found comfort in her painting, even if it was at three in the morning.

She picked up the brush and began to work on the painting already on the easel. It was the girl from her dream and she found comfort in painting her as she had been in the beginning. How she looked now was not something to be shared or painted. It was too harrowing. Hopefully when she had finished the painting the dream would pass and sleep would return.

This wasn't the first portrait of an unknown person Saoirse had painted. Her library was full of anonymous smiling faces, young and old. Saoirse felt a connection with each and every one and never had the heart to part with or paint over any of them. The blonde would join the others in the library and in time more restful sleep would return.

Her strokes were slow and steady as she added honeycomb highlights to the girl's long golden hair. Her hair was like sunshine; unlike Saoirse's auburn tangled mess. The picture was nearly finished. She stood back to admire it in the half light. She was a very beautiful girl, and Saoirse was very proud of her representation of her: her youth and enthusiasm oozed from the sparkle in her eyes. She smiled, and breathed slowly. Calmness had returned.

From the corner of her eye she saw the first flickers of light peeping over the horizon in the distance. September sunrise, it must be about half six. She had done it again, painted all night.

She loved this time of day, its stillness. Thankfully today was Saturday; she could make up for the lack of sleep with a glorious dream-free catnap later. She loved the weekends. All she had to do now was get through that dreaded visit from Sean at eleven. Her grandmother had seen to the problem of her mother by suggesting a surprise weekend away with her father. Gran knew how to save her. She smiled lovingly and pulled the robe tightly around her.

A small tap disturbed her from her trail of thought and the smell of freshly brewed coffee drew her eyes to the door. Standing in an old-fashioned, flannel nightgown and robe, her grandmother was like a character from one of the many books she had read: petite, with long grey hair and a face that carried on it the stories of her eighty or so years. Saoirse didn't know how old her grandmother was; she didn't like to celebrate birthdays and always said it was rude to ask a lady her age. It was just one of the many secrets her gran held close to her heart, but had promised to share in time. That was all irrelevant though, as right now her grandmother was carrying her favourite mug filled with fresh coffee and she knew they would spend the next hour or two on the window bed, chatting and telling stories.

She loved her grandmother, but could she tell her what she was dreaming? Would it scare her? Would she think she was crazy? Her dreams were really starting to frighten her and their content was so graphic and disturbing that she was starting to question her sanity. Her grandmother was the only one she could turn to. She would have to tell someone, and if they continued, it'd have to be soon.

'So this is the latest addition! What's she called?'

'Gran, you know I never name them.'

'Just thought you might decide to change things, name one maybe. She's beautiful. She looks very familiar, you know,' her gran always did this, tried to find people she knew in the paintings, tried to get Saoirse to name them. She obviously didn't know where the images came from, because if she did she would never have asked her to name them, never made her make that intimate connection. She would probably have run screaming.

She stared at Saoirse intently now, a knowing in her eyes that Saoirse could not understand. She came closer to the painting and asked again, 'Are you sure you don't have a name for her?' She had never done that before, never pressed about the pictures and their inspiration or names. Again she looked at Saoirse, waiting for an answer. She was very serious, too serious. Something was wrong, but Saoirse couldn't read the expression on her face.

'Do you recognise her, Gran?'

'No, no,' she broke away from her gaze and her mood shifted instantly, 'I just thought such a beautiful face should have a name. Breakfast is almost ready, so don't be long,' said Gran as she bustled out of the room.

What? Breakfast so early and no long chat... what was up? There was something wrong. Her grandmother could never normally resist the opportunity to tell her wondrous stories of Irish legends and war goddesses.

Saoirse's heart rate increased and she felt that strange and uneasy feeling she felt after her dreams; a cold sweat began to gather at her temples. A chirpy shout from the kitchen two storeys down brought her back to reality with a pleasant bump. It always amazed her how her frail grandmother's voice carried all over the house with such ease and grace.

The kitchen was filled with morning sunshine, the table was set with flowers and cutlery for two, and homemade American pancakes cooked gently in the pan on the range. Her grandmother always had the fire going, and Saoirse loved its warmth, even now on a sunny September morning. There was just something so comforting about it.

'Happy birthday, chicken, I wanted you all to myself to celebrate this very special birthday. Sit up there and we'll start on these pancakes.'

The fear she had felt earlier evaporated. This was her grandmother: happy, cheerful and all hers. She settled herself in the chair next to her and they both tucked in. Her grandmother made the best pancakes, light and fluffy with no need for accompaniments. Munching into her second pancake, she spotted the box on the table. Her grandmother saw her and her eyes lit up.

'What's that?'

'It's your birthday present!'

Saoirse's heart sank a little, it wasn't a book, and she had been secretly banking on another for this year's gift. Her grandmother pushed the box towards her and she took it in her hands. It was beautiful on second glance, delicately carved walnut. On the lid was a beautiful young woman with long flowing hair, standing on a cliff top. On the four sides were landscapes, cliffs and the ocean and on the back part a castle. Saoirse knew the place: it was her grandmother's home place, Dunluce in the North. She very often spoke so fondly and vividly about it, and it was carved painstakingly on the wooden box. It was magnificent, an heirloom for sure, at least a hundred years old. She didn't ask if it was, there was no point, her grandmother wouldn't tell her.

'Open it, chicken!'

Open it? Saoirse had thought the present was the box. It was exquisite. How could anything inside live up to the container? She tried to open the stiff lid clumsily. With a pull and a small bit of a grunt the lid gave way and revealed a red velvet interior. The box looked far smaller on the inside than you would have expected, but sitting quite snugly inside was the most beautiful silver comb. Another exquisitely crafted piece, half-moon shaped sterling silver with thick prongs and a beautiful ornate handle. Waves inset with three sapphires – her birthstone – were hand gilded across the top. It was truly breathtaking; but surely it belonged in a museum and not to a nearly sixteen-year-old with a head of unruly hair.

Her grandmother saw her expression, and taking the comb in her frail hands, she turned Saoirse in her chair, undid her loose plait and began to comb her hair. The comb ran smoothly and effortlessly through her long locks. Saoirse's scalp had been on tenterhooks a second ago, but now she relaxed into the calming sensation of having her hair combed. How could that little comb run so quickly and pain free through the wilds of her hair? It felt sensational and as Saoirse relaxed into the repetitive strokes, her grandmother started her stories.

'So, I suppose you better get dressed, chicken. You can't really entertain Sean in your pyjamas.'

Saoirse looked up, where had the time gone? It was nearly ten o'clock.

'Thanks Gran, it's absolutely beautiful. The box would have been enough, but the comb is just amazing. Where on earth do you find these things?'

'Some day you'll know. But remember this one thing for me: inside of everything lies something far more meaningful and powerful. Inside of you and me are our souls, our true beings, but the things I have given you also have souls, true meanings you have yet to find, you just have to look at them in the right way.'

Ever the cryptic! Saoirse hoped someday all these mysterious clues would fall into place and she would finally know her grandmother. For now, all she knew was that her grandmother had moved to Cork from Dunluce, before her father was born. She recalled vaguely hearing about illegitimacy or unsympathetic parents. They had never taken her to Dunluce, and they never talked of relatives. Saoirse's grandmother had never been back, but her father had been several times in the past few years, flying visits that never lasted more than a week and were always unplanned and hastily decided upon, much to her mother's disgust and constant disapproval. Her mother had never gone and refused to let him take Saoirse. Saoirse found it strange at times that she knew all about her mother's family, but nothing about her father's. Who was he visiting and why wasn't she allowed to go with him? But her grandmother liked it that way and Saoirse would never upset her. Curiosity or no curiosity, she respected her too much to push her.

She picked the box up from the table and placed the comb back inside. It was her grandmother's. This was her history and all she would know of herself for now. It didn't matter anyway, she loved her regardless.

3

Right on the bells of eleven from the cathedral, Sean's knock came at the front door. Saoirse had spent the last hour tidying her already very neat study and trying to rack her brains for answers to the inevitable questions she was about to face. Sean greeted her with a smile and an awkward hug. His strong athletic frame easily wrapped around her and she fitted snugly under his arms. His sandy hair was short and his skin sallow. It was awkward... but for her alone; Sean seemed very comfortable, in himself, and with everyone and everything. Saoirse would have loved if she had just an ounce of that comfort, that security of knowing who you are and being okay with that. She had been even more uneasy with herself of late, especially since this dream began; it really had affected her to the core.

'Are you going to let that boy in, or are you going to make him stand outside and work on that project from there?' Her grandmother appeared from the kitchen behind her, with a tray and a smile.

Immediately Sean sprung around her and took the tray from her grandmother, 'Let me carry that for you, Mrs O'Donnell.' The manners, her grandmother would love that, and he seemed so genuine about it.

'Why thank you, Sean. You are so like your father, you know. I was so sad to hear of the passing of your mother, she was a good woman. I hope that wayward sister of yours isn't giving your father too much trouble, he doesn't need that at the moment.'

Both Saoirse and Sean stood in a little bit of shock. Saoirse had only just met Sean at school. He had no idea who Saoirse's grandmother was, so how did her grandmother know so much about his family? Her grandmother was very much a home bird, she rarely went out, and when she did it was solely to do a bit of shopping or to buy some books. She didn't gossip, she didn't talk in general outside the four walls of No. 4. How did she know the Fitzgeralds?

'That tray is for you, fresh coffee and scones should help with the work. Enjoy!' With that she disappeared back into the kitchen with an ease that defied her advanced years.

'I suppose you'd better follow me,' her voice betrayed her again. It was weak and almost inaudible, but he heard her and followed her up the stairs to the top floor. She could see he was impressed by the house. Its Victorian grandeur was impressive; living here had made her immune to its beauty, but it was nice to see it in his eyes. She pushed the heavy door to her study open and let him in before her with the tray. She had set two chairs on either side of a large mahogany desk that took pride of place in the centre of the room. The rest of the room was shelves, and one cupboard. There were two windows in this room that mirrored the two in her bedroom, but these looked out on the roadway below and had curtains to block out the street lights. Today it was bright and airy, even with the seas of books surrounding them. Sean placed the tray on the edge of the desk and sat on the chair facing the door. She was glad as it was not her chair, but the one she had brought up from her dad's desk on the next floor down.

'Very nice house, Saoirse! Your parents must be loaded!'

'You'd think so, I guess, but we're not really. Dad is a history teacher and my mum is a legal secretary with one of the solicitors here in Cobh. The house belongs to my gran, but we've always lived here with her.'

'She's from the North is she? I love her accent. How does she know me? Didn't want to be rude downstairs, but she seemed to know a lot about my family and I haven't a clue who she is. I don't think I've ever even seen her before. Maybe at mass, perhaps?'

'We don't go to church.'

'You're Protestant?'

'No. Well, I don't know really. We've never practiced any religion, to be honest. It's funny, I've grown up in the shadow of the cathedral but, you know, I've never been inside.'

'Really? Do you know, in the last minute I've learned more about you than I did in an entire double class during the week!' He smiled warmly. 'It wasn't that difficult now, was it?'

It was true, perhaps it was because she was in her own environment, or because she was getting to know Sean, but she felt a little more open today, a little more forthcoming with answers. But then again the questions had come in conversation rather than formally, perhaps she would clam up when they got down to the real stuff. It was only then that Saoirse realised Sean had not brought any bag, note book or pen. He saw her looking quizzically at him and somehow pre-empted her question with an answer.

'I saw how difficult you found it at school to answer questions, so thought it might be better if we just got to know each other casually first. So I didn't bother with the books or forms.'

How did he do that? How could he have known what she was thinking? Perhaps living with four sisters had given him an innate ability to read women. Whatever it was, he seemed to be very good at it. He poured coffee and handed it to her, then took a cup himself and sliced a scone in half and added butter, but no jam. He strolled to the window, scone in one hand and coffee in the other. He watched the street below, and munched on the scone. Approving noises showed his appreciation for her grandmother's cooking and Saoirse sat hugging her coffee in awe at his ease and confidence.

'So while I have you at your ease and a little chatty, let's get to know you a little more, Saoirse O'Donnell.'

Okay, she could do this: just answer his questions. She was at home, comfortable, in her own room, at her own desk, in a chair that knew her oh too well. She took a long satisfying drink of warm coffee and a deep breath; she could do this.

'Okay, what would you like to know?'

'Favourite colour?'

'Ah that's easy! Midnight blue.'

'Now that wasn't so bad was it?'

She couldn't help but giggle, it wasn't that bad. She really could do this. He started with easy questions, small talk questions like favourite time of year, favourite food, and built up to questions that required a little bit of debate. Sean liked the Coronas as did Saoirse but they couldn't agree on their favourite song or album, and had finally agreed to disagree.

She'd told him all about her love of books, *Wuthering Heights* being her favourite outside of her grandmother's and she had admitted that she loved to paint. It was easy, Saoirse didn't feel uncomfortable, in fact she felt very much at ease chatting, but that was about to change.

'What frightens you the most?'

She sat stunned, not knowing how to answer. Things had been going so smoothly. She knew what scared her: her dreams, where they were going, their frequency, how graphic they were. But she hadn't even been able to tell her grandmother about her dreams. And she was the one person she had always been able to talk to about everything. How, then, could she tell this practical stranger about a dream she still hadn't even come to terms with herself? She felt the colour drain from her face, visions flashed through her head of the beautiful blonde girl. Her mind reeled and she felt a little sick. She needed a change of subject, and she needed one quickly.

'Would you like to see the view from the front of the house?' She steadied herself as she rose from the chair and placed the coffee mug back on the tray. She knew he would. He turned from the window and beamed like a little child. They crossed the landing to her bedroom, the door was ajar and as she approached it she saw the picture of the blonde on the easel. She had forgotten it was there and she saw Sean rush towards the window, but he stopped dead in the middle of the room. The abruptness startled her. He stood staring at the painting. She called his name, but he didn't turn. He didn't look horrified or scared; instead he was looking at the painting with a little smile on his face and a knowing in his eyes.

'How do you know Kate?'

'Sorry?'

'How do you know Kate, my girlfriend? How do you know her?'

'I don't. . .' Saoirse was confused. What was he on about?

'The likeness is uncanny. You've really gotten her, the little smirk and the dimple. And the highlights, they're only new you know, she only had them done in the last month or so, said she wanted something different. I prefer her hair natural, but whatever makes her happy.'

Saoirse began to panic; he was talking about the painting. He knew the girl! That meant he knew the girl in her dream. Her heart began to pound and a cold sweat broke out on her forehead. Visions of her dream flashed before her eyes: broken limbs, open wounds. . . an instinctual scream gained momentum in her lungs, she felt it rumbling and coming to the surface. She had this uncontrollable desire to reach out to him, to scream, to warn him. She gulped back her breath for fear she would actually scream. Why did she feel the need to warn him, and about what? Her and her craziness perhaps, but no, she felt she needed to tell him about the dream. Her mouth went dry and then suddenly filled with saliva, she was going to be sick, she felt weak and her knees began to give way. Sean turned just in time to catch her.

'Jesus, Saoirse, are you okay? You look like you're going to be sick. You look awful. Will I call your grandmother?'

'It's okay, Sean, I'm here.'

Her appearance behind them startled them both, but Saoirse breathed a sigh of relief. Her grandmother was ever her saviour. They sat her on the window seat and her grandmother opened the window and let in the sea air.

'I think you'd better go now, Sean. Saoirse is obviously not feeling very well. I'll show you out.'

She took him by the elbow and led him towards the bedroom door; he glanced at Saoirse at the window and then took a last lingering glance at the painting and smiled.

'Hope you feel better, Saoirse. I'll text you to see how you are later.'

And with that her grandmother whisked him away, down the stairs and out the back door. Saoirse watched him cross the gardens at the back of the houses and head down the steps that lead to the back of the local library and out onto the town square below. Her breath still caught, and her forehead was still clammy, what had just happened?

Her grandmother returned and sat on the window seat with her. She said nothing, but took her earlier gift from the desk, opened it, took out the silver comb and began to comb Saoirse's hair. Immediately her breathing began to calm and her heart rate stabilised. The combing was rhythmic and soothing, it cleared her head and her heart, and for the first time she felt she could open up about everything.

'What just happened, Gran?'

'I don't know, Saoirse, can you tell me?'

'He knew her. But then again so did you this morning. Who is Kate, Gran? And why am I dreaming about her?'

Her grandmother didn't answer immediately, she continued to comb Saoirse's hair and took her time with her answer.

'I don't know Kate either, chicken, but I did recognise her. You have to understand that you must be yourself, listen to yourself. Sometimes deep within us are the answers to all our questions, if we just listen carefully we can answer them from within. Don't be frightened, my love, we all grow up, we all change and we all grow into the people we are supposed to be. Now are you feeling a bit better? You look better. How about I make us a little lunch and you can have one of your cat naps this afternoon? I think you could do with one.'

She hadn't answered her question, but Saoirse did feel better. She would still have to face Sean again and explain her sudden illness. . . But he didn't have her mobile number, so she had until Monday to come up with a good excuse. Now she did feel better.

4

The weekend had passed rather uneventfully after the drama of Saturday morning. Saoirse had catnapped Saturday afternoon, and spent the evening watching movies, having her hair combed and sipping her grandmother's special cocoa. She had slept well – a deep dreamless sleep – and had woken on Sunday morning feeling refreshed and revived.

Her parents had returned in a flurry of good humour and little gifts from the weekend away around noon, full of the joys of life and madly in love as usual. She loved to see her parents like this. All too often her mother was far too serious and over-protective. She loved to see her carefree and giggly, her father had that effect on her. Gran had the opposite effect on her; her mother contradicted everything her grandmother said, and tried her utmost to keep her and Saoirse apart. Saoirse was yet to work out what it was that her mother so hated in her grandmother, because for the main part they seemed to get on well together. But when it came to issues involving Saoirse it was a different story. Saoirse hated to admit it, but she very often sided with her grandmother, and she felt that perhaps this added to the tension between them.

But Sunday was a good day. Her grandmother had cooked a family roast and her parents had enjoyed a glass of wine on the patio afterwards; the sun was still warm and their south facing garden was making the most of what appeared to be an Indian summer. Saoirse had sat with them, hearing all about the romantic weekend they had had, joking with them that these were not things to be sharing with their sixteen-year-old daughter, to which her father quickly responded, 'Ah, but you're not sixteen yet, honey! You have a whole five days. God I remember this time sixteen years ago,' he turned and smiled lovingly at his wife, he reached across the table and kissed her cheek softly. She blushed slightly, but the smile outshone the embarrassment.

Saoirse's mum was the beautiful Irish Caitlin, her skin was milky white, her hair the same beautiful auburn as Saoirse's and her eyes the purest green. She was breathtaking, especially on days like this, perfect days when she was happy and carefree. Saoirse smiled at her parents, they were very much still in love. They had met in college and had Saoirse very soon after. Life as young parents had been difficult for them, but they had gotten through. They inspired her, made her long for that kind of love. Her grandmother had promised her it would come when it was ready and that Saoirse was far too young to be even looking for a love like that already. This was the one thing they agreed on; neither her mother nor her grandmother wanted her to date. There would be plenty of time for that when she was older.

Saoirse had enjoyed the afternoon in the sunshine and had spent the evening finishing homework and preparing for school. Apprehension and anxiety began to creep into the pit of her stomach as she put away her books and packed her bag. She would have to see Sean tomorrow. Her sudden sickness would not be the issue, Kate would be. How would Saoirse explain to Sean that she had absolutely no idea who Kate was? Or that she had never met her before and had painted her because she had appeared to her in the most disturbing dream she had ever had? Saoirse took a deep breath. She found it hard to share the simplest of things; being an only child, her passions, and her ambitions, how the hell was she going to tell a guy she barely knew that? Crazy, crazy, crazy. The words dazzled in neon lights, blinking wildly in her head. She must be crazy. There was no way she could tell him the truth. So what lie could she come up with that would sound the most feasible?

She flopped down at her desk and opened her laptop. She typed Kate's name into Google and prayed something would come back that could explain the picture. 'Kate Smith, 17 Captain of the U18 Cork All-Ireland winning camogie team'. If Saoirse had believed in God she would have thanked Jesus. She was someone, someone Saoirse would know other than if she had personally met her. Now all she had to do was come up with a reason for painting her picture. Art. . . role models. . . school projects. . . Yes, she had it! She was painting a picture of Kate to include as part of her art project that presented positive role models for young girls in sport. Sean had missed Art last week because of a match; she'd get away with it until she could come up with something better. She breathed a sigh of relief. Now she could sleep.

Sleep came quickly but didn't last long. At half twelve she bolted up in the bed, her stomach churned, saliva gushed into her mouth and she rushed to the bathroom, panting she hugged the toilet bowl and hoped the nausea would pass. Her heart pounded in her chest and her head was spinning, her breath was quick and uneasy and tears streamed down her face. She had never in her entire life felt like this before: what she had just seen was unimaginable. She didn't even want to think about it. . . but she had to. Things had really changed now, she would have to start figuring these out, she knew people in the dream tonight.

The toilet was cold and the nausea seemed to be passing. She had to calm down: deep breaths in and out, in and out. She must have been on the floor ten minutes or so because when she went to stand her left leg was asleep and the painful tingle was a welcome distraction. She moved to the basin and splashed her face with cold water, checking her reflection in the mirror. Pale skin, freckled face, red eyes; she looked awful, as if she had seen a ghost. She pushed the hair back from her face and took another deep breath. Slowly she moved across the cool tiled floor, turned the light off in the bathroom and made her way in the dark back along the landing and into her room.

It was a dark night on the harbour, and very quiet. She felt like a storm was raging in her head and had almost expected it to be reflected in the water outside. She pulled on her fluffy robe and settled herself on the window seat. She pulled *Wuthering Heights* out from under her and placed it on the desk beside her. She loved that book. She loved the deep intensity of Heathcliff and Catherine's love, but found the idea of Catherine's ghost, of the afterlife and the entire unknown, a little unsettling. Why could true love not just be true love? Why did destiny and the supernatural have to come into it? Saoirse felt it was destiny and the supernatural that had ruined the love story. Life was so much simpler when it was just life. Her grandmother always laughed at her when she argued this point with her.

'Your destiny is your destiny, Saoirse, whether you like it or not. The supernatural exists, even for those who do not believe it. Just because you can't see or touch it, doesn't mean it doesn't exist. Everything happens for a reason, and sometimes that everything is given a little helping hand from destiny or the supernatural. Catherine and Heathcliff were no different. Destiny meant for their story to be the way it was. Remember you are born who you are and then you spend your life becoming who you are meant to be.'

Saoirse's argument to this had always been that it was fiction, from start to finish, a great but tragic love story, that was undermined by the appearance of Cathy's ghost.

They had argued this point almost as many times as Saoirse had read the book, which on last count was thirteen. The idea of Cathy's ghost haunted her tonight. It was too close to home. She picked the book back up and tucked it under her nose. She took a deep breath in and held it there. Love had great power, according to the book, even in the next life. Did that mean that her dream could actually have meaning in her own life?

The dream had been different tonight, very different; she had recognised people, specifically Sean. She tucked her knees up under her and stared out at the harbour. Had he appeared in the dream tonight, because subconsciously she now knew he was connected to Kate, or was the dream some kind of message or even something more sinister? Why did she feel she needed to talk to him? Why did she have this almost uncontrollable urge to find him now and tell him what she had just dreamt?

She grabbed her notebook from her bedside table and turned the desk light on. She sat at the desk and again looked out at the harbour. It was still quiet and still very dark. The painting was complete. She had nothing to keep her occupied tonight, so she opened the notebook and decided to write down what she had just seen, hoping that perhaps it would be cathartic and might release her from the dream's grasp. She took her pen in her hand and tried to find the words to explain what she had just witnessed. But nothing came. She couldn't write the words, nor could she recall the beginning of the dream. All she could remember now was the ending, that horrific image of the broken blonde girl, the image of Kate, lifeless and shattered. She shuddered; it was so real, so real that she found it hard to believe it was just a dream. The panic returned. She held the desk and tried to calm herself once more, tears began to form and her stomach churned. She was going to be sick.

'Are you okay, chicken?' The voice was barely audible, but she heard it, almost felt it brush her ear. She turned and there was her grandmother in her dressing gown and nightie, holding a cup of warm milk. 'I couldn't sleep either. Bad dream. I heard you up and figured you might need this.' She held out the cup and when Saoirse took it her grandmother reached over and took the carved walnut box from the desk and took out the comb. The sapphires caught the light of the desk lamp and twinkled ever so slightly. She turned Saoirse's head as she had done when Sean had left and began to comb her hair. Immediately Saoirse began to feel an ease wash over her. The same comforting and calming feeling returned and she settled into the motion.

'You know you can talk to me about anything Saoirse. There isn't anything that would shock me'.

Saoirse thought about it, her grandmother was up too, a bad dream she had said, perhaps she had had a dream like hers, maybe she would understand. But how could she? The things she was dreaming were far too disturbing; surely her poor grandmother would never understand them and she didn't feel the need to inflict the gruesome content of her dreams on her. It just wouldn't be fair. It was enough to have to deal with herself, without the guilt of knowing she had involved her grandmother.

'Just a bad dream Gran, I must have eaten too late or something. I'll settle now after this and I should be okay.'

Her grandmother looked at her softly, willing her to elaborate, Saoirse could see the look in her eyes, but she just couldn't, not now, not yet anyway. She turned fully and hugged her grandmother tightly. She was tiny compared to Saoirse's tall willowy frame and Saoirse engulfed her with her long slender arms. She held tight and whispered softly into her grandmother's ear, 'I'll be fine Gran, don't worry about me. Love ya.'

Reluctantly her grandmother gave into her, hugged her back and then withdrew. It was getting late, time Saoirse should be in bed, she had school tomorrow. Her grandmother waited till she had gotten back into bed and then like a little child she tucked her snugly into the large double bed, brushed the hair from her forehead and kissed her softly. She then turned to the desk, pulled the silver comb from her dressing gown pocket and placed it back in the box on the desk. She tapped it softly and affectionately. Then blew a kiss at Saoirse and outted the light. Saoirse barely heard her leave the room in the dark and before she knew it she was sound asleep.

5

Far too quickly day came and with it the alarm clock. She thought about hitting the snooze button, but she was so tired this morning that might just be too dangerous. Her mother hated it when she overslept and Saoirse didn't feel like another lecture from her mother. Yesterday had been so lovely and easy, she preferred to keep it like that. She dragged herself out of bed, and went to check out the harbour; quiet and still, a tanker in the mouth of the outer harbour sending up a little puff of grey smoke, but other than that peaceful. The weather was magnificent for September, the water like glass in the breezeless, pale morning sunlight. She tore herself away from the breathtaking view out the window, to inspect an entirely different view: the one of her very tired self in the bathroom mirror.

What greeted her this morning was so far removed from the swan she hoped she would one day see, that she covered her face with her hands and groaned. The afflictions of excessive height, pale skin, red hair and freckles were not enough, now to add to that she had deep, dark circles under her very red and puffy eyes. She thought it could only get better, but she had been very wrong. She splashed her face with water and decided her shower would have to wait until after breakfast, she needed coffee and she needed it badly.

She pushed the kitchen door open slowly and hoped her mother was not up yet. The kitchen was empty, but the coffee pot was on and steaming, someone was up. She grabbed a mug from the cupboard and put a slice of bread in the toaster. She poured a large mug and settled at the island in the centre of the kitchen. She was exhausted. She'd have to pull herself together before her mother got up; she'd kill her for being so tired.

A humming caught her attention from the French doors to the garden and she spotted her father sitting on the patio, cereal bowl in hand and coffee steaming on the table in front of him.

'Morning Dad, you're in great form this morning. Beautiful day, huh? Such a pity to waste it inside a classroom. Maybe we could take off for the day? I'll write you a note if you write me one?'

It was their running joke since she had started secondary school, one day they would both bunk off school together and do something fun. Saoirse knew it would never happen; they both were too good to do something like that. Plus her father loved his job: teaching was his passion, history his life.

'You look tired, sweetheart. Did you sleep okay? Gran said you were up during the night. She's gone back to bed, she's wrecked. Are you okay?'

'I'm fine, Dad. I'll go to bed early tonight. Is Gran alright?'

'Ah, she'll be grand; she goes through phases like this where she can't sleep very well. She tells me she's heard you up a lot recently, is that true?'

He looked at her lovingly, but in his eyes Saoirse saw something else, her father had never looked at her like this before, there was a realisation Saoirse could not comprehend. He saw something, something she didn't, and he was proud. Saoirse was confused, how could the admission of having bad dreams make her father proud? She thought it was kind of strange, but Saoirse saw definite pride in her father's eyes.

'Come here, sweetheart.'

Saoirse balanced on the arm of his chair and snuggled up next to her dad. He threw his strong arm around her waist and pulled her in tight. She was tall, but she always felt like her father's little girl. His strong athletic build had meant he was great at sports at school, but they never really interested him; his passion had always been Irish history and folklore. Saoirse always found it so ironic that he had been built to be an athlete, but had turned his back on it to be a nerd. He didn't fit the stereotype and she loved him all the more for that.

'You know you can talk to us about anything and anytime. Being a teenager is difficult these days, it can be confusing and scary.'

'Dad, are you giving me your teacher speech again? I'm your daughter not a pupil,' she giggled, there were times her dad treated her like one of his students, but that wasn't such a bad thing: he was a good teacher, and a good dad.

'I just want you to know that sometimes talking things through can help. Even if it's just discussing a bad dream. Your Gran has bad dreams too, maybe she could help.'

Saoirse's mother appeared in the kitchen and they both turned when they heard the rattle of cups in the cupboard. Saoirse jumped to her feet and tried in vain to make herself look a little fresher. Her dad watched her feeble attempts and grinned knowingly at her. 'Talk to your grandmother, you'll be surprised how much she may be able to help you! Please...'

He trailed off as her mother appeared at the open doors, showered and dressed immaculately as usual. She took a deep breath of the fresh morning air and stepped out onto the patio. Saoirse's father grabbed the chair next to him and pulled it out for her, he winked quickly at Saoirse and started off into a reminiscing conversation of what they had been up to this time sixteen years ago, four days before

Saoirse had been born. Her mother loved the story as it was all about their move into this house. She had lived in Cobh all her life and always dreamt of living in the Crescent. So Saoirse's arrival had coincided with another one of the happiest times in her life. She was distracted and Saoirse made her exit, flashing her father an appreciative smile on the way.

She practically crawled up the stairs, and into her bathroom. She checked her reflection in the mirror once more, no miraculous change, she still looked awful. Perhaps a shower would help. She turned on the shower and let it run, her mind wandered back to the dream from last night, flashes of Kate's broken body pierced her mind and she shook her head, they were replaced by images of a distraught Sean screaming and shouting. Again she shook her head, they were too disturbing, she couldn't spend the day thinking of them, she would have to find something to distract her. She stepped over the rim of the bath and into the shower, the water was just a little cool which was refreshing and she squeezed the citrus body gel into her hand, the smell filled her nostrils and gave her the slight feeling of morning stimulation it had promised on the bottle.

Once she had showered, she began the mammoth task of washing her hair. It hung limp and wet around her naked body. It was long and thick. She shampooed and thought about not conditioning it, but with curls like hers that would be asking for trouble. She would spend the day trying to tame it, and her hair was not something she wanted to have to deal with today.

She stepped down from the tub and back onto the bathroom tiles. The shower had helped, physically, if not mentally anyway. She took a glance at her reflection in the mirror, but the steam had fogged it up. As she wiped the glass with her towel, the image facing her startled her, her breath quickened and the hair stood up on the back of her neck: it was Kate. Just for a fleeting moment and then she was gone, replaced by her own pale reflection. She grabbed the sides of the sink and looked down, taking a deep breath. She looked back into the mirror, her own hopeful face that greeted her every morning was gone, replaced by a reflection she knew was her own, but that looked a little alien. There was a worry, a distraction clearly visible in her eyes, highlighted by the dark cycles beneath them. She looked older, and tired. People always asked you when it was your birthday did you feel older; this year was the first year that Saoirse could truthfully say she did. She definitely felt different.

She heard her mother was calling from downstairs, so she wrapped herself in a towel and walked to the landing. She peered down the staircase and could see her mother standing at the bottom. She smiled lovingly up at her, Saoirse must have looked someway better, because there was no lecture about how important sleep was.

'Hey honey, I'm off to work. I'm heading into town after work to meet your dad; we have a special present to buy for someone I know who has an important birthday Friday. Do you need anything from the city?'

'No thanks, Mum. Do you want me to organise dinner when I get home from school?'

'Not at all, love, your gran has a stew on the hob already; she must have been up all night again.' She tutted and looked a little annoyed, but then she smiled up at Saoirse again, 'Have a great day at school, see you this evening.'

Saoirse went back to her room and looked out at the harbour, it was beginning to come to life. There were two tankers now in the mouth waiting patiently for the pilot boat, and the launches for the naval base had begun taking the sailors to work. Another beautifully still and bright morning on the water. The boats' movements carved through the glass and sent ripples that echoed out across the entire harbour. The sun had begun to climb and the sky was cloudless.

'September!' Saoirse thought. 'Why couldn't we have had weather like this in August when I didn't have to go to school?'

She turned from the window and came face to face with Kate. She took a step closer to the painting and sighed. What was this all about? How could she have painted such a realistic painting without ever having met this girl? What would Sean say or think? She had her story; she went over it once more. Kate, the role model, not the dead beauty. What kind of freak was she? She sat down on the bed. Being a teenager sucked, life was too confusing and her nightmares seemed to make it all the more crazy.

She checked the clock on the bedside table, eight-fifteen, she'd be late and it was one thing she hated. She went to the wardrobe and there hanging, freshly washed and ironed, was her uniform. She thanked heaven for her grandmother and uniforms. The idea of having to choose a different outfit everyday would have made her life a living hell. Her uniform gave her anonymity, she could blend in and go unnoticed and she liked that. Not being part of a crowd didn't bother her, but standing out did. She liked life to gently pass by, without drawing attention to herself.

Once she was dressed, she grabbed her bag from her study and her phone from the desk. She felt a good bit better and took the stairs two at a time. Her grandmother was standing at the final step when she got there. She looked tired this morning, but greeted her with her usual warm smile.

'You okay? You didn't sleep very well last night. You know you can talk to me anytime about it.'

'Are you and Dad up to something Gran? He said the very

same thing. You didn't sleep too well yourself. I can smell the midnight stew on the hob!'

'Touché. I'm just worried about you chicken, that's all. I'm here anyway if you need me. Have a good day at school.'

She reached up to kiss Saoirse and Saoirse obligingly bent towards her so she could. Saoirse's 5'11" frame was nearly a full foot taller than her grandmother and at the bottom of the stairs they must have looked like a very odd couple. Her grandmother kissed her softly on the cheek and hugged her tightly and then left her go.

Saoirse popped her earphones in and closed the real world out, as she left the house and hopped down the front steps. Florence and the Machine filled her head and took over her mind. She loved her haunting sound, her power, and her lyrics. If only she had half her strength, she knew they were only songs but she found them inspiring. It was a welcome escape on the journey to school and made it all the more bearable. Saoirse needed it this morning. Lying was not her forte, but she could hardly tell Sean the truth.

She was there before she knew it, caught up in the middle of the Monday morning hype: the boisterous boys, the girls sharing the gossip from the weekend, pushing and shoving in the corridor, blocking the lockers, not seeing her. The phone was the greatest invention ever. Saoirse could block it all out, and not feel obliged to look at, talk to or even acknowledge anyone. She didn't have a class with Sean today, but something told her he would seek her out, dying to know about the painting. She had her story, but intended, today more than any other day, to keep her head down and try and stay as invisible as possible.

Lunch time came and still no sign. She had heard rumbling about his absence from the other boys in her class at break, but Florence had prevented her from hearing why he wasn't in school. Could she be this lucky? Could he really not be in school? Was she safe for now? It appeared so, the final bell rang at four and Saoirse was free, she practically skipped the whole way home. If she was really lucky maybe he'd be out all week.

She was that lucky, for once it seemed, Thursday arrived and went and still no sign of Sean. Maybe the birthday girl had gotten her wish, either way Saoirse didn't care, she hadn't had to answer any questions about herself or Kate and she hadn't had a dream all week. She got into bed on Thursday evening a very happy girl: tomorrow was her birthday.

6

It was a busy club, the music was too loud and the crowd too big for the tiny place. The music pounded in her chest and echoed around inside her head. Disorientated, she looked around, she didn't recognise anyone. Panic set in, what was she doing here? Another frantic glance and she spotted Sean and Kate in the corner, chatting and giggling in each other's ears, oblivious to the noise and the crowd around them. Saoirse moved towards them and was surprised that the crowd parted for her as she walked.

As she neared Sean and Kate, their mood began to change. Kate was becoming irritated and loud. Her face lost some of its serene beauty, as she stood and shouted at Sean. He looked lost, confused by the sudden change in mood. He went to grab her hand to get her to sit back down, but she dramatically pulled it away and in doing so swayed violently and stumbled into the couple standing to her left. More shouting followed, the music left Saoirse's ears and all she heard now was the argument, or rather Kate's shouting. She was not making much sense and Saoirse realised she was drunk. This surprised her. Sean kept his voice steady and tried to coax her to sit down, but to no avail. She was shouting something about Sean not loving her really and her only being a trophy girlfriend for the big rugby player. And then she heard her say she was glad he had torn his cruciate, that maybe that would be the end of his unwanted career and he could get on with being his own boring self. Saoirse glanced down at Sean and true enough his left knee was braced and his crutches were balanced against the wall behind him.

'Oh that's why he's been out! God I hope he's okay. That's a serious injury,' Saoirse thought. She remained about ten feet away from them, they hadn't seen her yet and she didn't feel it was the right time to interrupt. But she continued to watch them, a morbid fascination holding her there.

Kate was crying now and continued to shout abuse at Sean; he was getting embarrassed as the crowd began to turn to watch the domestic. Kate gained momentum and the abuse got even more personal, she criticised him for not standing up to his father, for not being himself and for always being such a bloody neat freak, that it irritated her beyond belief. Sean was broken, visibly, but he continued to try and calm her down and began to shift from the chair and attempt to stand. She grabbed his crutches and threw them across the dance floor.

'I'm leaving!' she slurred. 'Stay where you are, cripple, one of the lads will drop me home. It's over, I've had enough!' She took off far too quickly for her drunken state and collided with several people before disappearing through the back entrance. Sean attempted to get up from the seat, but his crutches had disappeared in the crowd and he was in no position to move without them. Saoirse went towards him to help him, but he motioned at her to follow Kate, which she did.

Outside she came to a stop at the back entrance of the club, where Kate was being sick in the alley. She never spoke, but looked at Saoirse with the biggest, saddest brown eyes. Saoirse flinched; she saw her dreams echoed in the pools of her pupils. She helped Kate to straighten up and held her at the waist to steady her. From around the corner a car appeared. 'Our ride!' she smiled, almost wickedly and Saoirse felt uncomfortable.

The car stopped and the door opened on the passenger side, she climbed in the back and Kate got into the front. She couldn't tell what make the car was, she was never that interested in cars. She couldn't tell who the driver in the front seat was, but the radio blared and as soon as they left the restrictions of the city streets he sped up and soon they were travelling extremely fast. It was all happening so quickly that once the street lights faded Saoirse couldn't tell where they were and the landscape flew by so quickly she couldn't distinguish anything.

She leant forward in the seat and caught a glimpse of the driver in the rear-view mirror. She didn't recognise him. Kate, in the passenger seat was obviously still upset, but she seemed happier now and less drunk. They were chatting, flirting even. Saoirse couldn't believe her, she had only just crushed Sean in the club and now here she was chatting and giggling with a random guy. He was telling her how hot she was and how all his friends wouldn't believe he'd had her in his car. He sped up, obviously trying to impress her. She was delighted, thriving on the attention and encouraged him, egged him on. They hit a country road and Saoirse reached out to tell him slow down. But Kate turned up the music and the guy put his foot down. It was as if she wasn't even there.

She must have passed out; because all she could comprehend was that they must have crashed. The sound had been horrific. She had never heard a bomb go off, but she imagined it would have sounded similar. It was followed by an eerie silence. Slowly, as if in a fog, she became aware of several sounds: a dripping noise, repetitive and slow; a cracking noise like ice cracking under foot in the winter... and screaming. At first the screaming seemed like it was in the distance coming towards her, but then she realised it was directly in front of her. It was high pitched, horrifying and surprisingly male! Saoirse blinked, and rubbed her eyes.

Her body ached, but not physically, more mentally; her head was heavy.

She leant forward again and looked into the front of the car. It no longer existed, not in the form it had when she had leant forward to tell them to slow down. The windscreen was gone and the dashboard a mess of crumpled plastic. The steering wheel had disappeared behind an air bag and the driver's blood was smeared all over it. He was flung back in his seat, unrecognisable. It was him screaming and those screams echoed around the empty country road. Saoirse reached out to touch him, but stopped short when she caught a glimpse of Kate.

The image was familiar. Eerily so. She had seen this broken doll before, and she knew instantly what this meant: Kate was dead. Her neck was at an awkward angle, her mouth slightly open and her eyes wide, but empty, her beauty wiped away and replaced by the cold face of death. Saoirse touched her face, it was still warm. She wasn't sure what she should do, so she reached up to her eyes and closed them. The driver saw her do this, and his screams reached hysteria and he began to hyperventilate. Saoirse turned to him and went to put a reassuring hand on his shoulder. It was then she realised the clean pink pyjamas she had put on going to bed were still unwrinkled. . . she wasn't there at all, this was another dream.

Saoirse wasn't sure what was happening. She was dreaming, she knew that. There was no way she would have come out of that crash unscathed if she wasn't. But this was the first time she had not woken screaming from one of these dreams. She lay there, silently. Her heart still pounding. What was she supposed to do? She opened her eyes. And screamed. There was a figure at the end of her bed.

'Shh, chicken, you'll wake your mother and she'll have my head.'

'Gran! What. . . How long have you been there?'

'About five minutes, Saoirse, I thought you'd wake sooner, but I guess it takes some time to figure out. Tell me about the dream.'

'Figure what out, Gran?'

'Ah, Saoirse, never mind that, tell me about the dream. I need to know about the dream.'

Saoirse looked at her grandmother, and for the first time in her life her grandmother looked her age, whatever age that was. Her eyes were full of concern.

'Why is the dream so important, Gran? And how do you even know I was dreaming?'

'Those things you'll learn in time, but for now can you just tell me about the dream, please, chicken, it's important.'

Saoirse could see how serious she was, and so described in detail the dream she had had and all the dreams she had been having the past couple of weeks. She felt relieved to have told someone and for them not to have freaked out. Her grandmother didn't bat an eyelid. Instead Saoirse had felt as if she was reporting an accident, and her grandmother had been taking her statement. When she had finished her grandmother looked relieved, which had surprised Saoirse.

'You look relieved, Gran. I've just described the horrific death of a girl I didn't even know existed until last week, but now know does and you look relieved. She's not just a figment of my imagination, she's real and I've just seen her die. That's just weird, Gran, and you look happy.'

'So you're telling me that Sean never got in the car tonight? Is that right?'

'No, Gran, he didn't. I've only seen him in two or three dreams, but he always looks well and happy, whereas Kate changed over time.'

'That's good,' she genuinely looked relieved, she slumped down in the bed next to Saoirse and let out a sigh. 'Conor has been through enough over the last few years and in my dreams Sean had featured strongly but not clearly, so I wasn't sure.'

'Gran, your dreams? You have them too? You've been dreaming about Kate and Sean? I don't understand...' Saoirse began to lose control of herself; what was this all about? Her cryptic grandmother was having similar disturbing dreams of real people's deaths. What was wrong with her family? Were they some evil force that caused all this, was she part of some freakish family who heralded the death of poor innocent souls? She began to cry, irrationally, she didn't know why she was crying and she couldn't control herself. Her grandmother went to the desk and picked up the carved box, took out the comb and returned to the bed and began to comb.

'I can only say so much, chicken, the rest you must find out for yourself. Don't panic, I know what you're thinking: are we going to cause Kate's death? But it's not like that, not like that at all. I can't explain now, but what I can tell you is that you must follow your instincts, go with what your gut tells you, even if you think it's the wrong thing, you must follow your gut! The voice inside is always the one with the most wisdom. My dreams are similar to yours, but never the same, we will always see the same outcome, but the lead up will be different. You're closer to their age so you see it more clearly, and from their point of view. For me, I'm old; I see Kate and Sean's families' reactions. Thankfully tonight I didn't dream of Conor and now you've confirmed it: Sean doesn't die.' She smiled, but how could she? She was happy Sean wasn't going to die, but accepting of Kate's death. Saoirse was disgusted.

'Why does Kate have to die, Gran? Can we do something to stop it?' She was more than a little panicked now. Maybe the crash was going to happen tonight and maybe she could stop Kate from getting into the car. Maybe she could do something. But. . . why was she seriously considering rescuing a girl she didn't even know was in danger, purely because she had had a dream and her elderly grandmother had told her what she dreamt was true? She was confused, exhausted and bewildered. She held her head in her hands, defeated.

'Saoirse, my love, we do not have that power. Even if we see how someone is going to die, they don't always die in that way. The form of death may change, but the death itself is still just that: death. It will happen, with or without our input'.

Saoirse closed her eyes, and hoped she would wake from this part of the dream. Her mind couldn't quiet comprehend what it was her grandmother was trying to tell her. She willed herself to wake up to an empty bedroom, but when she opened her eyes again, she felt the comb sailing through her hair.

'It's hard to take in I know and I'm just sorry I can't tell you everything, but if I did, we would be worse off. You have to listen to your soul. Let it guide you. Now sleep, chicken, the next few days are going to be tough.'

Her grandmother finished combing her hair and that strange calmness returned. Gran tucked her in and placed the comb on the bedside table, rather than the desk. It gleamed in the moon light from the window. She tapped it fondly and ran a finger across its spine.

'Where did you get it, Gran?'

'A friend gave it to me for my sixteenth birthday back home. It had always been with her for as long as she could remember. Its special, Saoirse, so take good care of it and it'll take good care of you. Good night, chicken.' She kissed her softly on the forehead and slipped nimbly from the room.

As soon as she was gone, Saoirse got back out of bed; the

harbour called. She picked up the comb and perched herself comfortably on the window seat. She pulled her dressing gown around her and began to comb. The moon danced on the harbour. Saoirse loved this peaceful time, she felt alone, just the water and her, and she felt it could wash away everything. Or at least she had thought that in the past.

She'd always had bad dreams, always painted pictures, watched the ocean, calmed her soul, but things had changed in the last few weeks. Nameless faces had become people she knew, dreams seemed like they could become reality, and her grandmother, for once in her life, had started to open up, albeit to create so many more unanswered questions. What was happening to her? She passed the comb through her long auburn hair and marvelled at the ease with which it moved and the peace it brought. She was tired, the ocean brought no peace tonight, but perhaps sleep would.

Just as she stood to return to her bed, a pair of eyes caught her attention in the garden below. She moved silently closer to the window pane to get a better look. They were looking right up at her, glinting in the moonlight. Her heart raced.

She had never seen a fox before, and hadn't expected to see one in her garden. The moon caught the beautiful red of its coat. It was staring right at her. She looked deep into its eyes, mesmerised. It held her gaze for two or three minutes, then it looked towards the bright moon, gave out a single yelping howl and was gone. The hair stood up on the back of her neck, and a pleasant shiver ran through her. What in the world was happening? This was the strangest night of her life. But she was calm and felt like she could finally sleep. She climbed into bed, wrapped the duvet around her and sleep overcame her almost immediately.

7

Saoirse woke of her own accord, no shrill from the alarm clock, no shout from downstairs, and for once, mysteriously, given the night she had experienced, she felt rested. All too often lately she had woken stressed and uneasy, but this morning she was calm, her mind quiet, her body re-energised.

She stretched her long lean body, curled her toes and smiled. Even if the events of last night made absolutely no sense at all, she felt better. She hadn't accepted anything or understood what was going on, but she felt at ease, and she wasn't going to question it, just yet. She got out of bed and walked to the window. Watery morning sunlight greeted her. September was such a beautiful month this year, far better than the summer had been, it was still warm and had been dry for weeks.

She smiled: today was her birthday. She glanced at the cathedral clock to her left, 6.45. She was up early. In fifteen minutes the bells would start their hourly cycle and while she would hear the first round of bells, generally the rest would fade, unnoticed, into the background noises of everyday life. The cathedral rose above her small harbour town, and although it played such an important role in the pictures of her life, she had never in all her sixteen years been inside its daunting oak doors. It was a beautiful building and Saoirse found it strange that her natural curiosity had not taken her inside. She smirked: she was truly a funny fish.

A tap on her door brought her back to the room. It was her grandmother, a little sheepish and tired-looking. 'You okay, chicken?'

Saoirse should have had so many questions. But something inside her told her this would work itself out, that there was some kind of resolution coming and there was no need to panic. The calmness was intoxicating and Saoirse loved it.

'I'm fine, Gran. I still have so many questions, but for now I think its best we leave it. Mum will be watching like a hawk today; I'm sure she wouldn't approve of the conversation we had last night.' As the words parted her lips, it suddenly became very clear why Saoirse's mother had always been so cold and uncooperative with her grandmother, she was trying to deny whatever this all was. She had been so awkward because she knew what might be coming. Saoirse felt guilt wash over her. She had always been so hard on her mother, she always sided with her grandmother, and yet all along her mother had been trying to protect her. From what, she still didn't really know.

She looked at her grandmother. 'Yes, Saoirse, she knows. But she always secretly hoped you wouldn't be affected. She tried to protect you from it all and she was doing a pretty good job, but we can't hide from the truth. You can't run from what you are. It always wins out in the end.'

'What is the truth, Gran? What has she been protecting me from? Who. . . or what. . . am I? And why is she not the same? God there are so many questions, but I don't even want to think about it now. Can we just put things on hold by any chance?'

Her grandmother smiled weakly. 'I'm just so sorry I can't explain things more clearly chicken, but I would be putting you in so much danger if I did.' Her grandmother had never looked so old. She sat on the corner of Saoirse's bed and sighed heavily. 'You must work this all out for yourself, but I have given you the tools to do that: you're surrounded by them, I've made sure of that. And Sean will help.'

Saoirse spun from the window and stared at her

grandmother. 'Sean? Why...?' That feeling returned to her stomach: nausea, combined with a weakness in her knees and now it had been joined by the feeling of extreme heaviness in her head. Surely this was a dream. There was no way the insanity of the past few days could actually be true? Saoirse began to panic, either her grandmother was absolutely crazy... or perhaps it was just her. Maybe she was imagining this whole scenario. Maybe it was all in her head and the stress of going back to school after the summer break had taken its toll and kicked her over the edge. In the middle of it all was Sean. She had only just met him, but since then everything had changed. Maybe it was him; maybe this was all his doing?

'Gran! What does this have to do with Sean?' She shouted this and immediately regretted it. She startled her grandmother and knew she had attracted the attention of her mother downstairs, because she immediately heard her shift from the kitchen table and move across the kitchen to the end of the staircase. Saoirse heard the panic in her voice as she called up to the third floor:

'Saoirse, honey, are you alright?'

Saoirse's grandmother sighed, and looked at Saoirse dismayed. 'We're going to get it now!'

The footsteps echoed up the staircase, it was clear that Saoirse's mum was taking the steps in twos. It was barely thirty seconds before she was standing breathless at the doorway of Saoirse's room. Immediately Saoirse saw the realisation and despair in her face. Her body physically crumpled, her face dropped.

Looking at Saoirse grandmother, she whispered in despair, 'You win. I really hoped you wouldn't.' She sighed heavily. Saoirse's grandmother moved along the bed and held her daughter-in-law in her arms. It was clear there was no victory. As Saoirse watched two of the most important people in her life comfort each other on her bed, she began to realise that something immense was taking place. But what it was she didn't know. Today she had no idea who she was, or even what, she was. How could a simple recurring nightmare have changed her life so profoundly? She had no answers, but she had a feeling that her life would never be the same again.

She turned to face the harbour, looking for comfort and escape. She pressed her forehead against the cool glass and took a deep breath. She thought she knew what she was, but even the idea of it was ridiculous. She had read, time and time again, about figures from Irish folklore, and characters from the books her grandmother had given her. She had questioned whether anything like this could ever have existed and wondered how it would feel to be a part of their world. Surely she couldn't contemplate that world existing in reality? She wouldn't dare believe. Could she?

She turned again to face her mother and grandmother, who had begun to compose themselves on the bed. Even saying the words seemed so ridiculous. She couldn't bring herself to say it out loud; it was just too far-fetched. She lived in the real world, a world of science and logic. This was just too weird, even for her, but Saoirse's grandmother and mother looked at her in a way that made her think there was definitely something amiss. Her mother's look scared her. She was such a practical person; she would never let her grandmother get away with all this if there was nothing to it.

'It will take you some time to figure out,' was all her grandmother could muster. 'Take your time.'

'What the hell? Gran, this must be some kind of joke. I can't believe it might be. . . I might be. . .'

Saoirse sat herself down on the window seat and took a deep breath. Her mother stood up and came to join Saoirse at the window. She stroked her hair gently, rested her chin on the top of her head and whispered softly.

'I really hoped I could spare you this. I really hoped you weren't. . . like them. Oh Saoirse, love, your life would have been so much easier if. . .' She stopped, but her breathing gave her away, she was crying softly. Saoirse turned and looked up into her mother's beautiful face. Her eyes said everything: she looked defeated, but the love was there. 'I'm sorry Saoirse, I shouldn't be upset, today is your sixteenth birthday and, in more ways than one, the beginning of your adult life. I love you no matter what and I'm here for you. I'm just sorry I can't help you more. I just wouldn't know how. I have always found it so hard to grasp this whole thing, let alone believe it. Your grandmother has to help you with this now.' With this she hugged Saoirse tightly and then released her, turning to face her mother-in-law. 'Please do everything you can to help her. I need you to protect her.' She was pleading.

Saoirse's grandmother joined them at the window. She took Saoirse's mother's hand in hers and nodded. The two women looked at each other, no words were spoken but you could see that an understanding was exchanged between them. Her mother turned and kissed Saoirse on the head again.

'Best get a birthday breakfast ready,' she said, trying to muster some enthusiasm. But it was glaringly absent. Saoirse turned and caught her arm as she moved away.

'I love you Mum,' was all she could think of saying. Her mother smiled warmly turned and headed out the door and down the stairs. Saoirse's heart melted, she had unknowingly chosen her grandmother over her mother and her mother had graciously admitted defeat and bowed out with dignity.

What would happen now?

8

The morning had passed in a daze.

Saoirse felt lost, lost at sea, with no one to explain or even hear her out. What the hell was happening to her? She wanted her protected world back. She wanted her boring, normal life. This new, mysterious one, where her dreams were actually reality, was not for her. She lifted the book she had received last year from the shelf and placed it on the desk in front of her. She ran her fingers over the ornate cover and opened it. The smell wafted up and filled her nostrils; mysteries. . . and somewhere the truth. . . lay inside, but where?

Inside the front cover, on a crisp, cream page her grandmother's calligraphy pen had scrawled a message. Saoirse had always read these and then flicked eagerly onto the next page, overly keen to begin the book. Today she paused. What great insight could she find in those words that would calm the chaos in her head?

'A year makes you older and wiser, but always remember that the thoughts and dreams of our childhood are precious and true,' she had signed and dated it too. Her grandmother had always been mysterious, but Saoirse had never paid any heed to it. Today she thought she should. She rose from the desk and pulled out the other four books from the shelf above her. She had a total of five books now. Oh, how she had looked forward to her sixth, but to her dismay, this year had brought no book. She stared at the five books, each one had a beautiful ornate hand-bound leather cover, similar, Saoirse now noticed, to the beautiful wooden box that held her silver comb. On closer inspection she realised that they were practically identical, and Saoirse wondered had they been made by the same person.

None of the books had titles or authors, but each one had its own distinct cover, depicting one of the stories held within it. This first one had a picture of the Giant's Causeway and Fionn standing proud on it. She had loved this book especially, probably because it was the first one. She remembered receiving it so clearly.

After her birthday party, which had comprised of her mum, dad and grandmother helping her to blow out the eleven candles on her lemon drizzle cake, Saoirse's grandmother had snuck them both upstairs and produced the book, wrapped in crisp brown paper with a lemon coloured bow, from her dressing gown. She had stroked the book lovingly as she passed it to Saoirse. She remembered tearing the paper open and gazing in awe at the book. She had never seen a leather-bound book before. She remembered running her hands across it and feeling the smooth skin beneath her fingers, and then instinctively she held to the book to her nose. The aroma that engulfed her nostrils that day had stayed with her always. It was like sweet perfume. It took her to a place of freedom, to the places she read about inside the books and it gave her comfort.

She had never questioned why she got such ease from reading these books, but now she noted that the sense of ease and release she got from the books was mirrored in the feeling the comb brought to her. She looked at the books again and then rose from the chair and went to fetch the comb from her room. It sat on the bedside table, the box open and the comb snugly tucked inside. Picking up the box, she couldn't resist.

She sat on the window seat and gazed out across the harbour. It was late afternoon, but the sun danced on the still water outside. The town was busy, it was Friday afternoon and traffic was chaotic as always on the narrow streets below. Saoirse turned towards the cathedral as the bell chimed four. She combed gently, and smiled. She still couldn't believe she had not ventured inside. Maybe she would someday, Sean was Catholic, maybe there would be a reason in this project for them to visit. Her stomach turned, and an old familiar pang of fear hit her with a smack. Sean, Kate, the whole mess. She combed harder and the ease returned. She loved the feeling it gave her, the emptiness in her head. She could comb and sit without thinking: it was ecstasy. Books, craziness and reality could wait. She moved from the window seat and the busy world outside, to the comfort of her bed, she pulled the pillows up behind her and propped herself up comfortably. She knew sleep was imminent and an afternoon nap seemed so much easier to deal with than the reality of her life.

9

When Saoirse woke she was still propped up on her pillows and the comb was firmly wedged in her right hand. The evening was closing in fast and the harbour and town below were beginning to quieten and the sun cast long shadows across the garden.

She remembered the fox she had seen last night and smiled. It was like it had known her; an understanding glance between old friends. She hadn't questioned that, and thinking about it now it was as absurd as the rest of the mess that occupied her mind. She shook her head and looked down at the spot where she had first seen the fox. She was startled immediately, because there stood Sean waving ridiculously up at her with a crutch, and a grin on his face.

Panic gripped her. What was she going to say to him, why hadn't she been in school? She felt sick to the core. Cold sweat began to bead on her brow.

'Hi, I'm a freak that can foretell death, what you think about that? Oh, and by the way, your girlfriend is going to die soon. I've seen it.' Nausea grew in the pit of her stomach. The house was empty. Perhaps she could just pretend there was no one at home. No, he had seen her at the window, why else would he have been waving?

The back door rattled under his knock. She took a deep breath. She would have to answer it. One step at a time, she told herself, she had to open the door first. She turned from the window and placed the comb back in its box on the bedside table.

'Coming,' she called. He would never hear her from here,

but the knocking stopped and she took her time on the stairs and crossed the kitchen slowly, watching him through the French doors, inspecting the patio. She slowly opened the door and startled him a little.

'Thought you were hiding on me! How are things?'

How could he be so relaxed and cool all of the time? She could never dream of being so calm or collected. She grinned at him, and stood back, inviting him wordlessly into the kitchen. He bounded in past her with ease – crutches were obviously not a hindrance to him – and settled himself on a stool at the breakfast bar.

'It's been a bit of a trek up from town, never realised how steep those steps from the library are, any chance of a drink? I'm parched!'

Saoirse was still standing at open door, awkward and panicked as always in company.

'Of course, what would you like? We have tea, coffee and I think there's some lemonade in the fridge.'

'Oh, very posh! I'll try some of the lemonade please. Can't believe how warm it still is, but hey, I'm not complaining. So you weren't at school today?'

It was a loaded question, Saoirse could tell he was fishing for something, but she couldn't read his intentions. She quickly flipped the question.

'You haven't been in school for quite a while Sean, and you spot me the one day I'm out. What's your excuse? And don't use "oh poor me on crutches".'

Ah, the sarcasm had returned and it was biting, but it made her feel better. He looked a little taken aback at first, then smiled and looked at her intently.

'You're a funny one, Saoirse. I did my cruciate, which meant a bit of a hospital stay and eventually will mean an operation when the swelling goes down. But for now I'm on a bit of rest, and fourth year isn't really the most demanding of school years, so I'm taking it easy. Went in today to see you about our English project – if we are ever to get it done – and lo and behold you weren't there. Typical! But it got me thinking and I remembered something you had said last week. . .'

At this he produced a small package from his coat pocket, wrapped in brown paper with a pink ribbon tied around it. He beamed, as if he'd finally gotten something on her and declared in a large booming voice

'Happy Birthday Sweet Sixteen!'

Saoirse was stunned. She didn't know what to do. She was completely overwhelmed, tears welled up and a very large lump formed in her throat. She had never gotten a gift from anyone other than family before. She was speechless and stood there gaping like a fool. He saw her surprise and smiled. He made his way clumsily around the island towards her. Before she knew it she was enveloped in his arms, his smell intoxicating her. His warmth was disorientating. Her head spun. What was he doing? Why was he holding her? His aftershave was fresh and masculine, light on the nose but it lingered in her head. His arms were strong and they gripped her tightly and the lump in her throat exploded into her stomach and her legs gave way.

The darkness spread through her mind, but once she let go it was pleasant, a gentle falling into peace like a warm embrace and then she felt like she was being carried away. Maybe the ground had opened up and swallowed her and she had escaped the embarrassment of the situation. She felt calm in the darkness, at ease. Could she stay here? Could she never open her eyes and face reality and just exist in this dark peacefulness? A little voice inside her, answered in her gut and she knew she had to open her eyes and face him. She prepared herself for the mortification.

She opened them slowly, but she was no longer in the

kitchen. He had her laid out on the window seat in her room. How had he made the stairs with so much ease with his knee? He saw the shock in her face and answered her unvoiced question.

'You never know your own strength!' and he winked. He helped her to sit up and handed her a glass of water. His face showed his concern and she could see a question brewing.

'Go on, ask me whatever it is. I can tell you want to ask me something.'

'I can understand it might be difficult for you, but. . .'

'Sean, get to the point.'

'I'm sorry, Saoirse. I just wanted to know are you sick? Mam fainted and had dizzy spells a lot before we found out she had cancer and I just wanted to let you know that I was here for you if you wanted to talk.'

Saoirse closed her eyes tightly and took a deep breath. Who was this guy? And how pathetic was she? He had known her all of about two weeks, but in those two weeks she had spoken to him far more than anyone else in her whole entire life. She knew all about his family, his girlfriend and his hopes for the future. He had shown a genuine desire to be her friend, and had gotten her her first ever birthday present and she repaid him with her immature, social ineptness, that she now realised mimicked the symptoms of a cancer patient.

'Saoirse! Breathe!'

He shook her gently. She had taken a deep breath and forgotten to let it go. She opened her eyes again and decided it was time to come clean, at least a little bit. He deserved that.

'I'm not sick Sean, but thank you for the concern. I just can't handle social interaction. It upsets me and makes me uncomfortable. It's not that I don't want to interact – I do, but I just never have. Mum always kept me pretty sheltered growing up and you are a lot of my firsts! I have never had a full blown conversation with anyone at school, except you. I have never told anyone anything about my family, except you. I have never invited anyone into my home, gotten a present from anyone or shown my paintings to anyone but you. I'm finding it very difficult and I don't know why. But I'm so sorry if I gave you the impression I was sick, Sean, that was never my intention.'

The relief was surprising, but not fulfilling, she had told the truth, but not the whole truth, and by the look on his face he knew she was holding something back. There was a connection; she had not been imagining it. She felt this boy sitting in front of her knew what she was thinking, well, in some way knew that she was keeping something from him. It was a compelling desire and it was so powerful she knew that even though what she had to say to him was utterly ridiculous, she had to tell him. She steadied herself on the window seat and readied herself, and just as she was about to speak, he crossed her.

'Tell me, where's the painting of Kate gone?'

'I put it away with the rest of them.' Her answer was short and cold, she wasn't ready to talk about Kate, she'd have to build up to that.

'With the rest of them? How many are there?'

'A few.'

'Can I see them?' His voice had genuine interest, but these were her paintings, they were extremely personal and were full of her anguish, she wasn't ready to share them.

'Maybe some other time,' she tried to make it sound casual, but it was forced, as always.

'Can I please take another look at Kate's at least? I really can't believe just how like her it looks. You have a talent, Saoirse; you shouldn't be ashamed of that.'

She had a talent alright, one that he had no idea of and

one that she was even afraid to admit she had herself, but in an effort to change the subject and to stop him asking her questions, she got up and went into her study. From the large mahogany wardrobe, she pulled out the painting of Kate. As she did so she dislodged several of the other paintings and they came crashing out onto the floor. She quickly shoved them back into the cupboard and was jamming the door closed when she heard his heavy footsteps. She handed him the painting and secured the wardrobe door. She didn't want him to see the others.

He held the painting in front of him and smiled. 'She's gorgeous, isn't she?'

Kate's broken body, the awkward angle of her neck, her empty, open eyes swirled in Saoirse's head. She shook it, trying to dislodge the images, but they remained there, nagging her, pushing her. The nausea developed in the pit of her stomach and worked its way up her throat. Her grandmother's voice echoed from behind the gruesome image, 'Tell him, you have to tell him. It'll be your only release.'

'Sean...' She couldn't do it. How ridiculous would she sound? But the picture boomed in her head now and the smile on Sean's face was haunting.

'What?'

'Sean, there's something I need to tell you about Kate.'

'Ah, so you do know her. I thought you might. No one could have done such a fantastic painting without knowing the person.'

'I don't know her, Sean. I've never met her. That's the thing... I... I dream about her.' She'd said it, or at least part of it. She watched his face intently trying to gauge his reaction. He had a glint in his eye, but the reaction seemed positive.

'I do too!' he said slyly, winking.

'Sean, I just told you I never met your girlfriend and that I dream about her. Don't you find that a little strange?' She'd raised her voice without even realising it and now the look of shock spread across his face.

'Saoirse, I dream about people I don't know all the time. There's no big deal. You probably saw her around somewhere and subconsciously remembered her. It's a great painting.'

This irritated her even more. It was a big deal, her life had been completely changed over the past few weeks over this girl and the dreams she was part of. How dare he dismiss them? Anger grew inside her and burst out of her mouth like an explosion.

'She's going to die. I've dreamt about her death over the past three weeks. She dies in a car crash and soon.'

The words hung there, like letters etched in the air, floating around the room at first and then swarming, around her, around him. They echoed loudly in her head. She watched his face, no reaction. He stared intently at the painting and then looked her straight in the eye with a sternness she had never seen in him before.

'That's not funny, Saoirse. You should never joke about something like that and you certainly didn't strike me as the type of person that likes mean jokes.' He was cross, she could see that and she could also see how much he loved Kate. This was going to be so awful if her dreams were true. 'I think I'll go. Have a nice birthday.'

He placed the painting on the desk and turned to leave,

'Wait, let me explain.'

'I don't know how you could explain that, Saoirse, and to be quite honest I'd rather forget you ever said it. Maybe you need to get out more.' The tone in his voice hurt her deep in her heart. She was disgusted, at herself more than anything, and dejected, she let him go. She returned to the window seat and listened as he crossed the kitchen two storeys down and then opened the French door. She slipped off the window seat and crouched on the floor peering over the cushion as he crossed the garden. She wanted to see if he was still upset, but she didn't want him to see her looking. He crossed the garden quickly, and disappeared down the steps on the far side. She was more upset now than she had been all day. Why was life so complicated? She had actually thought her dreams were true, that she could predict death and she had foolishly shared that with someone. Perhaps her mother was right to have locked her away from people all this time. It was easier and it certainly hurt less. That look had been painful: a feeling she had never felt before. It still rattled around her heart and drained the life from her. She looked at the comb and her bed, and decided they were all the companionship she needed.

10

Her mother woke her shortly after eight, with a gentle shake. She said nothing, but held her. Saoirse gave out a sigh. They must have sat there for ten or fifteen minutes because there came a loud call from her father below that dinner was getting cold and he sounded a little irritated. Her mother held the comb in her hand and looked at her questioningly. Saoirse nodded and her mother began to comb. The relief was instant, it always was. She relaxed and even allowed herself to smile.

'We'd better go down, sweetheart. Dad's made your favourite and he's waiting.' She kissed her tenderly and helped her up from the bed. She did feel better, she felt like there was less weight on her shoulders.

As she entered the brightly lit kitchen it became apparent she had missed out on quite a lot during the day. Chinese lanterns hung from the ceiling and all around the walls were enlarged photos of her blowing out the candles on each of her fifteen birthdays. The table was set for the four of them. In the centre sat a large chocolate birthday cake, decorated with paint brushes, an easel and a canvas, and of course sixteen candles. Her father and grandmother were already seated and her mother ushered her into her father's seat at the top of the table. The joy and excitement in their faces was contagious and the worry and confusion of the day melted in to giggles, retold memories and delicious food.

They must have sat for hours chatting, eating and laughing because before Saoirse knew it the bells from the cathedral were ringing twelve. The night had escaped them, but in such a wonderful and happy manner. Saoirse shivered as the bells rang and her grandmother was quick to wrap a shawl around her shoulders. No-one wanted to get up, it was too enjoyable. There seemed to be an unspoken consensus that another cup of tea was called for so that the night would continue. Her grandmother did the honours of reboiling the kettle for what must have been the tenth time. It had been such a wonderful evening, and thankfully tomorrow was Saturday; Saoirse could stay in bed. She sighed and snuggled into the shawl and the comfortable seat. She wondered if she could freeze time in this moment: the love, the comfort and the surety of her family was intoxicating. Not like the utter confusion and pain of earlier in the day. If only she could, perhaps a birthday wish could come true. . .

Her answer came in a frantic loud banging on the French doors. All four of them jumped at the sound. But both her grandmother and father settled quickly, her grandmother taking her shoulders and her father heading towards the door. Saoirse's face looked panicked: who would be calling at this hour of the night? Her mother's face reflected hers. But her grandmother remained calm. The banging continued and increased and finally Saoirse's dad opened the door. Saoirse couldn't see who was standing in the doorway, as her father kept them shielded from her view. All she knew was that it was a man. His voice was hysterical, high pitched and breathless between sobs. He was trying to force his way into the kitchen, but Saoirse's dad held him by the shoulders.

'Let him in son. He's had an awful fright. He needs us.'

Her grandmother's voice was calm and assertive, and Saoirse watched as her father stepped aside and let Sean enter the kitchen. Saoirse blinked with fright. This didn't look like the Sean that had left her hours ago. Instead a broken, white-faced sobbing boy stood in front of her, barely able to stand, gripping her father's elbow. His crutches were nowhere in sight and he was soaked with sweat. One look in his eyes told Saoirse that her life was forever changed. She saw the pain, the fear, the anger and she saw Kate, the lifeless broken Kate. She stood from the chair and walked towards him, she felt a strength she had not felt before and she felt she knew what to do. She took his arm and guided him to the chair she had been sitting on. She settled him and took the shawl from around her shoulders and wrapped it around his. She turned to the stove to make a cup of tea but her grandmother was already finishing, putting a drop of what looked like whiskey into the tea. She handed the cup to Saoirse and she in turn handed it to Sean.

'Drink this, Sean. It won't make you feel any better but it will warm you up.'

Sean did as he was told and the sobs quietened. He hung his head over the cup and Saoirse and her family gazed at him with astonishment and anticipation. Saoirse looked to her mother and was met with saddened eyes. Her thoughts were etched on her face: the legends were true. There could be no other reason why this boy was in her house in this state, at this hour. She had to accept what her daughter was, and Saoirse saw that her mother had.

Sean was quiet now, too quiet. The hysteria of a few moments ago had left him and he sat dejected, elbows resting on his knees, his head held in his hands. Saoirse rubbed his back and he looked up at her with dark, bloodshot eyes. Saoirse saw the pain, the fear, the anger but also the questioning. He said nothing but held her gaze and she continued to rub his back. She knew they had to wait for him. When he was ready he would break the silence. It wasn't for them to question him in this moment; it was up to him to open up.

'How. . . ?' It surprised them all. It was shaking and low, but they all heard it. He stared at her, searching for answers and when none came he scanned the room and looked at these people he didn't really know. 'How?' this time it was stronger and more demanding, but still they didn't answer him. Sean moved to stand. Perhaps they would answer if he stood and questioned them. But before he could stand, Saoirse had taken his shoulders and forced him to remain seated. He looked her straight in the eyes and pleaded, 'How?'

'I'm not sure what you're asking me, Sean, and I'm not sure I can answer you or give you the answers you're looking for.'

'Saoirse, none of your bullshit shy and cryptic crap tonight please. Kate is dead! You said she would be and now I want to know how!' There was an irritation and anger in his voice that they all felt. Saoirse looked to her grandmother and she nodded gently at her. The truth would have to be told. . . but did Saoirse know the truth? Was she really part of the legends? Could it really be true? One look at Sean's grief stricken face told her it was, and she now had to face her obscure reality and help this boy who had just pushed his way into her life and turned her world upside down.

'I can foretell death,' she said it with a clear, yet unconvincing voice. He looked at her unimpressed, the answer wasn't good enough it seemed. She took a breath. She started again, this time calmer and more assertive. She was admitting this to herself just as much as she was admitting it to him. 'I am a banshee, Sean. I can foretell death. I have no power over it, only that I can warn people and prepare them for its arrival. I know it sounds ridiculous, I am still trying to get my own head around it, but it seems to be true. I am a banshee.'

Now the real relief came. She had told the whole truth and she felt all the better for it. It was as if a weight had been taken from her shoulders, and as she looked around the room she was surprised by the reactions she saw in the faces of the people in her kitchen: her grandmother stood proud and smiling, as if she'd arrived home with an A grade paper; her father had a mixture of worry and pride, he stood tall at the island while her mother had concern and disbelief huddled at the counter. Sean, however, seemed to not have taken anything she said in. He stared at her with a blank expression she could not read. The grief and anger was gone and he looked as if he was somewhere else. The room was silent and Saoirse wasn't sure what she was supposed to do now.

Her grandmother spoke first, 'Sean, I'm going to ring your father, I'm sure he'll be worrying about where you are. Can I have the number please?'

Sean took his mobile out of his coat pocket, searched for the number and then handed it to Saoirse's grandmother. 'It's ringing.' His voice was barely audible and he dropped his head to his hands again. Her grandmother took the phone to the hall and Saoirse could hear her grandmother talking to Conor on the phone. It seemed he was on his way and would be there soon.

Saoirse bent to kneel in front of Sean and touched his hand lightly. He looked at her, with confusion in his eyes. She touched his face and looked deep into those eyes. She had never had so much physical contact with a male in her entire life; bumping into boys in the corridors in school was uncomfortable and awkward, but this felt right. Surely it shouldn't; she was comforting a friend who had just lost his girlfriend and she was enjoying the intimacy it entailed. She shook her head and looked away. Guilt wracked her mind.

'Saoirse why you? Why me? Why did you dream about my girlfriend? Was it because we got put together in English class?' His voice was weak and broken, pleading. He took her hand and looked her in the eye. She had no answer for him; she had no answer for herself. She had no idea why she dreamt about Kate, no idea why she dreamt about any of the people from her dreams. The only answer she had was that she dreamt about them because they were going to die.

'Sean, I'm sorry, I have no idea. Kate is the first person from my dreams that I know actually exists. Until I met you I had assumed the people from my dreams were figments of my imagination. I didn't even know what I was until today, tonight even, when you called and brought the news of Kate's death. I'm sorry I don't have a better answer for you, but that's all I know.'

'There are more? How many more?'

Saoirse didn't get time to answer. Sean's dad appeared in the hallway behind Saoirse's grandmother. He entered the kitchen with authority; he was a tall, strong man and oozed confidence. She saw where Sean got his charm and his looks. He greeted Saoirse's parents and then took Sean by his shoulders. He hugged him tightly and comforted him. Sean broke down in his arms and wept like a baby. His father nodded at Saoirse's dad and the pair of them practically carried Sean to the front door.

Saoirse's grandmother took her by the hand and sat her at the kitchen table next to her mother, then went into the hall after the others. Saoirse turned to her mother, who looked shell-shocked. 'There's nothing more we can do tonight, honey. Perhaps we should go to bed.' She leant forward and hugged her daughter.

'But Mam, did that just really happen?'

'It did.'

She held her close and sighed heavily. Saoirse wasn't sure what to do, but the thought of her bed and more importantly her comb allowed her to agree with her mother and she headed towards the door. She could ponder all of this with the comb and her bed upstairs.

11

Saoirse had spent the weekend confined to the house. She felt claustrophobic, fenced in by a fear of the unknown that lay ahead of her and the reality that lay outside her front door. Friday night had been dream-like when she woke late Saturday morning, but the morning papers and the neighbours had confirmed it had been very real. Kate's death had made the front pages of the all local newspapers: everyone was talking about it. She had tried to contact Sean, but to no avail. He didn't answer texts and his father said he had spent the weekend with Kate's parents helping with funeral arrangements. He said he would pass on the message, but she heard nothing. So, in frustration and confusion, she had locked herself in her study and stared blankly at the books in front of her. But she found no answers in them.

Monday arrived eventually and her mother had found the mercy to leave her stay at home. She couldn't face school. She still had things to come to terms with and couldn't deal with people's grief: she felt intrinsically linked to Kate's death. She positioned herself on her window seat with a large mug of coffee after everyone had left the house and was set for an hour of mindless gazing at the harbour, when she spotted the crowd. They were in their hundreds, piling orderly into the gaping, dark hole at the entrance of the cathedral. Saoirse found it strange that she had not thought of Kate's funeral and that it would be so close to her home. Never once over the entire weekend had she thought of the burial, that this was what Sean was helping to organise.

She was ashamed. She had spent the weekend thinking of herself and her role in this, she hadn't thought of all the other people involved. She was so self-centred, how could she be so selfish and heartless? She hung her head and stared at her cooling coffee.

When she looked up again, she caught a glimpse of students from the local schools, dressed in uniforms forming a guard of honour at the cathedral gates. A group of camogie players, in their playing gear, guided a black hearse through the gates and stopped with it in front of the entrance. From the window where she sat it was like a silent movie. Saoirse could see the sobbing, see the grief, see Kate's friends who had to be helped inside. All her life she had lived in this house and this was the first time she had seen a funeral so big, so sad and so moving. She was drawn to it. She saw the funeral director signing orders and then she saw Sean appear from the black Merc behind the hearse. He wore a dark suit and tie and he looked tired, older and somehow different. Her heart broke. She could see his pain, and placed her hand on the window so it touched his head.

Almost as if he felt it he looked towards the house. She saw the pain, the grief but she also saw that he had felt something, he looked at the house searching the windows for her and when he saw her, she was startled by his expression. There was a pleading, a cry for help. She held his gaze trying to let him know she was there for him, hoping he would know that. He smiled ever so slightly, but then the connection was broken and the funeral director ushered him towards the coffin. He joined a group of five others and they slowly lifted the coffin and linked arms across their shoulders. Within seconds they disappeared into the dark and the crowd piled in behind them.

Saoirse sat staring at the empty space outside the cathedral. Thoughts whirled through her mind and she was full of questions. She had never been to a funeral; she had never had to deal with death. Her grandfather had died before she was born and her mother's parents had died before she was married. She had never really understood death, but then she never had had to deal with it, so why would she? She had never been inside the cathedral, but because they were not Catholic she had no reason to be. In fact they had no faith of any kind in their lives and now she began to question what she had been missing, if she was missing anything at all?

She had just watched hundreds pile into the church. Perhaps this very public display of grief helped them in some way. She made up her mind. She dressed quickly, barely checking her appearance, and hurried down the stairs. She pulled the large front door closed and took one last look at the cathedral from this safe distance. She took a deep breath and started to walk; she knew she had to do this.

Before she knew it she was standing at the intimidating oak doors. The sound of the choir drifted out and mingled with the whispers of the locals gathered at the back of the church. Saoirse wasn't sure what to do next. Should she make her way inside or remain perched on a step at the back with the gossiping ladies? Initially she thought it best to remain outside, these women had stayed there for a reason, perhaps there was no room inside. She couldn't tell how many people the cathedral could hold, but she had seen the crowds and presumed it was full. But the whispering soon irritated her, 'Drunk driving. . . massive fight. . . disgrace. . .' It was all too much for Saoirse and her anger drove her to find refuge inside.

She pushed past people standing on tip-toe trying to get a look and found her way to an empty space in a long wooden pew next to an elderly white haired man. She smiled briefly at him and he motioned for her to sit down. She squeezed her narrow frame into the tiny space available and sighed heavily. The old man reached out and gently tapped her knee, then went back to the rosary beads in his hands.

She looked around her. Never before had she seen anything like it. She had seen churches in art books and on TV but nothing could compare to the space and height she was now experiencing. The ceiling rose above her, carved and moulded with figures of saints and scholars, flowers and crosses. The plaster was met at its end with dark wood, equally as beautiful and crafted. The contrast was crisp and this dark and light was mirrored throughout the great space. Here and there were hints of gold, red and green but that was it. The colour was simple, but breathtaking. Simple, that is, until a change in sunlight outside illuminated the stained glass window high above her. Colour erupted through the congregation and a red dusty sunbeam caught the photo of Kate placed on the coffin at the front of the church. She was glowing in a red hue and her beauty was even more apparent; the loss was too much for some people in that moment. Wails and sobs erupted from the congregation. The whole effect was surreal, and Saoirse found it hard to believe that this was reality and not one of her vivid dreams.

From where she was sitting Saoirse could not really make out the front of the church. She could see the coffin in the centre aisle: it stood alone, a tall burning candle at its feet, draped in a Cork flag and bearing Kate's beautiful face on top. But other than that all she could see from here was the back of countless heads. She searched to see if she could see Sean's, but she could not. She started to feel uncomfortable and claustrophobic. So many people. Such a heavy, emotional atmosphere. A high pitched voice soared above the bowed heads. A red-haired young woman was standing at the pulpit now. The sound was emanating from her. It was out of this world. The soprano was pale, red-haired and similar in build to herself, but Saoirse could never dream of sounding like this. The lyrics were emotionally charged, but the sound was mesmerising, soothing and angelic. Saoirse relaxed back in the seat and looked up.

Around the entire building stained glass windows depicted the stories of the Bible. Saoirse had no idea who they were, but the figures and the pictures reminded her of the covers of the books in her study: great craftsmanship, attention to detail and beauty. Saoirse followed them from one side to the other and created the story for herself as best she could from the images. Her head tilted right back to view them clearly; she forgot where she was and why she was here. The old man next to her brushed her arm lightly and brought her back.

'They're beautiful, aren't they?' he whispered.

Saoirse just nodded. She wasn't quite sure whether it was appropriate to be having a chat, but the old man's demeanour was friendly and she was glad of the distraction.

'Would I be right in thinking it's your first time here?'

Again Saoirse nodded.

'Did you know Kate?'

How did she answer that? She didn't know Kate... she had never met Kate... so how did she explain why she was here? She didn't want to appear like a gossip, here to gape at the spectacle, but it wasn't like she could actually tell him the truth. *'Oh I predicted her death; I've been dreaming it for weeks.'* The easiest thing was to be as honest as she could be while still appearing sane.

'I'm a friend of Sean's. I'm here to support him.' It was the truth, or at least she hoped it was. She was his friend, she felt like they were going to be friends, but the events of the past few days might have changed that.

'Saoirse? You're Beibhinn O'Donnell's granddaughter? I'm Sean's grandfather. Myself and your grandmother go way back. No wonder you've never been here before!'

Saoirse was taken aback and a little unsettled by the knowledge the old man seemed to have of her.

'Very brave of you to venture in here on your own, your first time. Do you know your grandmother and mother are over there in the women's aisle?'

He was so laid back and casual, very much like his grandson. Even in this place, at this funeral, in the absurdity of it all, they were cool and calm. It was unsettling and comforting all at once. What was it about these Fitzgeralds?

She managed a weak, 'No,' and lowered her head slightly. She didn't really want them to know she was here. This was her decision and she still hadn't figured out why exactly she had come; she didn't need the inquisition when she got home. The old man squeezed her knee and smiled.

'I won't say a word, but mind you keep the head down. We're almost done here now and the congregation will be filing out in about five minutes. The coffin goes first. If you stay here, they shouldn't see you. Although neither will Sean and I'm sure he'd love to know you were here for him.'

Sean. She was here for him. He was the only reason she was here. Guilt consumed her, this was supposed to be about Kate, a beautiful young girl lost far too soon, and although for the past few weeks she had felt so attached and close to her, even living out her last few moments with her, she felt no true sorrow. She didn't really know her: she was a figure from a dream to her. Sean, on the other hand, was real. He had been the first person to hold her, she remembered his sweet smell, his strength and she flinched. How could she be wrapped up in herself and Sean when his heart was breaking? She took a deep breath and settled herself. She was here to support her friend, Sean. God knows he looked like he could do with all the support he could get when she saw him outside the church earlier.

Sean's grandfather touched her arm lightly again and

brought her back from her thoughts. 'They'll be leaving now. Are you going to go to the graveyard?'

Saoirse shook her head. This had been enough for one day. She felt like she would be a fraud to go and watch the coffin lowered into the ground. She'd had enough new experiences for one day. She had been here. She had paid her respects, if that's what you could call this. The old man squeezed her arm reassuringly and started to move towards the centre aisle.

'Perhaps that's best.'

At the front of the church there was a rumbling of movement, people standing, people sobbing and the funeral director whispering instructions to the people around him. The priest, whom Saoirse had not seen before, appeared from behind the altar in a black suit with a dark jacket and Bible in hand. Saoirse saw Sean rise from the pew at the front and join the five others from before. Slowly and solemnly they hoisted the coffin onto their shoulders, and carried Kate out of the church. He looked towards her as he passed, almost instinctively knowing she was there. Saoirse nodded. He lowered his head and continued walking.

Kate's mum and dad followed immediately behind the coffin, their faces said it all: they were devastated. Saoirse's eyes welled and she felt the pain. She gulped down the lump in her throat and tried to stay composed. It was not the place for her to cry. Behind them friends and family sobbed and huddled together as they filed out. Before she knew it Saoirse was left alone in the vast expanse of the empty church. She took a breath and relaxed into the wooden pew. Life had been awkward and uncomfortable at times at the beginning of September, but she would happily go back to that now if she could. Now things were a whole new level of crazy. She was some kind of mythical creature, she was a banshee that could predict death, and now that she had finally met someone she could open up to and perhaps even had a friendship with, she had blown his world apart by predicting the death of his girlfriend. Why was life so complicated? Being a teenager was hard enough. She closed her eyes and longed to be curled up on her window seat with the comfort of her comb.

12

A strong hand touched her on the shoulder, startling her. She automatically jumped to her feet. There was a man behind her.

When she turned she saw that it was the priest from the mass earlier. 'Are you okay? You've been here quite a while and I wasn't sure whether to disturb you or not?'

He was a young enough man, greying slightly around the temples, but fresh in his face. He wore the dark suit from earlier, but he had removed the white collar from around his neck and opened the top two buttons of his shirt. Saoirse was surprised at his youth; she had always pictured priests as old men with narrow minds who ruled with the iron fist of the Bible. But this man seemed different: there was an ease and openness about him. And his smile was warm and welcoming.

'Oh, I'm sorry,' she said. 'I hadn't realised I was here so long. Time got away from me.'

'That happens sometimes when we're under pressure or have a lot on our minds. Is there anything you'd like to talk about? It's not confession or anything, but sometimes a problem shared is a problem halved, as they say.'

His manner was easy and comfortable, his smile genuine and there was nothing forced about his question. Saoirse thought about it. But how could she share her problem, even half it? How could she tell a man of God that she could foretell death? That as far as she could make out she was a being from folklore, that she was an immortal creature heralding the deaths of innocent people. She was certain that if she told the truth the man was sure to think she was disturbed and would most definitely insist on her getting help of some sort. If she was honest, she questioned whether she needed help herself: surely she was mad. But she felt she couldn't lie to him. She lowered her head and took a deep breath and when she looked back up at the priest, he motioned for her to sit, which she did.

'Is it that bad, that even talking about it won't help?' His voice was caring and crisp, one used to articulating important messages to large crowds, but humble enough to be inviting and warm.

'I'm not Catholic.' It was all she could think of to say in reply. She didn't want to lie.

'I know you're not. I'm guessing it's your first visit to us, too. There's nothing to be worried about. We don't judge, contrary to the perception you might have. But it's understandable. We don't come across as the most welcoming. And we certainly aren't very popular at the moment.' He shrugged as he said this and Saoirse recalled the countless newspaper articles and reports on the Diocese. They certainly didn't have a good reputation at the moment, but Saoirse had always found it strange that people attacked the current priests for the sins of those before them. Surely they should be judged on their own behaviour.

'Can I ask how you know I'm not Catholic? Do we stand out or something?'

She was intrigued that he could tell her religion without her telling him: did he have some kind of religious radar that told him who was part of the flock and who was not?

'I know your Grandmother. She comes to visit now and again.' He said it with such affection that it was obvious she visited more than just now and then. Saoirse found it strange that her grandmother would have a relationship with a priest. Religion had been so obviously absent from her home life that she had assumed none of her family would have had any connection with it and she also assumed that priests had no lives outside of the church and the orders they had taken. But now that she thought about it they were people too, they had friends and families, they had a life.

'Oh, I didn't know she visited. I didn't think any of my family did. We have a distinct lack of religion at home and I just presumed. . .'

'I am a man of God, Saoirse, but I'm also a man. Your grandmother comes to talk to me, not necessarily the priest. Sometimes she has things she feels she needs to discuss that she just can't talk about anywhere else. And as I said before I don't judge, nor do I question. I listen. And over the years I've grown very fond of her. She is an amazing woman, strong-minded and strong-willed, but very open and accepting.'

Saoirse wondered how much her grandmother had told this man. Surely she couldn't have told him the whole truth. If she had, she was sure they wouldn't be having this talk so casually, and her grandmother would not have been a repeat visitor. But then again maybe she had, and he had taken pity on her. Maybe he thought she was a raving lunatic and had taken her under his wing, protecting a poor, crazy, elderly lady. Maybe she had been honest and he had believed her. Perhaps he was more open-minded than his counterparts, and had accepted that if God can exist then surely so could banshees.

She was finding this whole new identity thing quite difficult to get her mind around. Actually, that was an understatement. How can you accept the fact that you are what you read about in books as a child, that you are the person kids tell ghost stories about at sleepovers and then spend half the night awake in fear? How do you accept that your dreams are Death's calling cards, a little heads up for who has a visit to the mortuary in their not-so-distant future? And, even if you do accept that, how do you explain to others what it is you are? A priest was probably the last person she should be talking to, but he seemed as good as anyone at that moment in time. She felt alone, Sean had his own worries and her grandmother was too optimistic and cryptic for her liking. Maybe she had been right, Saoirse needed to work this out for herself. But she couldn't and she knew she needed someone. Maybe this priest was the answer.

'Saoirse, you've gone very quiet. Would you like me to leave you in peace?'

'No. . . please stay. It's just that, it's just that. . .' How could she put it into words, where should she start?

'I'm feeling very selfish today. I didn't know Kate. I know Sean, but just since the start of September really. We got thrown together for an English assignment. I've never really been a talker, to be honest I pretty much keep to myself. But Sean is lovely. He's brought me out of myself over the past few weeks. And then he called to my house and saw the picture I painted of Kate. I hadn't even realised that she was a real person, and since then everything has changed. My life has changed. Things will never be the same again.' She took a breath and sighed heavily. She was rambling and she knew it, but she was talking and she needed to talk. 'There I go again, all about me. I keep forgetting that a girl died, her life is over, her parents' lives have been torn apart and I'm worrying about myself. I'm ashamed of myself. I'm sorry.'

The priest was still sitting in the pew behind her and she had herself angled in the seat so her back wasn't turned to him but she wasn't facing him straight on. He lent forward and gently squeezed her shoulder. There was sincerity in his actions and, although she had already said more than she had intended to, she continued. She felt she could without being ridiculed or judged. She felt his sincerity and it gave her hope.

'I feel like I don't know who I am. I thought I was a nice, caring, normal person, but my dreams are so vivid and horrifying. Surely if I was the person I thought I was, I would try and stop what happens in them. Surely I should be devastated by Kate's death. I am sad, of course I am, but I knew she was going to die and I did nothing. What kind of monster does that make me?'

She looked at him pleading, longing for an answer, and then realised what she had just said. She had admitted she knew Kate was going to die. She searched the priest's face for shock, but found none, just that same sincerity that was in his voice, his touch.

'You must think I'm mad.'

'I know what you are Saoirse. Your grandmother has always been honest with me. I was the only one she could be honest with. My vows mean I cannot tell another living soul what she tells me. My religion also means that I am protected, even though I know the truth. She told me she had been searching for someone like me for years and had all but given up when, by chance, she met me in this very spot actually, after Sean's mother's funeral. She said it was relief at last to speak to someone, without putting herself or them in danger. She has battled with the same emotions you are battling now, for a lifetime. She says that she has always wondered whether she made the right decision moving here, away from her home place and who she was. But she says your father and you were worth every minute of hardship. You are her life, Saoirse, she adores you. She never wanted to draw this on you and was hoping you took after your mother; but then you started painting. She spent a long time here with me trying to decide how to handle this, what to tell you. But she's bound; she can only tell you so much without endangering you or her. I can probably tell you more, but she's been very clear on what I can and cannot tell you. You need to figure most of it out for yourself, its important you do that.'

Saoirse sat in disbelief. Here was a priest explaining her messed up world to her. Surely his religion should mean that he would dismiss this as lunacy. She was a lost sheep in need of psychiatric help and the firm hand of God. But he seemed genuine and he read her confusion and answered her unasked questions.

'I do truly believe in God, but in doing that, Saoirse, I have to accept that if He exists so must other things that we assume do not. I must allow everyone to find their own path, have their own mind. It is not my place to say what is real and what is not. I accept what I see and experience, and your grandmother has a gift, if you could call it that. She has never been wrong. I have been able to subtly prepare families for death because of her; she has helped to make life that little bit more bearable in horrific times for them. I know you think it's awful that you cannot help these people, but from my point of view when the Lord decides it's your time, then the decision is made. No one, no matter how powerful, can change that. Your grandmother and I have found a way of helping, in the small way we can. Although, with Kate, there was nothing either of us could say or do. No one expects that kind of death.'

Saoirse was overwhelmed. Reality was becoming clearer and it sat heavily on her shoulders. This man, a man of faith and integrity, was clarifying her confusion, fixing her reality and she wasn't sure she wanted to hear it. She wanted her window seat and the calmness her comb gave her. She still had so many questions, but it was beginning to look like the main one was answered: she was a banshee. Where she went from here was the next question. Then suddenly she remembered something the priest had just said.

'You said she didn't want to endanger us, and that you were protected. From what?'

He shifted uncomfortably in the chair, but answered her with the same clear voice.

'I'm not entirely sure, Saoirse. Your grandmother was very vague about that part of her life story. All I know is that your grandmother, and now you, are the only 'mortals' of your kind. She said she fell in love with your grandfather and that was not allowed. They had sought help to be together: that meant the secrecy and the move to Cobh. She said they paid a very high price to be together and that the price had not been completely paid. There were conditions, and her silence was core to them. She said if anyone ever found out about her that he would come to cash in on those conditions. She has never told me who he is. She said that whilst my faith may protect me to some extent, he was more powerful than anything she knew and she feared: even the Lord could not protect me from him.'

'So it gets worse? I feel as if I'm in the middle of some teenage horror movie and the boogie man could be on my tracks. Father, do you really believe all this?'

'Michael, you can call me Michael, Saoirse. I do. Your grandmother, as I said, is a wonderful woman. I do believe what she says and I know not to question her. If she tells me it's for my own protection, then it is. I won't go against her. I know it's been a tough few weeks and I'm not sure it's going to get any easier any time soon, but your grandmother has found her peace with this, I'm sure you will too. And I'm here if ever you need a listening ear.'

'I told Sean, you know. About Kate and what I think I am. What do you think he thinks of me?'

'Sean will get it; you just need to give him time. And

speaking of time, the next mass begins in ten minutes Saoirse, so I'll have to leave you. You can stay if you wish. If not, I'm always here. I live in number two, around the back. Come and talk. As I said I won't judge, I'll just listen.'

He stood to leave and as he did so he leant forward and squeezed her shoulder again.

'Talk to your grandmother, Saoirse, she needs to know you're okay with this. It was a pleasure to finally meet you. Don't be a stranger.'

And he was gone, disappearing through a door at the front of the church into the sacristy. Her life was getting more and more complicated, and at the same time things were becoming clearer and clearer. She had to sit down and make sense of all this. Her window seat called, she stood to leave and her legs were stiff, she had been sitting for far too long and when she exited the cathedral dusk was falling on the Crescent in front of her and No. 4. She shivered, the Indian summer was finally over, autumn and winter were on their way.

13

She took her time walking home. She knew she had lots to think about and work through, but she had spent days shut up in the house and hours in the church, she needed some fresh air. She decided to take the long route home through the town. She crossed the road and headed down the steep hill to the waterfront. The weather was cooler, and she pulled her cardigan tight around her. The light was fading fast, but Saoirse loved this in-between time. She made her way onto the main pier and stood at a railing facing Haulbowline Island. The sea air was crisp and calming, the lights of the naval base on the island were just coming on and the final launch, delivering men and women home, was just leaving the pier on the little island in front of her. She closed her eyes and took a deep breath. She loved the smell, the sounds, the breezes, and the ever-changing landscape of living so close to the sea. She could never move inland, she'd be lost.

She kept her eyes closed and listened. Letting her mind go blank, she soaked in the sounds of the harbour. A trawler was docking at the pier, the fishermen's voices sounded tired and disgruntled. Further out the smooth movement of a container ship easing through the channel, a sound she loved to hear in the dead of the night, its large awkward appearance at a complete contrast to the grace and fluidity of its movements. The pier faced the Titanic Museum and below it the restaurant was unusually busy for a Monday, she could hear voices, boisterous and laughing on the decking. Words floated here and there on the breeze and even from so close a distance she only caught a few. Saoirse loved to people watch, boat watch, anything watch and concoct stories to go with what she heard or saw. It would be a welcome distraction now.

She opened her eyes and looked across to the restaurant parallel to her, ready to create their story. The voices were suddenly swept away by the breeze, but when she saw the faces she gasped slightly. Sean stood with his father on the deck surrounded by what must be his rugby team. Large, over-trained young men, but all neatly dressed in black pants and white shirts. Sean had removed the tie he was wearing earlier and although he still looked tired and worn, he looked more relaxed and was laughing. Saoirse knew they were probably remembering funny stories about Kate, laughing and joking about her, the adults drinking themselves silly, but all in memory of the lost soul. It was a typical Irish wake.

Suddenly she became very aware of the fact that he might see her standing there, gazing at them. She wanted to talk to him, but now was not the time. She hurried in from the pier head and walked quickly across the square and up the steps by the side of the library. She couldn't remember the last time she had come this way, and marvelled at the beauty of the library building itself and also at her home. She stopped at the top of the steps and looked up at the Crescent encompassing her. It really was magnificent. She could see why Sean was so eager to have a look inside. She made a mental note to ask why Cobh and why this house, to add to the mountain of things she had to ask her grandmother about.

She took a deep breath and crossed the communal garden and then pushed the gate into her garden. Her mother and father were sitting at the breakfast bar drinking coffee, both looked worried. She was in trouble, she knew it. She pushed the French doors open and stepped into the muted light of the kitchen. Her mother turned immediately and Saoirse saw the look of relief in her eyes for an instant, and then came the anger.

'Where the hell have you been, Saoirse? I've been worried sick all day. You do realise no one has seen you since this morning? God I wish you'd take your phone. You'll be the death of me.'

Saoirse felt guilty. She hadn't thought that they would be looking for her, she hadn't really even thought about them at all. She had been too wrapped up in her own problems. She really didn't like this new Saoirse, so selfish and self-centred; she had never been so thoughtless. She dropped her head and her shoulders and in the lowest of voices she apologised.

'I'm so sorry Mum, I got carried away. I really didn't mean to upset or worry you. It's just I've had so much to get my head around and then there was the funeral. . .'

At this Saoirse's dad raised an eyebrow and her mother mirrored his reaction. Saoirse was surprised, where did they think she had been? She didn't have any friends and there wasn't far she could go without her phone or wallet, both she remembered now were sitting on her desk in her room. Where else could she have gone?

'Where did you think I was?' She was genuinely eager to know what they thought she had been up to for the past seven or eight hours.

'I really didn't have a clue, honey.' There was relief in her father's voice. 'I'm just glad you're back. Now all we have to worry about is your grandmother.'

Saoirse was confused, she had assumed the worry and stress that could be felt in the kitchen when she walked in was all about her, but now it seemed her grandmother was also on the missing list. Where had she disappeared to?

'Mum, I saw you with her leaving the church. Where did she go then?'

'She went to the graveyard with me, but said she was finding it all a little too much and went to sit at your grandfather's grave. That's where I saw her last, but that was at half two and she isn't answering her mobile phone either. Your father was just about to go out looking for you both when you came in. I'll be grey before I know it over the two of you, you know. Ye have me worried sick.' She sighed heavily and placed her head in her hands, resting her elbows on the breakfast bar. Saoirse's father went and stood behind her and wrapped his arms around her shoulders, kissing the top of her head lightly.

'Well, we have one back now; let me worry about my mother. I'll take the car and check to see if she's still at the graveside.'

Just as he picked the keys up off the kitchen counter the front door clicked and they could hear Saoirse's grandmother in the corridor removing her coat and hanging it in the closet. Her steps were slow, but sure, and she was fixing her hair when she entered the kitchen. Her cheeks were flushed from the cold, but Saoirse saw the tell-tale signs of tears that lingered on her face. Saoirse's grandmother looked up in surprise to see them all standing there looking at her and she dropped her head in embarrassment.

'I hope you're not all waiting around for me,' she half giggled.

Saoirse saw the look of anger in her mother's eyes and saw her father squeeze her arm lovingly, as if to say 'let it pass', which she did with another heavy sigh. Her grandmother moved across the kitchen and took the kettle from the stove. She filled it at the sink and returned it to the hot plate and came to join them at the island. Saoirse realised she was still standing at the spot she had been when she first came in and suddenly felt very tired. She pulled herself into the chair facing her mother and her grandmother sat up next to her. Two bold school girls here to make amends to the principal.

'I'm terribly sorry, love, I had a lot on my mind and I always find sitting and chatting with Ruairi is so therapeutic. I miss him so much, even after all these years, but always feel so close to him when I'm there. Although I reckon he only plants himself there when he knows I'm coming. I reckon he spends the rest of his time at home, roaming the cliffs and gazing at the sea like he did when we were young. That's beside the point, I'm sure I had you worried, disappearing for so long at my age and not answering my phone. But I had a lot to think about and I just wanted to be on my own.'

She sounded genuinely sorry and Saoirse's mother warmed to her apology. She visibly sat straighter and the slightest of smiles turned the corner of her lips. She looked at Saoirse and winked, she was okay and they were forgiven. The kettle boiled in the background and her father silently made a large pot of tea. He placed it in the centre of them and then brought over four large slices of carrot cake and some napkins. Saoirse looked at her grandmother and back at the cake. She was starving, they both were. Before he had the plate on the table, both had taken a slice and begun to devour it. He poured tea for them all and Saoirse relished the togetherness of her family. They all sat around the island and sipped tea and ate cake. It reminded her of Friday evening, before all this mess had really taken off. For now she was enjoying their comfortable silence, she knew it had to be broken shortly with questions, but it was bliss.

'So which of you ladies would like to explain to me first what exactly went on today?' Saoirse hadn't expected her dad to be the one to break the silence, but he was and while his tone was calm, there was an authority in it that meant he expected answers. Saoirse felt brave, warmed by the tea and full of cake. She raised her hand like a good student, a mocking gesture that did not go unnoticed by her father. He grinned and with his teacher's voice told her to proceed.

'I wasn't going to go anywhere. But when I saw all those people filing into the church I felt this compulsion to join them, don't ask me why. I've never been inside the church before, you know. I didn't really know what to expect. I wasn't going to go inside, but I ended up sitting next to Sean's grandfather.' At this her grandmother raised an eyebrow, but said nothing.

'The church was magnificent. I never even knew it was so beautiful and when the crowds left I found it was nice to sit in the peace and quiet. I must have fallen asleep or something, because it was only when Michael came along that I realised what time it was. I was away in another world.'

Her mother reacted this time.

'Who's Michael, Saoirse?'

'He is the priest that said Kate's mass. He found me at the back of the church after he had returned from the graveyard and was worried about me. He knows Gran quite well, perhaps even better than us.' At this she winked at her grandmother, who smiled back a little sheepishly. 'He left me with a lot of questions, Gran. Can you please help to answer some of them?'

Her father was surprised by this and looked at his mother with questioning eyes. It was clear he knew what they were, but there was intrigue in his eyes. Was there more to know?

'Mother, is it true? Do you know this priest?'

'I do. He's a very good friend to me, he gives me great counsel, especially when there is no one else I can turn to.'

Saoirse's father looked wounded by this: he was a good son, always there for his mother and here she was admitting to finding comfort and advice from a priest. She saw the hurt in his eyes and tried to rectify the situation.

'I turn to him because I could endanger all of you if I spoke to you. I'm sure he's explained what I asked him to, Saoirse, and made it clear that I am bound to what I can and cannot say. You know that what we are is not 'normal'. Very few of our kind still exist... and you and I, Saoirse, are even rarer. There are only two mortal banshees in existence: you and I. I was once a true banshee, but my love for your grandfather made me change that. It wasn't an easy decision to change, nor was it an easy process. We knew we had to make the sacrifices, but we did it to be together. At the time it seemed the right thing to do: we were young and in love. Ruairi was so strong and brave; he thought we could conquer everything. If he was here today I'm sure he would be saying the same thing now. But all I can say, Saoirse, is that it's very important that you are careful who you speak to about what we are. We can't have the world knowing we exist, because He might hear and come to take His revenge. It's complicated. He is a very powerful being and even discussing the conditions of our agreement with you might trigger His arrival. All I can really say is you don't want to meet Him, so please be careful who you open up to.'

Saoirse, her mother and her father stared open-mouthed in disbelief at her grandmother, who, in Saoirse's eyes, seemed to be aging by the second. Her body was visibly more stooped and fragile-looking than she had ever noticed before. Worry and stress were obvious both on her face and in her voice. Saoirse couldn't quite get her head around what her grandmother was saying. As if life had not become as complicated enough, she was now adding the threat of some supernatural being who would be listening out for her and eager to come and claim some kind of forfeit. Saoirse didn't know whether to laugh or cry. This was getting far beyond ridiculous and she needed to get out of here. She could see the confusion and weariness in both her mother and father's faces and really couldn't handle that on top of everything else at the moment.

'I don't mean to be rude, but I really think I need to go to bed. This is all getting too much for me and I need some space and time to think.'

She left them all around the island and headed up the stairs.

14

Saoirse didn't feel like watching the harbour tonight. Instead she lay on the bed, the silver comb running smoothly through her wild hair. Her grandmother appeared at the door and held up the cups, almost like a peace offering. Saoirse beckoned her in and pulled up her legs to make room for her grandmother at her feet. She placed the comb on her lap and took the warm mug gratefully in her hands. She loved her grandmother's hot chocolate. They sat in silence for some time, sipping from their drinks, a heavy air of tension between them. Saoirse finally broke the silence.

'I have so many questions, but I really don't know where to start.'

'Start anywhere, chicken, but I won't be able to answer them all. I only wish I could.'

Saoirse sighed, the cryptic grandmother had returned. Why couldn't she just answer her questions? She shook the annoyance out of her head and decided to ask the questions she had and see what answers she could get. At least it would be better than nothing. . . that is if she could answer any of them at all.

'Gran, I'll start simple. Why do I get such relief from combing my hair? It was always such a chore and now it feels so calming. I just don't get it.'

Her grandmother smiled, this was a question she could answer. 'As I said earlier, you and I are the only mortal banshees that exist. But that doesn't mean that banshees don't have souls or feelings. The gift we have is not one most people would want. Knowing that death is coming and that you can do nothing about it is a very traumatic and troubling thing. Banshees are recorded in history as wild and crazy creatures, bringing terror to people's lives. But no wonder they did. Half of them were crazy from the torment our gift brought them. Then a wonderful fairy called Aed invented the comb. He was a silversmith and made many beautiful things. And although the comb is very much a thing of beauty, it has a specific purpose: to calm the user. We are not the evil creatures we have been pictured as. The fairies knew that and took pity on us, the comb has been a sanity-saver for us and over the course of history it too has taken its place in the myths and legends. In later stories we are shown combing our hair in the week or so leading up to a death, far more serene than the wailing, terrifying banshees of earlier stories. Our most stressful time required us to be calmer: we had a job to do. Heralding death and accepting you can do nothing about it is very difficult, but with the comb we were able to be that.

'So your comb is a replica of the comb originally created by Aed. It is my comb, Saoirse. Most banshees are given one by their kin, but we no longer have any. That is my fault. But I no longer need mine; I have found my peace with who we are and seem to have fewer and fewer dreams of late. So, there we are, at least I could answer one of your questions. Hit me with another.'

Saoirse saw the delight in her grandmother's eyes: she was helping, she was answering, well, at least for now. Saoirse thumbed the ornate ridge of the comb in her lap. It was beautiful and Saoirse had known from the minute her grandmother had given it to her that it was of great sentimental value. She treasured it already, like she did the books. She knew her grandmother would not be here forever and this made these beautiful things all the more precious.

'How old is it, Gran?' It was immaculate. No dents or

tarnishing, but still Saoirse was instinctively aware that what she held in her hand was beyond old.

'Oh, if only I could tell you.' Saoirse's face fell, but her grandmother quickly continued. 'It's not that I know and I cannot tell you, chicken, it's that I don't know. My concept of age and time is greatly different to yours. Remember I was not always mortal. I existed for a long time before I met your grandfather. Since then our time was in some ways more like yours... until I had your father. Then my time became exactly like yours and I have to say I was sad to see myself age so quickly.'

Saoirse was intrigued. Everyone assumes their grandparents, their parents for that fact, are normal. They are born to parents, they are toddlers, they grow up, they meet someone, they fall in love, they get married and have kids. Time passes for all of us, for the most part in the same cycle. But her grandmother seemed to be suggesting that she was different somehow, that time had been a very different thing for her for a very long time.

'How old are you, Gran?'

'Again, Saoirse, if I knew I would tell you, but I don't. I never kept track, there was no need to because for most of my life I was eternal and there's no point in trying to keep track of that. But I know that since I met and married your grandfather I have been mortal for sixty-odd years. So, in human terms, I guess I'm around the eighty mark.'

She smiled, she was enjoying this. At last an opportunity to be honest and open with her granddaughter. It was so good to finally open up, but she checked herself, it would be too easy to say too much and get them both in trouble.

'Next question.'

It reminded Saoirse of Sean, and she hung her head. She wondered how he was doing, what he was doing and as if reading her mind her grandmother spoke.

'You have a connection to him, and that is completely natural, expected almost. Don't fight it, as it will just make things harder for you and for him. He will need to understand you and what you do, because you will play an important part in his life. But I can't give you any more information than that now, I'm afraid. Remember I have left you with the tools to answer those questions.' She said this with a determination that Saoirse accepted and understood it as not to ask any more questions about the Sean side of things. She had so many, but so far things were going well, she was getting answers. So she continued.

'Why are we in danger, Gran?' She realised that this was the most important question and perhaps one she should have asked first, but it came now and she hoped she would get a clear non-cryptic answer.

'As I said, I was not always mortal. I fell in love with your grandfather, which is unheard of for my kind. We had to make a deal with Him to be together, but it came at a very high cost. At the time we felt it was worth it to be together. This is one area, Saoirse, I cannot say too much about because it is too dangerous. I don't want you to get hurt or have to face Him. I don't want to face Him.'

There it was again: 'Him'.

'Who is He, Gran? And why are you so afraid of Him?'

'I can't even mention His name. I fear Him because of what He could do to me and what He will do to you if He finds out you exist. A lot of the information you need is in your books, you just need to find it.'

The delight was gone, the weary old woman from downstairs had returned and although she had a thousand more questions, Saoirse couldn't torture her grandmother any more. She was obviously tired.

'Gran, I have loads more questions, but it's been a long and very confusing day and I think I need to sleep. I might even go to school tomorrow.' She stood up from her bed, and for the first time in her life helped her feeble grandmother to stand. She cuddled her tightly, all too aware in that moment that her grandmother was mortal. She took in her smell and held her tighter.

'You're such an amazing young woman, Saoirse. Know that I love you and I'm very proud of you.' She sighed heavily and headed for the door, and just as she left almost in a whisper Saoirse heard her say, 'And thank you, you've plenty of questions, but you took pity on an old fool.'

Saoirse grinned, oh how she loved her grandmother. The thoughts of losing her were just too much to even comprehend. She needed her, she always had and always would and now more than ever. What would she do without her? She didn't want to have to think about it on top of everything else. She picked the comb up from where it had fallen on the window seat, settled herself at the window, the harbour at her feet and began to comb softly.

15

The smell of cinnamon was warm and welcoming and Saoirse realised that her grandmother had gone into winter mode. She always added cinnamon to the porridge in winter: it was her speciality. Saoirse loved the smell it left in the house and the warmth it left in her heart. Autumn was finally here.

'You've written off our Indian Summer, Gran, because of one day of mist and fog?' she said as she came into the kitchen.

'Oh Saoirse, I haven't really, but I felt I needed something warm inside me this morning. I have a desperate chill I can't seem to get rid of.'

Saoirse quickly glanced at her father, and he saw the fear in her eyes. Thoughts of sickness and death ran through her mind and Saoirse remembered the sinking feeling she had felt last night before she had gone to bed. She couldn't lose her grandmother, not now anyway; she needed her so much more now. Her grandmother saw her concern, 'Saoirse, darling, don't be worrying, I spent the day outdoors yesterday with just a cardigan. At my age that's crazy. Of course I'm going to have caught a bit of a cold. I was silly really. I'll be fine, don't you worry.'

Her father smiled reassuringly and nodded as if to say, 'There, she's told you herself, she's fine.'

A knock at the front door surprised them all and they looked at each other. It was a little early for their postman, but the letterbox slapped shut. Saoirse was still standing just inside the door, so turned and walked into the dimly lit hallway.

A single envelope sat on the front doormat, address down. It had been sealed with wine-coloured sealing wax. She got a little excited: they never got mail like this. She hurried across the hall and picked the envelope up. It was expensive, heavy paper, from what she could make out, and it was beautiful, a rich creamy colour. The seal was thick and the indentation ornate. She took a closer look and the image embossed in the wax was one of a horse's head. Saoirse liked horses, but this one was a little scary and, even though it was pressed into the wine wax, she could see there was viciousness in its eyes. She flipped the envelope over and was a little disappointed that the beautiful calligraphy lettering on the front was addressed to her grandmother. She rushed into the kitchen and handed it excitedly to her.

'It's for you, Gran, looks very fancy.'

Her grandmother turned the envelope in her hands and when she caught sight of the seal on the back her face visibly paled and the worried look appeared again in her eyes. She let out the slightest, almost inaudible, gasp. 'What is it Gran? Who's it from?'

Her grandmother tucked it inside her apron and turned back to the stove to stir the porridge without answering. Saoirse looked at her father questioningly and he shrugged his shoulders in response. She crossed the kitchen and stood next to grandmother and placed her hand gently on her shoulder.

'Is everything alright, Gran?' Her voice was gentle, but concerned.

Her grandmother turned to look her in the eye and smiled weakly. 'It's grand, chicken; it's just something from an old friend. I think I'll read it later in private if you don't mind. It's nothing to worry about.'

'How do you know it's from an old friend, you haven't opened it?'

'I know the seal on the back. Now if you'll excuse me, I need to go to my room. Breakfast is ready. Make sure you eat a good bowl if you're going to school today.' She ladled a bowl of porridge for Saoirse and then herself, she turned and handed it to Saoirse, squeezing her forearm gently and smiling as she left the kitchen with her own bowl. Saoirse looked at her father, who seemed distracted by his laptop and had missed most of the underlying tension that the letter had brought. Saoirse went and sat next to him at the island.

'Dad, do you think Gran is okay?'

'I'm sure she's fine, hon. She's a big girl, she can look after herself.'

'But did you see her face when she looked at the envelope? It certainly wasn't the reaction that you'd expect from someone getting a letter from a long-lost friend. She looked worried.' There was serious concern in her voice and her father heard it, he looked up from the laptop and smiled at her. His daughter was so beautiful, a wonderful combination of his wife and himself. He loved her big heart and the love she had for his mother: they had always been inseparable. He stood from the island and went to stand behind her. He wrapped his arms around her comfortingly and spoke gently in her ear.

'Your grandmother is a tough nut; if it is anything to be concerned about, I'm sure she'll be well able to deal with it. She wouldn't like you worrying or making a fuss you know.'

It was true: her grandmother would kill her if she thought she was worrying. Saoirse smiled at her father and finished her breakfast. She could hear her mother showering on the floor above and wanted to make sure she was ready to go by the time she came down for breakfast. She checked the clock, five to eight. She was early, very early, her mum would be impressed. She bolted up the stairs grabbed her school bag, checked the contents and then grabbed her phone from the desk and took one last look at the mist outside the window. It was an ever-changing picture, but she loved it.

Saoirse said her goodbyes to her parents in the kitchen, and popped her earphones in. She was early and had decided to take the scenic route along the town to school in the company of the Coronas. She pressed shuffle and Danny's sultry tones filled her head. She checked the screen on the phone and it said 'Warm.' She loved it already. The lyrics reminded her in parts of Sean and in others of herself. She drifted down the hill and along the promenade. *I never stop and think before I speak, but you said you like that about me. So tell me more, bare your soul.*' The words filled her head, her heart and her pulse raced. What was it about this guy? He didn't stop and think before he spoke, he didn't have to, he just always said the right thing. And all she wanted to do was bare her soul to him. Tell him everything, have him hold her like he had the day of her birthday. And she wanted him to keep her warm.

She stopped in her tracks and stared at the dull water through the fence of the park. The mist was lighter now and caught in her hair in little beads. What was she doing? How dare she? Sean had just lost his girlfriend, he barely knew her, she barely knew him, they'd hardly spent time together. She'd never had a boyfriend before; she'd never experienced this strange feeling. She needed to see him, talk to him, explain it all, in the hope that he would understand her and what had happened. And maybe someday he would keep her warm.

These feelings were so new and so alien, but they were growing and gaining strength. She hadn't had time or the energy over the weekend to deal with them, but the music drew her in and left her no choice. Her head spun and she fumbled in her pocket and turned it off. It was too confusing. She needed to clear her head, not fill it with new complications.

She stored her earphones and phone in her bag and started the ascent of the hill around the cathedral. It was twenty to nine; she was doing well for time. Michael was just getting into his car and gave her a friendly wave. The past week had been so unreal, this beautiful building had stood on her horizon for her entire life and she had finally ventured in and met a man of God who completely understood and accepted what she and her grandmother were. The world was certainly a far different place than she had thought, and while it scared the life out of her, it was beginning to settle in her head and not seem so bad. She waved back at him and smiled.

Rounding the corner, she headed up the hill towards the school. She picked up her pace and her lost her breath in the process. She was out of shape. Heading up the drive she had her head down protecting her face from the ever-increasing mist. She heard the final bell ring and hoped she'd be up the stairs to Room Eight before the teacher arrived. She ploughed on through the other latecomers and just as she was about to go through the side door, a strong arm grabbed her and pulled her to one side.

Hoping it wasn't the Vice Principal, Saoirse looked up, right into Sean's eyes. She stepped back in shock and he read her face immediately.

'You didn't expect me, huh? Sorry, Saoirse, I didn't mean to frighten you.'

'You didn't. I just didn't expect to see you today. Mum told me to not expect to see you for a while.'

He wasn't wearing his uniform; instead he had a green rain jacket and jeans on and wasn't carrying a bag. This unsettled Saoirse just a little. What was he doing here so?

'You not going to school today?'

'Does it look like it?' his reply was quick and sarcastic. 'Sorry, Saoirse, no I'm not. And I was hoping you'd agree to not go either. We have a lot to talk about, don't you think?'

Saoirse panicked a little, she had never ditched school before. She'd never been in trouble before. Things were going well at home with her mum at the moment, how could she put that in jeopardy by ditching school? But at the same time it was true, they had a lot to talk about and she wanted to spend time with him. There was only one answer, and she hoped her mother would understand. Sean needed her. It was the best excuse she had.

'Okay, where do you want to go?' She had hoped it would sound strong and in control, but her voice broke a little.

He smiled a wicked smile and Saoirse returned it with a meek one of her own. 'Come on let's go to your house.' He turned and headed out the drive. Saoirse stopped, her mum and dad would be out, but her grandmother was sure to be there. How would she explain this to her? Sean turned back to look at her and, as always, answered the unasked question.

'I'm sure your grandmother will be fine; she seems to get all this.'

Saoirse shrugged, he was eager and she didn't have the heart to tell him no. Her house it was.

16

Two mugs and a fresh pot of coffee sat on the island in the kitchen, beside them a stack of lemon cookies. Saoirse looked at them puzzled: who was her grandmother having over? She pulled off her damp jacket and hung it along with Sean's at the back door. They both sat at the island in silence for a minute or two. It was Saoirse's grandmother who broke the silence. She popped her head around the kitchen door and smiled at them both. The tired, worried expression still very visible, but her voice was light and cheerful.

'I have some errands to run this morning, should be gone till lunch. I've rung school to say you're not feeling well, so that's that covered.'

'But Gran. . .'

'Sorry, chicken, I have an appointment and I'm running a little late. The coffee is for you and I know Sean likes the lemon biscuits.' She winked playfully at him and was gone.

Saoirse turned to Sean and looked at him quizzically, 'Did you tell her you were coming?'

He shrugged his shoulders, 'No, but she seems to have known. Maybe she's psychic?' There was a touch of sarcasm in his voice, reflecting perhaps the strange news they had brought him in the past few days, but it was light-hearted rather than cynical.

'Or maybe she just knows us too well.' She must have heard Saoirse's conversation with her mother and decided Sean would want information too much to not come looking for her. She'd probably guessed he'd want to come here to see the other pictures. It didn't take a genius to work that out.

'Coffee?' He nodded. Saoirse poured two large mugs and settled herself back on the stool. She had to be open and forthcoming today, Sean deserved that, but she wanted to know he was alright first. She took a deep breath and looked directly at him. He was visibly tired and his eyes had the tell-tale signs of days of crying. She had to tread carefully, remembering this was not about her. It was very much about him and she had to be delicate. She had no way of understanding the pain he was going through and so could not presume anything or even offer any kind of advice or comfort. She chose the straightforward method. 'How are you?'

It hung in the air for a while. She didn't feel it was her place to speak first, after she had just asked the question. He sipped his coffee and looked out at the rain that was now falling heavily outside. She tried to remain relaxed, but it was just so uncomfortable. Should she talk, lighten the mood, offer more coffee? It was torture. She took her own mug in her hands and busied herself sipping it silently. Sean took a biscuit from the plate, but did not eat it; instead he turned to look at her.

'If I'm honest...' His voice was quiet and tense. 'If I'm honest, Saoirse, I don't know how I feel. It all feels a little unreal. The last week has been a nightmare. I'm just waiting to wake up.'

Saoirse smiled involuntarily at his mention of nightmares, she didn't mean to but she thought his analogy was very fitting. She had been having his very nightmare for the past few months and now that he was finally living it, she was free of it. It was strange how her release had been found. The smile wiped quickly from her face, she was free, but how could she be happy when he was in so much pain?

'You smiled, why?' There was nothing accusing or harsh about the question, in fact it was curious more than anything else.

She hung her head. Life was just so complicated. Sean was a grieving boyfriend at seventeen, Saoirse was coming to terms with the fact that she was a banshee. They were a whole new level of messed up.

Sean looked intensely at Saoirse and searched her face for answers. He stared for an eternity and Saoirse grew warm and uncomfortable under his gaze.

'Did you really dream about Kate's death? Did you really see what happened?' His voice was pleading: childish and needy. His eyes were heavy with tears and Saoirse's heart melted. She could do nothing but tell him the truth.

'Yes. For weeks. It got more graphic and detailed towards the end and I didn't sleep much. But now they're gone.'

He wiped a single tear from his left cheek and continued. 'I need you to tell me what you saw. I need to hear what happened.'

Saoirse wasn't sure if she should tell him about her final dreams, about the arguments, the other boy, Kate's behaviour. She couldn't hurt him even more. Doubt and worry swept across her face and he saw it.

'I know it's not pleasant, Saoirse. I was there up until after the club. But I want to know what happened when she got into his car.' His voice was more aggressive now, his words were pushy and it was only then that Saoirse realised he wanted to know if Kate had cheated on him before she died. She relaxed, he was tortured by ideas that he was mourning a girlfriend who had cheated on him. Saoirse sighed inwardly: at least she could erase that pain.

'She left the club after your fight and was sick in the laneway. She had obviously had too much to drink and wasn't herself. She wanted to go home, but was too proud to come back in and find you. She felt she'd made such a show of herself and you. A friend, she knew him anyway, at least I think, because when he drove around the corner she happily took the lift he offered and got in the car. He had wanted to go on somewhere, but she just wanted to go home. He tried to impress her with his driving but Kate turned up the music to block him and his driving out. It was very sudden. I don't know exactly what happened or what they hit, but she died instantly Sean. She wasn't in pain.'

Saoirse was embarrassed by the tears that fell from her eyes. It wasn't her place. He stood from his stool and walked around the island and sat next to her. He took her hand in his and squeezed it softly. She liked it. She gently took her thumb and stroked his hand. She felt the need to continue, but what else did she have to say? That was what she had dreamt.

'She loved you, Sean, she didn't cheat on you.' It hung there too, like her first question and she was sorry she had said it. It was not her place to say it or even think it. He squeezed her hand again lightly and looked her in the face, his intensity gone.

'I needed to hear that. Thank you. I had visions of her with that guy. Dying in someone else's arms, having betrayed me, betrayed us and it was killing me. I loved her.' He wept openly and Saoirse took his shoulders in her arms and drew him into her, stroking his hair. It felt comfortable and the right thing to do. There was no guilt in enjoying it, she told herself, she was helping a friend. He gave himself willingly and leaned helplessly on her torso and sobbed.

Time passed, how much time Saoirse could not tell, but Sean's sobs eased, until he was no longer crying, but was still enveloped in Saoirse's arms. She sensed he had stilled and slowly she released him and he sat up and looked at her, red eyed and weary.

'Saoirse, can I see the others?'

She knew that's why he had wanted to come to her house today. She knew he would persist and that for her own acceptance of herself she needed confirmation that only he could give: the pictures played an important part of that. But she was reluctant. Those pictures were so much a part of her and her fear, her pain, her anguish, was she ready to show them to him? She didn't really have a choice.

'Why so cagey?'

'Honestly, it's because there are so many, and they were painted out of fear and anguish. They were releases from nightmares I have had all my life, but they may relate to nightmares you have lived through, Sean, if Kate is anything to go by. Are you ready?'

He looked a little taken aback and a realisation spread across his face.

'You'll have a picture of my mother?'

'Probably, if what I am is real, I'll have a picture of anyone you've ever lost. That scares me Sean; there are more than ten pictures.' Saoirse realised for the first time that this popular happy-go-lucky rugby player that everyone in school loved and adored had been through so much pain in his young life. None of his admiring fans had a clue. She took his hand, the one he had held hers with, and led him upstairs to the study on the third floor. The paintings were still hidden in the wardrobe and she sat him at the desk and turned him to face the door and the wardrobe. She stopped before she opened it and looked at his face, trying to read his emotions.

'Start with your first drawing please, Saoirse. I'll no doubt have been younger and will probably less emotional about those ones. We'll build up to the inevitable.'

There was a distinct nervousness in his voice: he was as worried as she was. She turned and faced the wardrobe, she was about to uncover a whole lot of emotions for them both and she took a deep breath to settle herself. She opened the large mahogany door and flicked through the canvases. She drew out the first painting she had ever done, a boy of about five or six with bright green eyes. The painting was basic, but the boy's character was obvious in the childlike portrait. Saoirse's painting skills had always been good. The boy had his favourite teddy tucked under his chin. The bear had intrigued Saoirse as she had never seen one with a yellow dickie bow before.

Sean gasped and Saoirse quickly dropped the painting on the desk. Maybe this wasn't such a good idea after all, but Sean took the painting in his hands and marvelled at it.

'Joe O'Donovan, my best friend when I started school. That's Rufus, his bear. He died in a house fire when he was six.' Sean was moved, but not upset. 'But you know that, don't you? When did you paint this?'

'Just before it happened.' Saoirse dropped her head; it had been one of the nightmares that even after it had stopped she was secretly haunted by. She feared being burnt alive more than any other death. And she had seen so many other ways to die.

Sean grabbed her hand again and squeezed it, looking at her with pity. 'That is not a dream I would have liked to have had, and at such a young age. Awful. How did you cope?'

'I painted them as they were before. It helped.'

She pulled the next few paintings out, and with each one Sean explained his relationship to them and how each one had died. Each one matched perfectly with Saoirse's dreams and they both realised that it was happening: this was real, Saoirse was a banshee. She was Sean's banshee. Neither said a word, but they both knew it.

There were just two painting left in the wardrobe: Kate's and the picture of a beautiful brunette. Saoirse knew it was Sean's mum, but still she placed it on the desk like she had the others and allowed him to tell the story. He had not paused to ponder the actual painting on any of the others but he traced the lines of his mother's face slowly, his eyes filling with tears. He stroked her hair lovingly before he spoke.

'Mum always said she would be young forever,' his voice caught, 'I guess she was right.' A tear dropped onto the painting and he quickly wiped it away. 'She was diagnosed on my tenth birthday, but didn't tell any of us until a month later. She fought hard you know, Saoirse, four long years, but it took her in the end. It was peaceful, at home with dad, my sisters and me. God, I still miss her so much.' More tears fell onto the painting and he became annoyed with himself, brushing them quickly off the painting and his cheeks. Saoirse touched his shoulder softly and he turned and smiled at her. She was surprised.

'Can you tell me about her dreams, please?'

Saoirse returned his smile as she remembered these dreams with more ease and less dread. 'They were different: calmer, less nightmarish, a sadder movie. She was calm and peaceful, but she was also ready. She knew it was her time and, in the end, it was a release.'

'Can I have this one? Dad would love it.'

Saoirse had never thought about giving away one of her paintings, and she immediately became a little possessive, but she softened when she looked at him. Sean had returned to touching his mother's face and hair, smiling openly at the likeness. How could she not give it to him?

A door banged downstairs and the pair of them jumped. They had been wrapped in a cocoon for hours, neither of them had an idea what time it was and Saoirse saw the surprise in Sean's face when he checked his watch. Saoirse checked her own and it was nearly half past one. No doubt it was her grandmother downstairs; right on cue there was a call up the stairs that she was putting on soup and the pair of them were to be down in ten minutes. Sean looked at Saoirse and smiled.

'It's been a funny morning, Saoirse. I thought reliving the

pain that these pictures brought would be awful, but it's actually been quite therapeutic. I feel a bit better. Thank you.'

Then suddenly he hugged her tightly and she found herself willingly hugging him back. She took in his strength, his smell, his warmth. She hoped that one day he would be hugging her not because she had predicted his girlfriend's death or painted everyone he had lost. Not because this all meant that she was a banshee, his banshee, but because he wanted to, because he liked to. But for now she was happy to just be in his arms.

17

Three bowls of steaming vegetable soup sat on the kitchen table and a mountain of sandwiches on a plate. Her grandmother had laid the table neatly for the three of them and Saoirse was surprised that her grandmother was joining them for lunch. For some reason she had assumed her grandmother would have left her and Sean to it, but they all sat down together and Sean ploughed into both the soup and the sandwiches, his appetite returning after the ordeal of the last few days. When all three had finished, Saoirse's grandmother went to the stove and made a fresh pot of coffee and sat back down with them.

'Right,' her voice was matter of fact and firm. 'We have some things to discuss.'

Saoirse and Sean both looked at each other puzzled and then at her grandmother, her face stern and business-like.

'So, I'm assuming that this morning's session has confirmed that there is an unusual connection between the two of you?'

She looked at them both like a bossy teacher expecting straight and clear answers. They obliged and nodded quickly.

'But do you understand, Sean, what this connection is?' There was a slight break in her tone, but her face remained stern.

Sean looked at Saoirse first and then back to her grandmother, 'Saoirse predicts the deaths of people close to me. I guess that pretty much sums it up, yeah?'

'But what is she, Sean? I need you to understand what she is.'

'She's a banshee, she's my banshee, she predicts death in

my life.' At this he looked back at Saoirse with searching questioning eyes, and then those eyes turned to Saoirse's grandmother. 'Why me, though? Why does she predict death in my life? I don't get that bit.'

'Okay so, Sean, that bit I can answer. Your father is from the Fitzgerald clan. An ancient Irish family of high kings and chieftains mainly from the Kerry area. Saoirse's 'talent' means that she must be linked to one of these families. If I had remained in the North it would no doubt have been an O'Donnell, but I put an end to that. I had assumed coming here to Cobh we would have no links with any of the ancient families and that Saoirse would never realise her power, as there would be no connection to be made. But after I met your father I knew that we could be in for trouble. I knew immediately who he was and what line he came from. Banshees are always linked to great families, I was the O'Donnell's banshee, and now Saoirse is the Fitzgerald's.'

Saoirse couldn't believe how open her grandmother was being today, Sean was getting far more out of her than she had since this whole thing began. She was slightly jealous. So Gran had come to Cobh to try and get away from the world she came from, and ultimately to prevent Saoirse from becoming a banshee, but where did He come into this? He seemed to be the key to all of this, but also to the fear and dread that was creeping into her grandmother's life.

'Gran, how does *He* come into all of this so?'

Her grandmother's sternness faltered and her worried face appeared instantly, but only for a few seconds. Saoirse could see her thinking of how to word her answer and she could feel Sean staring at the two of them. Perhaps she shouldn't have brought it up, but if she was Sean's banshee they were in this together and he needed to know just as much as she did.

'Who was the letter from this morning, Gran? And I don't

want "an old friend". You don't react like you did to a letter from a friend!'

The fear was clearly visible for Sean and Saoirse and it swept across the old woman's face like a thunder cloud, shaking her to the bones. Saoirse realised it was from Him and answered her own question.

'So it's from Him! What does He want? Gran, you've got to tell us, we need to be able to help, but we can't if you don't tell us who He is or what He wants.' Saoirse heard the pleading in her own voice, it sounded desperate, she was desperate. The fear and panic of losing her grandmother was growing rapidly once more. Whoever He was he was powerful enough to reduce the strongest woman Saoirse knew to this.

'Was it from him, Gran?' Again she pleaded.

Her grandmother nodded, but it was so weak and almost non-existent that Saoirse wasn't sure she had definitely seen it, but the look in her grandmother's eyes confirmed it. Sean looked at Saoirse confused and she dutifully explained about the exquisite envelope that had appeared on the front mat this morning. Sean was intrigued. Who was this guy and why send a letter? It was such an old-fashioned and slow way to deliver a message. All the time Saoirse's grandmother kept her head in her hands. When Sean and Saoirse had finished she took them both by the hand, this startled Saoirse somewhat, it was such a dramatic yet tender action, the news could be nothing but bad.

'He knows that Michael knows about me. How He does, I don't know. Michael has no idea either, but He knows. And that was against the conditions of our contract. Therefore I must pay the forfeit. If I don't do so before the first full moon of October then He will come and instigate the condition himself.' Her voice was meek and frightened, heavy with fear and dread, but also an understanding that there was no other option: it was part of a deal she had agreed to. 'I don't want him coming here; I don't want Him to know about you, so I have to fulfil his wishes myself.' At this a single tear formed fully in her left eye and hung to her lashes for a second or two and then dropped heavily onto her pale cheek. Another formed in her right eye, then another and another. Saoirse's heart was breaking, she had never seen her grandmother like this before, and it was torturous. Sean looked on confused but greatly moved. What was it that had reduced this poor woman to this despair?

'What is the condition Gran? Can I help you fulfil it? Maybe we can do it together?'

Although she continued to cry, her grandmother smiled and squeezed her hand tightly. She steadied herself and wiped her cheeks with a handkerchief from her cardigan pocket.

'This is one thing you cannot do or help me with Saoirse, my love. This is something only I can do. I must go home.'

It hung innocently in the air. Neither Saoirse nor Sean could see the big deal in returning to Dunluce. It was an easy task, one that they could both help her with. She read their thoughts and shook her head.

'By home, I don't mean a leisurely trip to Dunluce, I mean I have to return to my own world: sever contact with this world and return to what I was.' The despair grew and her voice weakened, the tears returned. Saoirse was finding it hard to comprehend all of this. Did that mean she would become a banshee again, a full blown immortal banshee? Did it mean that she would never see her again? Her mind raced and muddled, she couldn't put together the words to even compose a question or express what she was thinking. It was Sean that spoke instead.

'I'm sorry, I'm lost...' There was an innocence and genuine concern in his voice. Again Saoirse was moved by how caring and close he had become in the few weeks she had known him. Saoirse looked to her grandmother for her answer.

'It means that I must leave here, and I must return to Dunluce, but not in the way both of you are thinking. Remember, Saoirse, I told you I was not always mortal, but I am now. In order to return to what I was I have to live out my mortal days and release my soul back to immortality. Unless I do that, he'll come for me. . . and ultimately you.' Her eyes were full of sorrow and pain, and Saoirse slowly realised that in order for a human to release their soul, they had to die. Her grandmother had to die to fulfil her contract, and ultimately to protect her. Saoirse's eyes filled with tears and her chest caved under an enormous invisible weight. She was losing her best friend in the whole world. She began to cry. Her grandmother took her in her arms and cradled and rocked her. Sean spoke quietly again and they were both unsure as to whether he was asking a question or thinking out loud.

'You have to die, to release a soul!' He went quiet and shifted uncomfortably on the chair. What was he messed up in? His life had always had its fair share of misery, but this was ridiculous. He had just lost his girlfriend. This girl experienced all of his pain and sorrow, and now, somehow, their connection and existence meant that this old lady had to die to protect Saoirse.

Saoirse's grandmother held her tightly and smoothed out her hair. 'I have had a good life, chicken, a far fuller and greater one than I had ever expected. I have done things that were never imaginable when I came to be: I became a wife, a mother, a grandmother, all experiences that I could never have hoped for or dreamed of, but I have had them. I have seen you grow, become the beautiful young woman you are. My life is lived, I can't complain. I made a deal, I must stick to it and I want to protect you.'

Both of them cried softly and hugged gently. Saoirse wished she didn't know. It would be so much easier to deal with if it happened unexpectedly, which she thought was ironic: death was never unexpected for them. But it was hard to accept. She had never lost anyone before, she finally would know what Sean was going through, but when?

'So, Gran, how is this going to happen? How will you die? What are you going to do?' Saoirse couldn't believe she was asking these questions, she saw an uncomfortable look in her grandmother's eyes.

'I have lots of things to work out, my love. And I have another appointment this afternoon, so the pair of you will have to excuse me. I must leave.'

She stood, brushing down her cardigan and wiping her face once more with her handkerchief. She stroked Saoirse's head lovingly and kissed her gently. 'I'll be home in about an hour, we'll talk more then.'

Sean and Saoirse looked at each other, Saoirse's eyes were red and blotchy, her chest still heavy and her head ablaze. Sean wasn't sure what to say or do, so just sat there quietly waiting for Saoirse to take the lead. Saoirse was so overcome she couldn't think straight, but all she could think of was her comb and the peace it would bring. She needed her window seat and the calming strokes of her comb and she needed them now.

'Do you mind if we go back upstairs, Sean? You don't have to stay, you can go, you've been through enough I'm sure for today, for a lifetime, but I really need to go back upstairs.' She was exhausted suddenly and even the thought of climbing the stairs seemed like a mammoth task.

'I'll stay, Saoirse. I still have lots of questions, but more importantly I think we both need the company.' He leant across the table and squeezed her hand and she smiled, she was so glad he was staying.

18

Saoirse knew she should feel strange bringing Sean upstairs to her room, but they both sat comfortably staring out the window in silence and watching the busy harbour. Saoirse pulled the box from her desk and laid it on her lap. She thumbed it lovingly and opened the lid and pulled out the comb, Sean watched her intently and was intrigued by the box's intricacy. He had never seen anything like it before, it was beautifully carved from the most exquisite dark wood. He reached out to touch it and Saoirse handed it to him. He thumbed it in the same way she had, running his smooth skin against the carvings on the lid and sides, they were amazingly crafted and detailed. Each side telling a story, complete in its single image, but still holding so much more to tell. Each landscape beautifully recreated and tenderly carved. The box was fascinating: it was obvious it was old. He lifted the lid and examined the inside and only then did he recall that Saoirse had taken something out of it. What could be so precious that it was contained in a box of so much detail and beauty?

He looked up to see Saoirse lost in a world of her own, slowly and carefully combing her long wavy hair with a silver comb. Her beauty was breathtaking, her pale skin caught the weak sunlight highlighting her chiselled features, high cheekbones, dark eyes. Her hair hung softly around her shoulders and fell to her waist with each stroke. Her beauty was otherworldly, not commercial or ordinary but very much extraordinary. He had never seen her in this way before. He felt he was spying on her in a private moment, intruding on something, but she was oblivious to him and the world around her. In that moment he caught himself moving on. He quickly snapped the lid shut and with it the thoughts he had been thinking. How could he? What about Kate? How dare he? What kind of person was he? He was disgusted with himself, and turned away from Saoirse and the box and looked out the window at the world outside. It wasn't the same world he had left this morning; so much had changed in the past few weeks.

Saoirse relaxed. Her mind emptied itself as her attention drifted out to the harbour. Each stroke brought her further away and it was intoxicating. Life was so much easier when you didn't have to think, when you didn't have to accept the reality that had been forced upon you and all that it entailed. She forgot where she was, she forgot that Sean was sitting across from her: she was calm and at peace. If only she could stay there. The snap of the lid brought her back to her senses and she watched Sean's face recoil in disgust as he turned and looked out the window. This was obviously all too much for him, they had ruined his life and not content with that they were involving him even more in whatever mysteries Saoirse's life would entail. He looked so vulnerable and hurt, sad and confused.

'I am so sorry Sean. I wish none of this had happened.'

'Kate would have died regardless, my mum would have died regardless, maybe I'm the one who should be sorry for having you live through my pain.' He turned and looked at her. What kind of world were they mixed up in? Life was so complicated regardless. Who needed banshees and this guy, this Him, to add to it? His eyes were softer now, and he looked genuinely sorry. Saoirse smiled slightly and looked back out at the window, she wanted to ask him something but wasn't sure she should, she wasn't sure if it was appropriate, but she needed to know.

'Does it really hurt?'

Sean looked at her confused; he wasn't sure what she was asking. She saw the confusion and reworded the question. She needed to know.

'I mean, does it physically hurt when you lose someone? I have never lost anyone Sean, I have lived through your losses, but I didn't know any of those people. I have never lost someone of my own and I'm scared.' She was petrified more like, and she began to shake slightly, the world she had known all her life was crumbling around her and she was sinking fast. She didn't know what to do and was terrified of what lay ahead. Her grandmother had always been her rock, her person to turn to, and now she was faced with having to do it all alone.

'I don't know what I'm going to do without her, Sean. I need her so much; I don't want to lose her.' She broke down, and wept uncontrollably. She couldn't imagine life without her grandmother, and now she was being forced to not just imagine that, but face the reality that before the first full moon in October she would be gone. It was all just too much. Sean shifted across the window seat and took her in his arms and gently rocked her. His arms were strong and warm, and brought some comfort, but there was no release from this. She would have to live it out. 'Does it hurt?'

'It does,' he whispered gently in her ear, 'It hurts like hell, and although some people will tell you it will pass, it doesn't, you just learn to deal with it. When mum died, I honestly thought I would curl up into a ball and die, the pain was so much. My heart ached and it felt like my chest caved in on it. I thought I was the only one hurting because around me everyone was busy, organising, telling stories, laughing. I couldn't understand it. Mum was dead; I wanted wailing, collapsing, rivers of tears, because that's how I felt. The truth is Saoirse for everyone grief is different: the pain you feel is unique to you and how you deal with it is unique to you. My sisters needed to organise, my father needed to be strong and remember, I needed to curl up. Everyone is different, but my God it hurts, it hurts everyone.'

He hadn't sugar-coated it in any form, and she was grateful for that. She needed to hear the truth. She held his arm that was wrapped around her and rested her chin on it. Her sobbing calmed and she pulled herself together. He had that effect on her, almost like the comb and almost as if he could read her thoughts, he released his grip and took the comb from her hand.

'So this is what goes in the box. It's beautiful. I have never seen anything like these before. They are absolutely exquisite. What are the carvings and where did you get them?'

Saoirse was glad of the change of subject and while her breath still caught now and then, she was feeling calmer. 'It's my sixteenth birthday present from my Gran. It's her comb. Each banshee has one, created by Aed to help ease the torment banshees experience before a death. Combing helps to calm the mind.'

'That figures. You were away in your own world there earlier as you combed. I thought it was strange considering all that was going on.'

Saoirse laughed involuntarily. Sean amazed her, he was so accepting and matter of fact about all that was going on, Saoirse was still finding it so difficult to understand. Maybe her grandmother was right, she did need Sean to help her work all this out. Maybe she would not have to do it alone. He seemed so open to it and grasped it far quicker than she did.

'You're sobbing one minute, laughing the next. What's so funny?' His voice was amused.

'I know I'm sorry, it's just that you seem so accepting of all this weird stuff. I just told you my comb was commissioned by the King of the Fairies and you just take it at face value, no problem. I find it hard to believe myself and you just seem to take it on board so easily. Wish I was as accepting as you.'

'Saoirse this morning you showed me pictures of everyone I have ever lost and told me the manner of each of their deaths. Each one was spot on, down to the very last details. How could I question any of it now?'

'But Sean we're talking fairies, banshees, a 'Him' we have no idea what he is. If I exist that means all kinds of other creatures we assume are folklore exist too. Do you not find that strange? Or at least hard to accept?'

'Saoirse, you have a gift, a talent, whatever it is, you have it, it's very clear and obvious to me. Your grandmother is petrified of whoever wrote that letter and that comb definitely works wonders on calming you. You have to look at the facts, strange and all as they might be, but the facts are the facts and you have to dare to believe. If you exist then most definitely others do too.'

'That must be what the books are for.' She said it out loud, although she thought she had said it in her head, and he looked at her puzzled.

'What books?' He was intrigued and sat up and away from her quickly. She hadn't realised they had remained so close since he took the comb. It had been so comfortable. She turned and faced him. He was eager, he wanted to know about the books and she could tell she wasn't going to be able to fob him off. She sat onto the ledge of the window seat and composed herself, wiping her face quickly. She stood and looked down at him, some of the weariness had disappeared from his face and she saw a glimmer in his eye. He was fascinated by all this.

'The books have been gifts from my grandmother since

my eleventh birthday. I'll show you. They're in the study.'

He sprang up and out of the room and was sitting at the desk in the chair before she even got to the door. The paintings were still out in front of him, he was looking at his mother again. Saoirse took them and stacked them neatly back in the cupboard leaving his mother till last. She left her on top and decided she'd give it to him on his way home. She took the books from the shelf above the desk and laid them out before him. He marvelled at the carvings on the leather covers, just as she had. She was glad he appreciated them as much as she did and her heart warmed even more when he took one and held it to his nose to smell. He smiled.

'Oh, the smell of an old book is so much more powerful and intriguing than a new one.' He winked at her playfully and went back to the book, running his fingers across each of the covers and spines, inspecting the intricate details of each image. 'They are very like the pictures on the side of the box.'

'I know, I noticed that myself. I reckon they must be done by the same person.'

'Talented, to say the least, if they can work on leather and wood in such a beautiful way. How old are they?'

'I have absolutely no idea. They are my grandmother's I'm assuming, and from what I'm sure you've seen, getting an age out of her would be very difficult. She's been in Cobh nearly sixty years, but she says her time before that is very hard to gauge because she thought she didn't need to keep track, time was endless. So your guess is as good as mine.'

He looked intently at the books and then opened the cover of the first; he inspected the writing inside, flicking through the pages. It was very old, obviously, but it was in great condition and made from extremely durable paper. It would be very hard to tell how old they were, and a trip to an expert was most certainly out of the question. They seemed to come to this conclusion simultaneously, and both began speaking at the same time.

'But. . .'

'You know. . .'

They both smiled, Saoirse nodded at Sean to go ahead.

'You know we can't find out how old they are. It would be too risky.'

'I was thinking the same myself. Gran said the comb is hers. Therefore the comb, box and possibly the books are all fairy creations, which means we'd certainly raise the alarm if we went to get them checked out. I've been thinking that it's not the actual books themselves anyway that I'm supposed to study, it's the stories. She was very adamant that I read them, and read them well.'

Sean opened the first story from the first book and looked at the title, then looked at Saoirse.

'Have you read them?'

'Yes, all five books several times.'

'And what are they about?' He looked down and the beautiful text in front of him: the book was thick, a very substantial read, it must contain a hundred stories.

'They're folklore. You know, stories of fairies, leprechauns, banshees, changelings, merrows and then there's stories from the legends of the High Kings of Ireland and their dealings with the other worlds. There are hundreds of stories, each one told beautifully, almost from an eye witness kind of perspective. . .' Saoirse suddenly stopped herself, snatched the book from Sean and opened it to the first story. She read a few lines to herself, then closed it again and sighed. Why hadn't she seen it before? It was so glaringly obvious. Sean was confused and sat waiting for an explanation. None seemed to be coming so he coughed questioningly.

'I have read these books so many times, assuming they

were well-told stories of folklore and mystery...I loved them because they were so graphic, but at the same time because they were so alien. Nothing like the characters exists in our world and I was intrigued, swept away by the stories and the settings, I don't know why I didn't see it. I'm normally such a perceptive reader.' She tutted to herself and opened the book again to look further.

'Saoirse! What? What did you not realise? Come on, you have me hanging!'

'Oh sorry. They are just that...they are eye-witness reports. Each story is told from the perspective of one of the characters. Each one describes a real event, an encounter with a particular creature from folklore. This one tells of how he met a young woman who was distressed on his way home from the market. She was stood on the narrow river bridge on the way out of town. He had tried to comfort her but she was hysterical, she said there would be nothing but sorrow for them all. He left her combing her hair and singing a haunting song. She frightened him and a worry grew in him for his family at home: his wife had taken ill in the days before and he had gone to the town to get medicine from a visiting doctor. A sorrow entered him after meeting the woman on the bridge, one he couldn't shake until he got home and found his mother-in-law in tears at the door. He knew immediately his wife was dead and the lonesome figure on the bridge was the banshee.

Each story tells of people's encounters with creatures from our folklore: good, bad and indifferent. They're all beautifully descriptive and entertaining. I had always assumed my grandmother was like my father, a history nut, loving our storytelling tradition, instead she was showing me the encounters humans have with the other world and how they perceive us. For the most part, unfortunately, they weren't well received.'

'So all these books tell us who else is out there.' Sean's voice was calculated and focused. It surprised Saoirse. What was he thinking? 'So we could make a list of the creatures we assumed did not exist from these. . . and maybe find out who He is?'

Saoirse hadn't even thought of it. Her grandmother was most definitely right, she needed Sean. And from his enthusiasm it was clear that he was fully on board and ready for work.

She looked down at the five books and recalled the hours she had spent reading them over and over again. There were hundreds of stories, it would take days to go through them all. And what if He wasn't in any of them? She couldn't recall anyone that had stood out, that could remotely have the power to instil so much fear in her grandmother. She sighed, it seemed impossible.

'Saoirse, two heads are better than one, I'll take two of the books home with me and work on them. We'll make a list of the creatures we find and see what we can come up with. It shouldn't take us too long if we're both working on it. I'm not at school for another few days, so I can work through the day and call you at night and check in. It would be a welcome distraction.'

He was eager and it was infectious. Maybe they could find out who He was themselves and be able to save her grandmother. It had to be worth a try, there was nothing else she could do. He gathered two books from the desk and stood, ready to leave.

She felt disappointed he was going, but he had spent the best part of the day with her, how could she complain? She loved being around him, he kept her calm and spoke so much sense. She felt guilty wanting him to stay with her, just so she felt better. Sean had his own stuff to deal with at the moment, she had to leave him go. She turned to the wardrobe and took out the top two paintings: his mother and Kate. She placed them on top of the books and smiled at him.

'I think these belong to you.' She felt she was doing the right thing; perhaps they would bring him some closure, peace even. She squeezed his hand and smiled again.

'Thank you, Saoirse. Does it sound very bad if I say I'd rather just take my mum's picture? I don't think I could cope with having Kate with me just yet. It's too raw at the moment to be constantly reminded. My mum, on the other hand, would be a comfort: I've grieved her and I know my dad is just going to love it. You really have a gift. These pictures are so beautiful and so true to them. Thank you for today, Saoirse. It really has been such a help and I know this probably sounds terrible, but this quest to find Him is a very exciting and welcome distraction.' He squeezed her hand and gave her back the painting of Kate, which she took and placed on the pile in the wardrobe once more. A pang of guilt swept over as she secretly delighted in the fact that he had not taken Kate home.

As she pushed the large oak door closed behind him, they both paused and smiled, realising that they shared a strong connection. They were in this together.

19

Saoirse woke with a start, checking her phone, it was 2.15am. An incoming text message had woken her from her sleep. The evening had flown past: her grandmother was secretively busy in her room and Saoirse had been on a mission of her own in her study. She had been worn out from the emotions of the day and had slipped quietly off to bed at around ten o'clock. The text had startled her. She sat up in the bed and opened her inbox.

You awake? First book done, going to start second now. S.

What? He had an entire book read and finished. That was some going, but Saoirse worried that reading them so quickly would mean they might miss something. Sean must have been worn out enough after the events of last week; he really needed to sleep. She waited. How was she supposed to respond to a text like that and at this hour? But she had to respond, if she didn't perhaps he would think she wasn't taking this seriously and ultimately he was doing this for her, but what should she text back? She really wanted him to take care of himself and she didn't want to be the reason he would get sick.

- SLEEP!!!! You need a clear mind to read these books; we're looking for maybe the slightest of clues. Please sleep Sean, it's late.

- Ah so you are awake.

- I am now! But I wasn't.

- Lightweight ;)

- Sean, please. You've had a really tough couple of weeks, go to sleep. We can talk in the morning.

- God, never realised you could be so cranky, must remember you don't function well without sleep.

Saoirse laughed out loud, little did he know. She had spent weeks awake after the dreams of Kate, his mother and all who came before them. Lack of sleep was a condition she was all too familiar with and one she felt she had learned to deal with quite well.

Much to her dismay she was very much awake. She climbed out of bed, pulled on her robe and wandered to the window. It was a surprisingly clear night, considering the day it had been. The harbour was still and dark, the town sleepily lit in a glow of amber, with not a stir in the streets or on the water. She tucked her legs up on the window seat and wrapped the robe tighter around her. It was actually a beautiful night. Sometimes being rudely awakened paid off, she thought, as she smiled at the vista in front of her. She loved this window and the view her bedroom on the hill afforded her. Her phone rang, breaking the peace and startling her. She fumbled to quickly answer it before it woke the house.

'Hello?' She knew it had to be Sean, but she was surprised that he would call her at this hour.

'Saoirse, you okay? You didn't answer my last text and I was worried I had offended you.' His voice was timid and concerned. Saoirse didn't know whether to jump with joy or be angry he was ringing so late. She looked towards her bedroom door, half expecting her mother or father to appear at it, but there wasn't a movement in the house.

'Saoirse?'

'Sorry, Sean, I'm here. Just wasn't expecting a phone call, and I'm sure neither was anyone else in the house.' She settled herself against the window pane and listened to the crackle on the phone. His signal must not be good. Her uninterrupted view of the harbour also meant she had excellent phone reception.

'I'm sorry, I just thought I'd upset you and that's the last thing I want. I know I should be sleeping, Saoirse, but to sleep means to dream and those are not pleasant at the moment. Being awake is far more bearable.'

He sighed heavily, there was a despair and weariness in it. Saoirse wasn't sure how to respond, not wanting to dream was something she knew all too much about, but for Sean his dreams were so much more personal. She dreamt of the deaths of people she didn't know, he was dreaming about someone he loved. It was a total different thing. She sighed.

'God, Saoirse, I'm sorry, I'm doing it again, speaking before really thinking. Of course your dreams are probably worse than mine. It was insensitive of me, I'm sorry.'

Why was he such a nice guy? Why was he being so thoughtful and caring? He was the one going through hell. Yes, Saoirse had her problems, but she hadn't lost anyone, not yet anyway.

'Sean, don't be sorry. Yes, my dreams can be awful. But I don't know the people in them, it's like watching a very real and terrifying movie, but once I'm awake I can detach myself from them. You don't have that luxury, when you wake up Kate is still gone: it's reality. I'm the one who should be sorry, Sean, I should be more understanding.'

There was a pause, both of them trying to think of what to say next. Then Sean began to giggle and Saoirse joined it: it was infectious. There was no reason for them to be laughing, but they continued until Saoirse was almost out of breath.

'Can I ask what we're laughing at, because I'm totally lost?'

'I have no idea. I guess this whole situation is just so absurd. I've spent the last five hours trawling through a book all about things that I had dismissed as a child along with Santa Claus and the tooth fairy. I've been taking it very seriously and noting as I go along. You do realise that if we go by what society thought decades ago, you are some crazed old hag with a high pitched voice that brought nothing but terror to the people she visited. I think you look quite good for an old hag!'

That was pretty funny, Saoirse thought. She didn't look so bad at all: her insecurities about her appearance seemed ridiculous now. Things could have been a whole lot worse, if she was to go by the legends. She giggled again.

'It's funny alright, I guess. I hadn't even thought of that. It is pretty absurd. I've never even thought about what people think banshees are, and come to think of it now, I'm glad I haven't. It doesn't bode well for me really, does it?'

She giggled again, picturing herself sat on a bridge frightening the life out of anyone who passed. Sean laughed as well. It was such a comfortable and wonderful sound, Saoirse relaxed back against the window and smiled. It was late and while she normally spent these quiet hours on her own painting or gazing at the harbour, having company was a very pleasant surprise. She liked it. A lot.

'You still there?'

'Sorry, Sean, I am. I was just thinking how strange the last few weeks have been. But they've been great too! I know that sounds ridiculous, because of the terrible things that have happened, but Sean, I've never had someone to talk to and, given all that's going on, I have to admit I'm. . . so glad you're around.'

'It's nice alright. I feel like I've known you for a lot longer than I actually have. I feel like you know me, like you know the real me, not the popular rugby player that's the life and soul of the party, but the mixed up teenager that's a little bit lost and lonely. I don't think I could cope with Kate's death if it wasn't for the welcome distraction of your crazy life.'

He sighed heavily. There was relief in it and Saoirse echoed its sentiment. Maybe it was true, maybe there was some strange, ancient and mysterious connection that had drawn them to each other, they were both glad it was there. It was nice to have someone to share the burden of their new reality with.

'I better go, Saoirse, don't want to be exhausted tomorrow. We have work to do. I also don't want to worry Dad. He is worrying about me enough already. Now you get off that window seat and get back into bed.' There was a sly chuckle on the other end of the phone as he hung up.

Saoirse was about to ask him how he knew she was sitting there, but the beeps told her he was gone. She smiled contently and hugged her knees up to her chest: life was crazy, but it had some good in it. She stood up and gave the harbour one last glance. The red fox in the garden caught her eye as she turned and she smiled at that too, it returned her gaze and then was gone.

Life, she was discovering, had a wonderful and mysterious side to it. She was beginning to accept that it was not all it seemed to be at first, but that the mystery brought with it a certain amount of happiness.

20

Saoirse woke the next morning surprisingly refreshed and upbeat.

She swung her legs out over the bed and greeted a bright morning outside with a big stretch and a smile to match. She stood at her window and inspected the world outside. She remembered the fox from the night before and looked down to where it had stood and was surprised to see her grandmother standing in the very same spot. At that moment, she looked up at Saoirse and smiled. Things were getting stranger and stranger. She took a breath and remembered the mission herself and Sean were on. She couldn't just let her go without a fight.

Saoirse threw her robe on and checked the cathedral clock, five past seven. She had time to dress after breakfast for school. She turned to leave, but her phone beeped on the bedside table and she grabbed it excitedly, knowing it had to be Sean.

- Morning! Gonna head to school this morning, see you at the gate before, we can work on the books together in double English and during break and lunch. S.

She smiled ridiculously, she knew if she could see her face now it would be one of those cheesy grins that was both goofy and infectious. Sean was going to school; she was going to get to spend more time with him. . . intimately. She caught herself again. She shouldn't be contemplating romance with a guy who had just lost his girlfriend. But it was nice to dream. She sighed heavily; it would be nice to have him hold her, kiss her lips softly. Her grandmother's voice woke her from her fantasy and informed her that two storeys down coffee and porridge were waiting for her. She smiled and shook her head. She'd have to shelve those emotions. For now, her grandmother and working out who He was, was the task in hand. Sean was committed to it, she also had to be: she needed her grandmother, and she couldn't get distracted. She popped her phone in her robe pocket and headed for the kitchen.

She was greeted by her father and her grandmother, busily chatting in the kitchen; they paused mid-conversation to wish her a good morning and then continued. Saoirse picked up her bowl from the table and ladled a large spoon of her grandmother's cinnamon porridge into it from the pot on the stove. She practically dropped the now full bowl when she heard what they were talking about: her dad was discussing her grandmother's will and how the solicitor would be fine with the arrangements they had made.

'What? What in the hell are you talking about?'

'Saoirse, please don't talk to myself or your grandmother like that.' Her dad was angry.

Saoirse's grandmother touched her son's shoulder lovingly and smiled gently at him. She turned to Saoirse and with much love and affection spoke calmly to her granddaughter.

'Saoirse, chicken, it has to be done. I have lived a long and more than full life. I have nothing to be sad or sorry about, I have had my time and I have loved every minute of it. I have the opportunity to ready myself for what is to come. Most people don't get that, and I am going to use that to my benefit. I want to make sure you and your father and mother are looked after. Our family fortune is a little tricky and I don't want anyone to have to go rooting around, so my will has to be straightforward and above board. There are also things I want to do before my time comes and things I want done afterwards. I need you all to help me with these, so I need you to be strong.'

Her voice had been strong and cheerful throughout, but it wavered ever so slightly as she finished. She looked Saoirse lovingly in the eye, crossed the kitchen and took her in her arms. She kissed her softly in her familiar way on the cheek and squeezed her tightly. Saoirse held back tears and breathed in her grandmother's smell. She always smelt so floral; Saoirse had loved the smell since she was little and loved the story behind it. Her grandmother's perfume was created from the beautiful cranesbill flower and its foliage, all native to her beloved Dunluce. Saoirse had yet to see the perfume in a shop and as she had gotten older she had tried to get it in many of them, she had hoped to surprise her grandmother with it as a present. Saoirse could never understand how her grandmother continued to have a bottle of her beloved perfume when she had failed to find it for sale anywhere. She took another deep breath and asked softly,

'Where does the perfume come from, Gran? You can't leave me and not solve that puzzle for me.' She tried to sound upbeat, but it was forced, and inside she felt herself losing the battle with her tears.

'Now that is something I can half answer for you. I have a supplier from home that calls from time to time and hand delivers it to me, in fact I've had a delivery of late, would you like a bottle of your own?' She giggled playfully as if there was some mischief at play between her and the supplier. Saoirse thought hard about who had visited her grandmother lately or who her grandmother had gone to visit. She drew a blank and looked back at her grandmother in a puzzled way. She giggled again and her face lit up, genuinely loving the secrets.

'You have to think outside the box, Saoirse, everything is not as it seems to be, surely you're getting that now.' She winked playfully and squeezed Saoirse's arm affectionately.

'Breakfast, chicken, that porridge is going cold.'

She spun Saoirse towards the island and pushed her gently. Saoirse's father smiled at Saoirse sympathetically, he seemed as lost as she did. Saoirse sat herself down and racked her brain. Outside the box. . . maybe she should chat to Sean.

'So do you want a bottle, chicken?'

Of course she wanted a bottle. The perfume was far too sweet and floral for her to ever want to wear it, well at least not until she had reached her sixties, but Saoirse wanted the smell, she wanted to be able to smell her grandmother even when she was not there. She had always had a strong emotional connection with scents, they brought her comfort and warm memories, and she knew she would find comfort in that smell long after her grandmother was gone.

'Oh I'd love one please, Gran.'

'I'm putting together some stuff for you, so I'll add a bottle of that too,' she said, as she practically skipped out of the kitchen. Saoirse shook her head annoyed. Her father reached across and took her hand. She looked up to see him as irritated and upset as she was.

'We have to support her. I know it's difficult, but we don't have her for much longer. We have to make the most of that time. There's no point in us feeling sorry for ourselves and ruining our final memories of her. I want to live our last few weeks with her to the best of our abilities. She won't be here forever, so let's enjoy her now while we can.'

'But what if we could stop it, stop Him, Dad? Are we just going to give up without a fight?'

Saoirse was pleading with him; she had never known her father to give in.

'Mother tells me there is no fighting Him. She says she's happy for things to go like this. And she wants to protect us. Saoirse, you are my only daughter, I need to protect you too. If Mother passing is going to help that, and she's ready for it, I have to accept it. Please don't make this any more difficult than it is already.'

Now he was pleading and Saoirse could feel his pain soaked in every word. She loved her father so deeply, she couldn't argue with this heartfelt plea. She lowered her head, and sighed heavily.

'I won't, Dad, I promise.' But it was said in the most unconvincing way. She finished her breakfast in silence. She needed to talk to Sean.

21

He was there waiting, as he said he would be, outside the school gate, school uniform immaculate and looking fabulous. She blushed heavily when he spotted her and smiled broadly. She had to stop this, it was ridiculous... but at the same time it was so nice. He spotted her blush and gave her the cheekiest grin. He amazed her, how was he so strong, so together, after all he had been through?

'So Ms Saoirse, how are you this morning? Tired?'

'No I'm good. You?'

'Not too bad at all. I actually got more sleep last night than I have in the past week. I felt tired going to sleep and my mind had been preoccupied so at least I slept.'

Saoirse smiled, it was good to know that he was sleeping better; she couldn't even begin to imagine what it must be like for him at the moment. Kate had been such an important part of his life. She was beginning to feel she had to look out for him, care for him, mind him. All she wanted was to spend time with him, to see his smile and she had a growing desire to be in his arms, to be held tightly and to feel his lips brush hers. Her breath got caught in her chest and she shook her head.

'Penny for them?' he was smiling amusedly at her, his eyes full of curiosity and fun. She dropped her head. Now was not the time to be thinking of him in this way, but she couldn't help herself and she most certainly couldn't tell him. She couldn't believe that all her life she had been longing to have this feeling. But now, when she had finally found someone that had ignited a spark, it was at the most awkward moment in a life that had been uncomfortable at the best of times. Her face burned red with embarrassment, frustration and guilt.

Caught up in a tangle of her thoughts and sinking fast, she forgot where she was, and only Sean's touch on her fallen cheek brought her back, back with a jolt. Electricity ran from her cheek throughout her body, exciting her and intensifying her confusion. As she looked up, she was taken aback by Sean's expression; she thought she saw that same confusion echoed in his eyes. He broke their gaze quickly and nudged her playfully in the ribs.

'Whatever it is snap out of it, we have a lot of work to do and I have a few questions. English is first and we have a double in the library, we might even manage to get an extra class out of Ms Cremin to catch up on the project under the circumstances.'

She looked at him with shock, he was taking advantage of Kate's death, she hadn't expected such a cold response, but as she looked at him, she saw his pain, he had said it, but regretted it instantly.

'That's awful isn't it? Oh Saoirse, I know it's been such a short few days, but there are times when I already find myself moving on, forgetting for just an instant. I'm heartless, aren't I?'

She felt the pain in every word; he was questioning himself, just like she was questioning herself. Life was throwing some serious curve balls at them at the moment; maybe they were just overwhelmed by it. She surprised herself when she felt her hand take his and squeeze it tightly. They were soft but strong: she liked it.

'Sean, I have no idea what it's like to lose someone close. . . although I'm about to find out, if we can't work out who He is and what to do about Him, but I can imagine everyone has moments when they forget. Surely Kate would want you to get on with things. You can't lock yourself away from the world and pretend nothing happened; you have to get out there and get living. I think that's the best thing to do. Show her you loved her by living.'

'I hope you're taking personal notes, my dear Saoirse, because that is very sound advice! I may or may not be repeating that to you very soon.' He now squeezed her hand and pulled her towards him, drawing her into his arms and wrapping them around her. It was as if he knew what he had just said would start her crying. Sean was right, her grandmother would be leaving her shortly and she had to accept that: she couldn't live forever and that had always been the case, or at least in Saoirse's eyes it had been. She had to get on with it, but there was still a glimmer of hope, a chance to prolong the inevitable, hidden somewhere in those books and she and Sean were going to find it. His closeness was comforting, reassuring and blissful. Being around him was heaven and hell, but it was worth it.

'Saoirse, Saoirse. . .'

Back with a bang, they were still standing at the school gates and people were beginning to stare at the pair of them hugging. Sean looked visibly uncomfortable, a little embarrassed and Saoirse's low self-esteem reared its ugly head. She thought he was embarrassed to be seen with her, her stomach flipped and her head swam, the nauseous feeling returned and she could feel the darkness coming: at least he would have an excuse for hugging her, he had been holding her up because she felt faint.

He grabbed her by the shoulder and whispered sternly in her ear, 'Don't you go fainting on me, I need you. I need you to act normally, as if you were just comforting me. Please, if you care about me, help me look like an alright guy, not the one that's already moved on to a new girl five minutes after his girlfriend died.' His voice was pitiful and it was mirrored in his eyes. He wasn't embarrassed to be seen with her, he was embarrassed that it looked like he had already moved on. Saoirse righted herself and caught him as strongly as she could around the shoulders, she squeezed him and then patted him on the back in the way that men do when they try unsuccessfully to show emotion, and then she let go, turned and walked towards the side entrance. Sean was sniggering slightly beside her.

'What? I think that was very good consoling!'

'Oh, is that what you were going for? Saoirse please don't ever harbour desires to be an actor, that was awful. But don't ever change, because you're hilarious as you are.'

They both laughed heartily, and then stopped just as quickly. Moving on was tough, timing was even tougher; they both seemed to be struggling with it.

The library was bustling when they got there, but people stopped and stared when they saw Sean. Saoirse knew people were shocked to see him, she guessed no one had expected him to be back for weeks, maybe even months. He acknowledged them all with a nod or a hello and as he moved across the room the bustle returned with whispers and murmurs no doubt about Sean. He approached Ms Cremin at the main desk with a small smile and a polite hello. It was clear she didn't know what to say to him. He politely asked for the double class and an extra one to work on the project and Saoirse saw her nod in agreement and almost sigh with relief as Sean turned and walked away from her. Sean walked past Saoirse and towards the furthest corner of the library, turning briefly to beckon her.

'It'll be quieter here and we can look at the books without anyone seeing them. I don't feel so bad about Ms Cremin, because technically we are working on the project.'

'And how do you make that out?'

'These stories are all part of your history as such, and we are trying to save your grandmother by looking into her past. It's about you and your family. Fits the brief as far as I'm concerned.'

He pulled his two books out of his bag and held the first to his nose, inhaled and winked at her. Saoirse pulled out one of her books and placed it on the desk in front of her. They were magnificent, unlike any of the books around them. But there were hundreds of stories in them, would they ever get through them and decipher anything that would help in time? Saoirse began to panic.

'Sean when is the next full moon?'

'Jeez, Saoirse, we never checked that!' His voice echoed her own panic. He pulled out his iPhone and googled it. 'October 16th, that gives us three weeks, Saoirse, we don't have much time. We'd better get cracking. So what do you think we are looking for?'

'I have no idea, Sean. I've read these books a few times, but don't remember anything about a creature or being that would have my grandmother willing to face death instead of meeting Him. There are dark beings in the books for sure, but to be honest I would have thought the banshees were the darkest and most foreboding of all of them. But now I see that differently. Maybe reading it now, knowing what I know, might help me see other things.'

'I've made a list of the creatures I've read about in the first book, maybe if we divide them into two lists, good and evil, we can narrow it down.'

'Good idea, are there many?'

'Lots of stories, but generally you have banshees, leprechauns, merrows and fairies. There's talk of pisogs too, but they were never linked to creatures as such, more omens to warn people. I did find that there was a mixed bag of stories, though. Sometimes the stories showed the beings working to help humans, but there are other times when they seem to be so menacing, out of character almost. The eye witnesses always seem to see a negative in the beings, but looking at it in some ways they are doing things for the good of the humans around them. Pretty much like you, Saoirse, warning of coming deaths, saving people from peril. I did notice, too, that in some of the most troublesome stories there are animals that seem to appear in unusual places: black horses appearing in village squares and farm yards, goats and rabbits in places and at times that you wouldn't expect. When these animals appear the stories are always that little more sinister, there is a greater darkness.'

'What if we link the two?'

'What do you mean?'

'I know I love books, Sean, and I know my grandmother said the answer lay within their covers. But modern technology could lend us a little helping hand. Let's Google the words.'

Sean typed the words *black horse, goat and rabbit* into the search engine and they both stared at the screen waiting. . . There it was. The first result and from Wikipedia, the answer they had been looking for: *puca*. They looked at each other and then back at the screen. Sean clicked on the link. It couldn't be this easy, could it? But there it was, in black and white. The screen on the phone was too small for them to read the whole article, so they quickly stashed the books in their school bags and headed to the computer desks at the other end of the library.

Saoirse pulled up the same webpage and they both read hungrily through the article. Was this really the Him her grandmother was so afraid of? The article explained how the puca was both a creature of good and evil, depending on what stories you read and what area of the country you were in. It was so vague, but Saoirse's hair stood up on her neck and arms to the extent that even Sean noticed and brushed her arm ever so slightly.

'I guess that answers that question.'

'I don't know, Sean. He doesn't seem that scary from these reports, does He?'

'Yeah, but he's a shape shifter, look here. That means he can take any guise. . . so maybe a lot of his dreadful deeds are not attributed to him. Your subconscious reaction seals it for me. We just have to work out how to tackle him now, and I'm assuming we'll have to go north to find him.'

'Woah! Slow down there now, Sean, we don't even know if this is actually who we're looking for. Maybe the first place we should go is to my grandmother see if we really are on the right track.'

He looked disappointed, almost: she had robbed him of a great adventure. But he agreed and they decided to return to the books to see what else they could work out from them before they went to talk to her grandmother at lunch. It couldn't come quick enough.

22

er grandmother must have had a sixth sense because the island in the kitchen was set for three when they burst into the kitchen, full of chat and questions.

They were starving after a morning of frantic research and wolfed down the soup and sandwiches. When they had finished, Saoirse's grandmother cleared the plates and set three cups of coffee in front of them. She looked ready for an interrogation. But to begin with she had her own questions.

'So how is the research going?'

She seemed a little annoyed, but Saoirse knew this was because she had asked her to leave this and let her get on with it. Saoirse was a little nervous. How was she going to react to the fact that they thought they had solved the mystery and, with her confirmation, all they had to do now was to come up with a plan? Sean answered her grandmother.

'It's going very well, we think. What can you tell us about the puca?' He was slow and deliberate in saying the word puca and they both watched her intently for her reaction. Her ashen face and caught breath confirmed they were on the right track. She slumped at the counter and looked defeated. Saoirse took no joy in having solved the riddle, she couldn't bear seeing her grandmother so vulnerable. But she needed to know more. They knew who He was, but how did they stop what was about to happen?

'What do we do now, Gran?' Saoirse's voice sounded a little more pleading than she had hoped and she knew immediately from the look on her grandmother's face that she would not be getting an answer, or at least one that was of any help to their mission.

'Leave it be, chicken, leave it be. If not for me, for your father. Bringing Him into your lives is the last thing I want. He will want things, and if he doesn't get them he will take them at any cost. If you love me, you'll leave this. Sean, I beg you: leave this be. Let an old woman die happy without worry or regret. Please.'

She gripped Sean's arm and looked deep into his eyes. She was begging. Saoirse could see him melt under her gaze and he turned to look at Saoirse with a look of defeat. She had hit a soft spot and Sean was helpless.

They all sat silently for a moment and then Saoirse's grandmother lifted herself from the stool with great effort and wearily stood up. She straightened her cardigan, as she always did, and then turned to the both of them and softly said, 'Let it be.' And left the kitchen. Sean and Saoirse looked at each other, not sure what to say or do next.

Moments passed, both mulling over what they should say. Saoirse felt extremely uneasy, she had never defied her grandmother before, but could she really leave this now? Could she just let her grandmother die without a fight, especially now that she knew who she was fighting, even though there was so much more to find out? She pulled her fingers nervously in indecision, cracking the knuckles on each finger slowly and meticulously.

'Saoirse! You'll get arthritis. Will you stop. It's horrible and it really irritates me.' He sounded annoyed, but not so much about the fingers, Saoirse knew it was more about what was happening. He had so welcomed the distraction of this quest, this adventure, but her grandmother had just nipped it in the bud. There was going to be no more losing himself in research, no more mysteries to solve, which meant a return to reality: to loss, death and mourning. Saoirse realised she was in the same position, only she was waiting for the last part rather than already experiencing it.

'I can't leave it, Sean, I can't just let this happen.' She sounded defiant, but not enough to convince him.

'We have to, Saoirse. Your grandmother doesn't want this and perhaps she's right. We have no idea what we are getting ourselves into. Nowhere in the books have we found evidence to suggest the puca is the dangerous evil being your grandmother suggests he is, so maybe he is that powerful that people are just too afraid to speak about Him. Maybe they mention him in a positive light in order to get on his good side. If that's true He really isn't someone we should be messing with. I haven't known your grandmother very long, but I know her enough to know that He must be extremely dangerous to instil such fear in her. She's willing to accept death rather than face him, that says a lot. So if she says leave this, then I really think we should. I have had enough heartache in my life of late; I don't really think I could handle any more right now.'

He leant across and touched her softly as if to console her and it annoyed her, the whole thing set her alight and anger boiled in the pit of her stomach. She couldn't just leave this be, she couldn't just let go without a fight. He could give up that easily, it wasn't his grandmother. She'd do it on her own; she'd find and sort this, although she had no idea how. She nodded unconvincingly at Sean and he read her expression.

'Saoirse, you are the worst liar I've ever met! I can see your thoughts written clearly across the frown on your forehead. You have to leave this go, you have to do as she asks, as we all ask.'

'I can't, Sean, I just can't. . .' Emotions overcame her and she broke down and coughed out frustrated, tearless sobs. She couldn't accept that this was final. She could not accept it; knowing death was coming and feeling helpless to do anything. She let the emotion completely overcame her and sank into a depth of despair she had never experienced before. Sean held her on the stool and she let the darkness take her.

She opened her eyes to see her grandmother standing before her. There was a determined look on her face, and Saoirse felt sure they would get some answers. Her grandmother began slowly and assuredly.

'A banshee is an immortal being, according to some without a soul or even a body, but we do have souls, we do have bodies, although they may be different in some ways to ordinary folk. I fell in love with your grandfather not long after I first became his banshee and visited him before the death of his mother. His sensitive soul, his acceptance and trust of what I was telling him, was captivating. I wanted to be near him all the time, but without a death I didn't have a reason. Then when his aunt died and cousin took sick I had an opportunity to spend more time with him. We fell in love at the most inappropriate time, and it was impossible. I wasn't human and he was a well-to-do O'Donnell. The books gave us hope; we read stories of one so powerful He could help us overcome our impossibilities. He was the answer, but He was not to be dealt with lightly. Few knew where to find Him; others were too frightened to tell us. But in the end He came and found us, eager to broker a deal and rid Himself of another banshee, and more importantly another O'Donnell. He granted me mortality, but there came with it a heavy price. We had to leave the North, never tell anyone that He had done this for us: our secret was to die with us. We were never to return to Dunluce or contact those we had left behind. It was a difficult decision, as you can imagine. Your grandfather was leaving his family, I was leaving a community, but we were so in love and wanted to be together so much, that it was worth it.' She licked her lips ever so slightly to moisten them and although her face was worried, flashes of a smile hinted on her lips as she spoke of Saoirse's grandfather. 'As I said, we came here because it was so far south and unrelated to anything from my world that I could find. I had your father about ten years after we moved down. We had never expected children and had been quite content to just be together. It had never been part of any arrangement and to this day I'm still not sure whether He even knows whether your father, or you, for that matter, exist. I'd like to think he doesn't, but I couldn't be sure. He will have no interest in your father, Saoirse, but you, on the other hand, I'm sure He will be very interested in. Sean, be careful and mind this precious one. I'm warning you both now, He will come and He will want answers. . . and more.'

And with that she hugged them both and left abruptly. They knew no more than they had when she came in, but both somehow knew that time was running out and they weren't going to find answers. Not here and now, anyway.

23

Saoirse had spent the last week and a half frantically searching archives of Irish folklore with Sean in a vain quest to find some answers, but all to no avail. She was defeated and sat on the window seat and watched the clear dark night on the harbour below her. It was clear time was running out. October was closing in fast and she traced the pale crescent moon on the window pane in front of her and sighed heavily. She had spent days trying to find any information she could on the puca: where she might find one, how she might make contact. This evening she had given up in despair. Who was she kidding? She had no clue what she was doing. Without her grandmother or Sean, she was lost at sea. Although, in fairness, how in the hell do you get in contact with a mythical creature that, according to modern society, doesn't even exist?

Her grandmother had caught her this evening and been very upset. Saoirse had promised her she would cease her futile quest and had spent the rest of the evening on the window seat with her comb emptying her mind of the worries that crowded it.

The weather had returned to its proper cycle and the temperatures were dipping. The leaves had finally begun to change colour and fall. The communal garden below her was turning a beautiful golden and the oak trees at the far end of the lawn, near the steps to the library, were beginning to shed their leafy coats. The light of the crescent moon cast shadows across the garden and highlighted the naturally gathered piles of early fallen leaves. She would normally have loved this time of year and would have kicked her way through the leaves in the garden, but she had no mind for it of late. She had no mind for anything at all.

She pulled the silver comb through her long heavy hair, her mind calming with each stroke. She thought how wonderful it would be if she could spend the rest of her life holed up here on her window seat, wrapped in her robe, watching the dark harbour ebb and flow below her and numbed so wonderfully by the magic of the silver comb. Wouldn't it be fabulous to be able to block out the reality of the mess her life had become, forget about Sean's dead girlfriend, his dead mother, and the long list of other people he was mourning, to forget about the fact that she was a banshee, hard and all as it was to believe, and finally to forget the fact that, in the very near future, she was going to lose her best friend, and all because of some strange and mysterious contract her grandmother had made with the puca.

She had spent time with Sean in school over the past few days, but without the distraction of the adventure they had hoped to be on right now, Sean had returned to his mourning. She did her best to keep him occupied working on their English project, but the truth was she was as miserable as he was; she was already mourning her grandmother even though she was still very much alive and well. She found it hard to spend time with her without getting upset and so had resorted to spending her time on her laptop, searching for information on the puca and then lulling herself into numbness at her window with her silver comb.

Saoirse snapped out of her daze as the moon crept behind a large dark cloud and the garden below went black. A feeling grew in her stomach that she could neither describe or name, but it spread outwards and the hairs began to stand on her hands and neck. Her stomach churned and she felt uneasy, she didn't feel as if she was going to faint, but instead felt alert and apprehensive: something was happening, something big.

A howl, unlike anything she had ever heard, erupted from the garden below and she looked down to be met by the sad, yellow eyes of the fox. It howled again, a long and piercing sound that resonated in her head, but it never broke their stare. The feeling of apprehension grew in Saoirse's stomach and while she was in no way threatened by the fox below, she knew this was bad. It was an ally, she was sure of that, and the howl was one of pain, more than terror. And then it dawned on Saoirse: the fox was her grandmother's friend, probably a shape shifter. She had read so much about them of late, maybe it was a fairy friend that remained in touch all these years, and the bearer of the perfume, no doubt.

Saoirse moved to her knees and pressed her face against the glass to see the scene below better: was her grandmother there too? In doing this she broke her gaze with the fox and it howled again, a longer and more sorrowful sound. It was heart wrenching and Saoirse immediately knew her grandmother would not be there. She panicked, jumped off the window seat and flew across the room, down the two flights of stairs, across the corridor and burst into her grandmother's room.

Saoirse wasn't sure what she was expected to find, but her grandmother looked as if she was sleeping soundly. Something told her she wasn't. She stepped closer to the bed and sat slowly down next to her, she held her hand under her grandmother's nose in the hope that she would feel her breath. When she felt none she placed her hand on her cheek and the cold confirmed her worst fears. What erupted from her lungs was something uncontrollable and indescribable, but Saoirse was sure that the sound could be heard throughout the house and indeed the entire street. The fox echoed her from the window outside.

How long she continued to make this sound she unsure, but she was still wailing uncontrollably when her mother ran in, pulling her away and telling her to calm down. She caught her breath, and tried to loosen herself from her mother's grip and returned to the room, but her mother held fast and dragged her to the kitchen, sat her firmly on the stool at the island and handed her a whiskey and told her to sip. Saoirse did as she was told. The whiskey warmed her throat as it went down and then exploded into her stomach. She had expected to wince and feel sick as she had seen in so many movies, but she didn't. She liked the warmth and secretly desired the numbness it would bring.

Her grandmother's room was illuminated at the end of the dark corridor and Saoirse felt she was watching her father in a movie. He was sat in the same spot that Saoirse had been, and he was gently stoking his mother's hair. His back was to her but from the frequent heaves Saoirse could tell he was crying. Again she was overcome by guilt. All too often lately she had made it all about her, she'd forgotten about how this would affect her dad. As she looked up and saw her mother's ashen and tear-soaked face too. She held her hand out to her mother, who took and squeezed it.

'Oh, Mum, I'm so sorry for being so self-centred. I just. . .'

Saoirse broke down and allowed the tears to flow. Her mother pulled her from the stool and into her arms, and they sobbed, as they held each other tightly, letting go of so much emotion. They hadn't been this close for quite a while and Saoirse was disappointed that this reunion with her mother had to be now, when they both couldn't enjoy it and relish it, but when all that was to be felt was consolation and loss.

Saoirse lost track of time and couldn't gauge how long they had been embraced in the kitchen, when her father came in and joined them. They all stood hugging each other and sobbing. There was comfort to be found in it and none of them were ready to face the next step.

24

The doorbell startled them. Saoirse looked at the clock, it was half four, perhaps her cries had woken a neighbour like her mother had warned. Saoirse crossed the dark corridor, turned the outside light on and slowly opened the door. She did not expect who stood at the door, but they both seemed to already know what was going on and immediately took her in their arms and hugged her as they came across the threshold. Sean lingered on the top step outside, after Father Michael headed towards the kitchen to her parents. Saoirse looked at him questioningly, but she didn't have time to say anything, because she was sobbing into his chest before she knew it and he was gently stroking her hair and leading her upstairs. He sat her gently at the window, took the comb from its box and began to comb her hair.

With each delicate stroke Saoirse's sobbing calmed and eventually she was able to ask him how he and Father Michael had known to call.

'Your grandmother called me.' His voice was gentle and he paused slightly. 'She called this afternoon, said that she was a little nervous, that she had found you snooping again this morning and was afraid you'd stumble across the information you needed so she had decided the time was right now. She said I was not to tell you this until after... She said to wait till roughly half three, four this morning and leave home then. She had even spoken with my father and cleared it with him. I thought it was all a little too much, but as I reached the top of the hill I heard your cry and I knew she hadn't been lying. I knew it was your cry, Saoirse.

I have never heard anything like it before and it carried all the way to there, I'm sure you could hear it all over town.'

So her grandmother had spoken to Sean and his father, she'd told them she had chosen to die tonight and she had chosen to die because she had continued to snoop. It was her fault, and while she should have been feeling guilty right now the comb was keeping her calm. It wasn't just smoothing her hair but it was also keeping her thoughts straight. It didn't matter whether she had been snooping or not, her grandmother had chosen this path, it would have happened anyway.

Sean stopped combing and took Saoirse by the shoulders and turned her to face him. He looked her straight in the eye and pushed a stray strand of hair behind her ear. He was beautiful and Saoirse was putty in his hands. She could sit for hours here and stare into those eyes, even now when she should be mourning her grandmother.

'Saoirse, did you hear me? I heard you, I heard you from the top of the hill, I shouldn't be able to do that.'

Saoirse found this funny and smirked. He had been so willing to believe all the other fairy myths, and the fact that she was his banshee, why would he now think it was so strange that he could hear her wail at such a distance? Wasn't that wail one of the most distinguishing characteristics of an Irish banshee?

'I'm a banshee, Sean, what do you expect?' It was light-hearted and accepting. She was who she was and she was surprised at how light-hearted she had been under the current circumstances. She even gave a little giggle and a shrug of her shoulders. His hands were still holding them and at the giggle he pulled her towards him and he hugged her tightly and whispered softly.

'I'm here, Saoirse, I'm not going anywhere. I'm here whenever you need me.'

Saoirse sighed, but didn't cry. She had known this was

coming for weeks now, her grandmother had prepared her for it, but she had also left her with someone she knew would help her make it through. Sean would be there for her, not just tonight, but tomorrow and the day after. She may have lost her grandmother and best friend, but her grandmother had ensured that that position was quickly filled. She had a friend, someone to rely on.

'Thanks, Sean, I'm overwhelmed, but at the same time quite calm now. I'm not sure whether it's the comb or the fact that I know I have you. You know who I am. You know how I'm feeling, so I can just be me. And that's such a help. She was so peaceful looking you know, she looked as if she was asleep. It was the fox that tipped me off...'

'The fox?'

'I've seen it a couple of times lately. A beautiful fox, I had assumed it was just a town fox, I'd seen it before. But recently it began to almost make a connection with me, it would hold my stare as I watched it from the window, and tonight I knew when I looked into its eyes that something was wrong. Its howl clarified it for me, because when I ran down the stairs she had gone. The fox is a friend of my grandmother's, a friend from home. I'm reckoning it's a shape shifter, but we'll never know now.'

'Maybe that's the friend she had been meeting and organising with? Father Michael knew a lot too. I met him on the steps; he was sitting on the top one. He wasn't surprised to see me, He said he was just giving ye time before he called. I still think it's very strange that he's your grandmother's confidante, the Catholic church and banshees, it just doesn't seem to quite fit, if you know what I mean.'

'He's different, Sean. I spoke to him the day of Kate's funeral. He gets it: he doesn't question the existence of his own god, so he shouldn't question the existence of us. I kinda figured my grandmother would have arranged things with him, he's too tied up in all this, he knows so much and she would have wanted to protect him too.'

Saoirse sighed again, her grandmother had been busy today; she had been busy for the past few weeks. Saoirse wondered what she had been up to, but she was pretty sure they were going to find out soon enough. She jumped as a knock sounded on her door. She froze, clutching Sean's hand in hers. Who would be calling now?

The door opened slowly, revealing a shadowy man in the doorway. She blinked allowing her eyes to get used to the light from the hallway, then took a deep exhale. It was Father Michael. He stood meekly in the doorway and waited for them to invite him in. When she did, he crossed the room and took Saoirse's free hand in his, and squeezed it softly.

'She was a wonderful woman, you'll forgive me, please, when I say that I will miss her so much and I am feeling a little lost tonight. It is not my place to grieve, but still I am. I've lost a dear friend, but it is nothing in comparison to your loss.' He squeezed her hand again and dropped his head. Saoirse's heart broke for him, everyone was entitled to grieve and she felt the need to comfort him.

'Michael, you were her very dear friend, probably the only friend who truly knew her. You're allowed to be sad, we all are.' Saoirse shocked herself with her maturity and strength; she had expected to be a mess. She took his hand and directed him towards the window seat and he sat down beside her. 'I assume you have lots to discuss with me, instructions perhaps, warnings more probably from her, that you have been asked to relay. Now is as good a time as any to start.' She felt strong, she felt ready to hear what her grandmother had left in store for her.

'She knew you'd be eager, she knew you'd be expecting something, but she wants you to take your time. For tonight and tomorrow you are to be there for your mum and dad. That's an order, she said. It's Wednesday today, on Friday she is being cremated, after which I'm allowed to tell you everything. But between now and then, she wants you to mourn normally, and be with your family. She also said you'd try to convince me to give you this information earlier but that Sean was to stop you, and tell you to be patient.'

He winked at Sean and they looked at her sternly, but conspiratorially. The game was set. There was no sense in trying to get around it. Her grandmother had it all arranged. Even in death, she was still in charge!

'No way at all of getting that info now?'

It was said dejectedly, but Saoirse thought it was worth a try and they both answered in unison with an emphatic, 'No!' It was stern but playful. She pushed herself back into the window seat, so her back leant against the window frame, and pulled her knees up to her chest.

'I thought I'd be more upset, I thought I'd feel differently. Is there something wrong with me?' She looked to them both for answers, and neither answered immediately. There was a long silence where Saoirse heard her mother moving around the kitchen two floors below. Father Michael looked to Sean and then to Saoirse.

'It's shock, Saoirse, it's completely normal. I know you've been expecting this, but it's still a shock. Everyone deals with death and loss differently, no one way is right or wrong.'

'I've heard that before.' And she looked at Sean. He smiled reassuringly at her and came and joined her on the window seat. They all turned and looked out at the dark harbour below. In the distance the first glimmers of sunrise were beginning to creep above the refinery on the far side of the harbour. Saoirse heard the howl of the fox once more, clear and shrill, but far off this time. Sean squeezed her hand tightly and placed a soft kiss on the top of her hand. What happened now?

The answer was quick in coming. A loud bang at the front door announced the arrival of their local GP, Dr Kelleher. Saoirse heard Dr Kelleher's voice commiserating with her father, and realised that, other than the odd check-up, Saoirse really didn't know this man. She could count the number of times she had been to see him on one hand. She knew his voice as a friend of her father's. They had gone to school together. He and his wife visited now and then for dinner, always leaving with the promise to do it more regularly, and always failing. But James greeted and comforted her parents as an old friend, before switching to professional mode and asking to see the body. Saoirse heard another voice, which she assumed was the undertaker, as it sounded at ease in the situation that was evolving below.

Saoirse looked to the cathedral clock: it was coming up to seven o clock. Where had the last three hours disappeared to? And what would this new day bring?

25

Saoirse boiled the kettle for what seemed like the fiftieth time that morning. Father Michael had stayed until the doctor had finished and the undertaker had taken the body away. But since then there had been a stream of neighbours, in to pay their respects and spend time with the family. Most were inquisitive more than comforting, but Saoirse was polite to each and every one, and was in awe at the endless supply of food each of them brought. Her mother wouldn't have to cook for a month, especially when Saoirse realised her grandmother had also stocked the freezer with all their favourite meals.

The crowd slowed in the run up to lunch time and Saoirse had an opportunity to have a few moments alone in the kitchen. Sean had gone upstairs to ring his father and tell him he was staying for another while and her mother and father were in the study following instructions laid out by Father Michael.

Saoirse had briefly nipped into her grandmother's room before they had taken her and found it so strange. She couldn't describe the emotions she had felt, sitting on the side of the bed. She had held her grandmother's hand, now cold and rigid, expecting to cry and want to hug her, but hadn't felt like that at all. Inside she became very aware that this was no longer her grandmother: she had been released from this human form, and Saoirse felt that wherever she may be, her grandmother still existed. This just the empty shell. The feeling had been uplifting and given her strength and had surprised her mother, who had come to join her in the room. It was obvious to Saoirse her mother had expected her to be a mess and was shocked at how together she was and how optimistic she seemed. She hugged her tightly and whispered softly in her ear that if optimism failed, she was here if she needed her.

But sitting here at the window, sipping hot coffee and looking out across the lawn, Saoirse was optimistic. She remembered her grandmother said she had to go home, it was comforting to think that was just what she had done. She held the coffee mug to her face and inhaled deeply. She had gone. But she was also still here. She would always be here, in the smells of hot coffee, the taste of lemon cookies and cinnamon porridge. She crossed the kitchen and took a lemon cookie from the jar next to the stove and took a bite. Yes, she would always be here.

'Oh God, I'd love one! I'm starving.'

Sean was next to her and before she knew it, he had taken the remaining piece of cookie from her hand and devoured it. He reached across her and took a mug from the counter behind her and filled it with coffee from the pot on the stove. Saoirse inhaled his smell and closed her eyes briefly. That was another smell that would be with her always. Butterflies fluttered in her stomach, it was a feeling she was growing to enjoy. It meant he was close to her, and that was a good thing. It was the worst timing in the world, but at least it was happening. She might not be able to do anything about it at the moment, but maybe she could in time. She hoped Sean would be in her life for a long time to come. She sighed, and looked up to find Sean standing extremely close and gazing down at her, coffee mug cupped in his hands and held to his chin.

'Penny for them? You know you go into a daze when you're thinking, it's mesmerising.' He blushed ever so slightly and this sent Saoirse's heart racing. She smiled sweetly up at him: maybe this wasn't one sided after all. He put down the coffee, never moving his gaze and moved in closer. Saoirse could feel his warmth, although he wasn't touching her. He leant forward and for a split second Saoirse thought he was actually going to kiss her, but he moved to her ear and whispered softly, but with a voice that was loaded with pain and guilt.

'I have feelings for you, have done since the moment I met you. It was part of the reason Kate and I were fighting the night she died, she said I couldn't stop talking about you. Your grandmother told me not to feel guilty. She said that the connection was inevitable. Fate and destiny had brought us together, just as it did with her and your granddad. She assured me that no matter how hard I had fought it, it would have always won. I didn't think it would mean Kate dying, but your grandmother said that was Kate's destiny not mine. Saoirse, it's the wrong time for this, I know, but all I want to do is hold you. . . I better go. I'm sorry.' He panicked and began to draw away.

Saoirse grabbed his arm before he could move away and threw her arms around him and held him tightly. At first he was rigid and it was awkward, but he quickly melted into her and lifted her ever so slightly from the ground and hugged her tightly. Saoirse was in heaven, she never wanted to let go, she wasn't alone or imagining that there was a connection between them. She was glad too that she wasn't the only one having a crisis of conscience about the timing of everything and she was about to tell him all this when her mother walked into the kitchen and broke their embrace with a forced cough.

They broke apart quickly. Sean blushed crimson and excused himself to the bathroom. Saoirse looked at her mother annoyed, it was the first truly intimate moment she had experienced in her entire life, it had been wonderful, but it had been too short-lived. Her mother didn't look happy, and Saoirse realised that to her it was inappropriate, and the timing was certainly off, it was everything they were both worrying about, so Saoirse quickly tried to cover herself.

'I was upset and Sean was comforting me... that's all we were doing, Mum.'

'Why do you feel the need to explain, Saoirse? Perhaps because that's not what was really going on? Sean seemed more upset than you to be honest. Honey, your emotions are all over the place at the moment, as are Sean's. Now is not the time to be starting anything. One of you or both of you could get hurt.' There was annoyance in her voice, but there was also genuine concern, and Saoirse felt it was time to open up to her mother and be honest.

'But there's a connection, Mum, like nothing I have ever experienced before. I've never even really liked a boy before. But there's something about Sean, something special. The feeling I have when he's close to me, the fact that I know him so well, without really knowing him at all. I know the timing is lousy, Mum, I've been battling with it since Kate's death, but because I feel so strongly about him, all I want to do is hold him, protect him, care for him. I'm awful, Mum, I know, but it's how I feel.'

Her mother's annoyance melted before her eyes and she crossed the kitchen and held her daughter. She said nothing for a long time and then asked if Sean knew. She suddenly realised that he didn't, he had just poured his heart out to her and she hadn't had the opportunity to tell him she felt the same.

'I didn't get a chance to tell him, Mum. He just opened up and told me how he felt and how it was tearing him apart with guilt and I never got to tell him, you walked in right then...'

'Go talk to him, Saoirse, don't leave the boy hanging like that.'

Her mother squeezed her tightly and released her towards the hallway. Saoirse called Sean's name, but there was no reply. She ran the two flights of stairs to her bedroom and her study but there was no sign of him there either. Where could he have gone? She took her phone from her bedside table and texted him.

- WHERE'D YOU DISAPPEAR TO?

She waited patiently for a reply and settled herself on her window seat to examine the town below. She waited and waited. No reply. Saoirse checked the clock on the cathedral spire and a tall dark figure entering the church caught her eye. She'd know that stature anywhere. It was Sean. She grabbed her coat from the closet and bolted down the stairs and out the door. She climbed the steps on the other side of the road and headed towards the cathedral. Her steps were far too slow; walking just didn't seem fast enough, so she began to run. She didn't exactly know why she was running, or what she was going to say, but she quickened her pace and was completely out of breath by the time she reached the doors of the cathedral. She stopped on the steps, trying to catch her breath and then stepped into the darkness.

Sean was a few seats from the back, hunched over the pew, kneeling. She stepped into the seat next to him, and sat. He didn't move at first, and it wasn't until Saoirse softly placed her hand on his shoulder that he turned around, tears in his eyes and pain etched in his face. Saoirse's heart broke. What had she done? She pulled him up from his knees and he sat next to her on the seat, she took his hand in hers and held it tightly. She had to fix this. She had to tell him how she felt.

'I never got a chance to answer you. I know it's the worst timing in the world, Sean, I keep hating myself for the way I'm thinking about you. You've just lost your girlfriend, for God's sake, and all I want to do is hold you, not to comfort you but to hold you for me. It's just so selfish, but it's there and I feel it too. What are we like? We can't do this, we can't do it now, it's completely wrong and so inappropriate. Poor Kate. How would her family feel if they knew? I just feel so terrible about everything, but I'm secretly delighted you feel it too.'

She blushed heavily and hung her head, he took her chin and lifted her head, her heart quickened and she prepared herself again for what she anticipated would be her first kiss, but he held her face at arm's length and spoke softly and warmly.

'I know it's the wrong time, we can't do anything about this now, but maybe in the future. Maybe some distance for the time being would be better. . .'

There was resignation in his tone; she knew there would be no kiss. Just more waiting. Saoirse knew in her heart that this moment would pass and awkwardness would creep in. They had laid their cards on the table, but folded. The game was in stalemate and they were both about to walk away from the table. She didn't want that to happen, she couldn't let it happen. She couldn't just let him go.

'You'll stay with me through the funeral though?' She couldn't believe how pitiful she sounded. Her words dripping with desperation.

'Of course I will. I care about you, Saoirse, but I can't do *this*. . . us. . . I want to, but it's just wrong. I'll be here for you this week, but then we need to take some time.'

He held her hand still, and she knew he was right. It was the wrong time and Sean, being the person he was, would do the right thing. He couldn't hurt Kate's family or indeed Kate's memory by moving on so quickly. She hated it, but it was part of the reason she felt so much for him. She couldn't believe that in a short few weeks she had come to feel so strongly for someone. She had never had feelings for someone before and now. . . now she was in love and she couldn't do anything about it. She didn't know which was worse: never loving, or not being able to have him. She sighed heavily and it echoed around the dark cavernous space around them. They were alone. No one seemed to venture in during the daylight hours except for mass. It was the start of October so there were no tourists either. It was just the two of them, but the memories of loved ones stood between them. Saoirse let go of his hand and slumped back in the seat.

'Why is life always so difficult?'

It was intended as a thought, but Saoirse heard it echo around her and it was not Sean's voice that answered, but Father Michael's.

'God only knows. And I don't mean that literally.' His voice was light hearted and he giggled ever so slightly. 'Probably shouldn't say that considering where we are, or maybe it's just the thing to say. As a priest I would say that God has a plan, but your grandmother would say it's destiny. Life is difficult, because we are working towards what is meant for us. We just have to leave it to fate or faith, whichever you chose.'

They both looked up at him, unsure of what he had overheard, hoping it had just been Saoirse's last outburst. They need not have worried, because even if he had heard, Father Michael's face was not one of judgement, instead his smile was warm and reassuring. He sat into the pew in front of them and turned to face them. Saoirse was surprised that she hadn't realised how attractive a man he was for a priest. She wondered what had brought him to the priesthood, why he had never married. But whatever it had been, she was glad he was here now. There was something so settling and calming about his presence.

'You two have been through a lot lately, you're lucky to have each other to get you through. I have a bit of work to do in the sanctuary, but I need to talk to you both this evening before the cremation tomorrow. Will you be in Saoirse's at about six?'

'I was hoping to go home and see dad for a bit, but I can be back by six.'

Father Michael obviously had something he needed to talk to them about and it must be serious enough that he could not do it here and now. She noted a little sparkle of excitement in his eye. Perhaps, despite her grandmother's death, the adventure was still alive.

26

Saoirse sat in the kitchen, the house was quiet. Her parents were out, busy organising the funeral. It was strange without her grandmother there; it just didn't feel quite the same. The range was empty of bubbling pots and there was no hustle and bustle that came with the whirlwind of her grandmother's cooking. She cradled the cup of coffee in her hands and took comfort in its heat. She hadn't seemed to be able to get warm all day.

Sean tapped on the French doors and let himself and Michael in. Saoirse offered tea and the two men accepted. She busied herself with the kettle and cups and poured a jug of milk. The occasion seemed to demand a little formality. She placed the last of the lemon cookies on a plate and arranged it all in the centre of the island where the two had settled themselves.

Sean could not conceal the anticipation on his face; he was eager to hear what Michael had to say and took it upon himself to pour the tea. Michael could tell he was eager and seemed to deliberately stall, taking his time with the milk and asking for sugar. He winked teasingly at Saoirse as she rose to get the sugar from the cupboard.

'Ah, Michael, you're killing me! What's this all about? What did she want you to say to us?' His restraint was gone; he couldn't hold it in any longer.

Michael grinned wryly. He took another sip of his tea, and played with the lemon cookie in front of him, before taking a large bite. He took his time chewing, and when he had finally finished, he took another sip of his tea. Sean was about to burst when Michael cleared his throat.

'Sean, Sean, Sean. Patience is a virtue you know! I needed a little refreshment before we began. I've been busy all afternoon with the list of chores she left me.'

Sean looked deflated, he clearly wasn't going to get the information he wanted immediately, he was going to have to wait and listen. Saoirse sat and looked at the two men in front of her. How strange the situation must look. How strange her life had become!

Two months ago she knew neither of these men, but now they seemed to be the only friends she had in the world, and other than her mum and dad, they were the only people who knew who and what she really was.

'Michael, can we get on with this please. What is it my grandmother has left for us to do? What other questions has she left unanswered?'

'Saoirse, don't be cross. This final bit isn't so stressful, or confusing, but it is an adventure of sorts. She wants you and Sean to take her home.' A smile spread across his face and his tone was bright: he saw this as a good thing.

'She wants us to take her home?' Saoirse didn't get it. 'She wants us to take her back to Dunluce? And how are we going to do that?

'She knew Sean had got his driving licence a few weeks ago, she booked everything and has it all organised.'

He pulled a large folder from his satchel, which Saoirse only spotted now. He opened it and emptied its contents onto the table. Sean looked at Saoirse, with mischief in his eyes. He'd been wanting an adventure up North. And now they'd have one.

Everything was booked and organised: return train tickets from Cobh to Dublin, connecting to Belfast, a camper van, of all things, and a small envelope with both Euro and Sterling notes inside. Among all these things Saoirse found a set of hand-written instructions, one set for her and one for Sean. Saoirse looked at Michael with disbelief.

'Is this for real? She wants us to take her home to Dunluce on our own? And Sean is going to drive a camper van from Belfast out there. She's nuts.'

Saoirse's realised she had referred to her grandmother in the present and this realisation caught in her chest. She was gone, she had known she was going and had spent her last few days organising this mad adventure for herself and Sean. Crazy and all as it may seem, her grandmother had thought it important enough to spend her last days on it, and Saoirse could not disrespect her grandmother by not fulfilling one of her dying wishes. She went to open her set of instructions, but Michael grasped her hand softly and stopped her.

'More rules! I'm sorry, but I'm not to know what's in the instructions. All I'm allowed know is that you are travelling to Dunluce, after that she requested that you tell me nothing. My safety depends on it, particularly if He turns up.'

'Turns up where?' Sean had been quiet, taking in all the paperwork on the table in front of him, but the mention of 'Him' grabbed his attention immediately. There was a spark in his eyes, he thrived on the danger. Saoirse hoped that was a good thing, and not a recipe for disaster.

'Your grandmother said He may appear at some stage. She thought that perhaps He may show up at the crematorium to make sure she was really dead, but she is almost certain he will show his face in Dunluce. At that stage he will have a fair idea that you exist, but she's hoping He won't realise what you are.'

'There's a lot of hopes and expectations there, Father. Could we be in danger? Could Saoirse be in danger?'

'As with everything of late, I have no straightforward answer. I am assuming that His presence anywhere will bring with it some elements of danger for Saoirse, but her grandmother thinks your presence might defuse the situation in some way. To be honest she was slow to tell me anything. She said I knew far too much already for my own good and she didn't want to put me at any more risk. She certainly was an infuriating woman; God rest her soul. All I wanted to do was put her mind at ease before she left, and let her know I would try and protect you, but she didn't want to hear it. After tomorrow I'm to steer clear of you till you come back.'

He looked quickly at his wrist watch, and shuffled nervously on his feet. He touched the satchel's flap lightly and then checked the clock on the wall. He seemed very ill at ease, and both Saoirse and Sean looked at each other confused.

'Michael, are you okay?' Saoirse was perplexed.

'I have confessions, right now! I've never missed them before, I'd better go. I really wish I could stay, but duty calls, I suppose.' They could see the disappointment written all over his face, followed by a flash of realisation. 'I guess she probably timed my visit deliberately. She knew I couldn't miss confessions, and she knew I wanted to know what was in the instructions, even though she had asked me not to. She was a clever old woman, your grandmother. A mighty clever woman.'

She had beaten him from the other side and he graciously accepted defeat. He reached into his satchel and Saoirse watched, mesmerised, as he pulled out one last treasure. Its quality and craftsmanship could be seen from a distance in its deep smooth, luxurious pile. It was mink grey, subtle but warm. Saoirse instinct was to reach out and touch it and looks had not deceived, it was sublime to the touch as her fingers ran softly over the folded material.

'What is it?'

'It's yours. Well, it is now. She said it was hers, that she has had it for quite some time. It was made around the time of your books, in the same workshops. She said it was now yours and that you would know when you needed it, but to make sure you brought it with you.'

He handed over the folded material, and then reached out and pulled Saoirse towards him and kissed her forehead. Saoirse was surprised that she didn't feel awkward or uncomfortable. His gentle kiss brought with it a warm comfort.

'She loved you beyond belief. You are an extraordinary young woman; she knew that greatness was your destiny. I hope you keep me in your life so that I can witness that. I loved your grandmother and will miss her deeply. I would hate to lose you too.'

Saoirse hugged him tightly and smiled broadly at him when she released him.

'How could I not have you in my life? I need a voice of reason. I'm certainly not going to get that from Sean!'

They laughed and looked towards him and he feigned disgust and disbelief. It lightened the mood and they all welcomed that.

'I'd better go; I've pensioners waiting to confess their mortal sins. I'll see you both tomorrow at twelve. I know as a priest I shouldn't envy, but I would love to be heading off on this adventure. But your grandmother insists she knows best.'

He squeezed Saoirse's arm affectionately and slapped Sean on the back as he headed towards the French doors and then disappeared into the darkness, leaving Saoirse standing in the middle of the kitchen with the grey material and Sean sitting at the island studying a series of tickets and maps. Saoirse gently placed her treasure on the island and stroked it softly and lovingly, before turning and heading to the counter.

'What are you doing? Aren't you going to see what it is, read the instructions?'

'Oh I am, but I have a feeling that this is going to be a long night, I'm making coffee first.'

Saoirse looked up from her third cup of coffee and caught Sean looking at her in a daze. He looked away, embarrassed, and quickly got up and poured himself another cup from the pot. They had been sitting here for hours. Saoirse's parents had come and gone. Dinner had been heated and eaten, without them ever moving from the island. You would think that the instructions had been long and cryptic, but they were anything but. Concise and to the point was all that you could say, no major information given, some slight differences in the details but for the most part they were the same. They couldn't figure out why she had written two separate sets when one would have done.

Saoirse looked at Sean, busying himself with the coffee pot. What had she gotten him into? She tried to keep her mind on the trip, but all she could think of was holding him, feeling his arms around her. She knew that contact would bring with it a release quite similar to the numbing effect of her silver comb, but Sean was untouchable, and it was killing her. She had been sitting there for the last two hours contemplating the awkwardness and tension that this trip was inevitably going to entail. A trip to the North alone with Sean! How could it be enjoyable, carrying your dead grandmother's ashes, knowing that you were being followed by an unknown force that was of great danger to you? And that you'll be in the company of a boy that is completely off limits to you. Life truly sucked, but it would make a good book, she giggled.

Her laugh was louder than she expected and it echoed in the stillness of the kitchen. Sean whirled around from the stove and spilled coffee all over himself and the floor.

'What? What's so funny?'

'God, Sean, you've made a right mess!'

Saoirse jumped down from her seat, took some kitchen roll from the counter and went to bend down to mop up the mess on the floor. Their heads collided mid-stoop with a light thud. In that instance they both inhaled deeply. His smell got her every time, she weakened at the knees and as if by instinct Sean took her by the elbows and righted her. Caught in the moment, caught in each other's gaze, the world fell away. They knew this wasn't something they would ever be able to fight completely. There was magnetism between them. Sean leant in to her ear and whispered ever so softly.

'If only it was another time another place, I would kiss you now Saoirse O'Donnell, I would kiss you long and hard and show you just how I'm feeling right now. Believe me, it will happen, but not just yet.'

He stood back from her and then like Michael had done before him he kissed her gently on the forehead. This kiss however brought no comfort, just a frustration and desire for so much more.

'I'd better go, before we do something we regret. I'll text later and call first thing. I think a break from these instructions and fresh eyes might help us work it out. Even though there doesn't seem to be anything to work out!'

He turned and was gone. Saoirse was left in the kitchen, alone, unsatisfied and confused.

27

The comfort and familiarity of her window seat and the numbing bliss her silver comb brought gave Saoirse comfort as she sat and watched the harbour bustle to and fro. It was a cold, clear night. She shivered and looked to the bed towards her robe, but then her eye fell on the grey folded bundle which lay on the desk beside. Saoirse reached out and took the smooth, grey mass into her arms; she could feel the warmth already. She had not yet unfolded it and now seemed like as good a time as any to see what it was. She shook it out and the soft, sweet aroma of her grandmother's perfume danced in the air around her. She brought it to her nose and inhaled her grandmother's scent. The fabric was soft and welcoming, the smell homely and unmistakeable. She sighed heavily and pulled the luxurious cloth around her. It was a cloak, smoky grey, soft to the touch, like the fur of an animal and she instantly felt warm and comforted. It had a calming effect quite like the comb, but this had more warmth, a hugging sensation rather than a numbing one. She pulled the wide hood up over her head and was enveloped by the comfort it brought her. Her phone rang. She let it. It could wait, she needed this time.

An hour or so must have passed, and when she refocused, she heard a soft tapping on her bedroom door. She turned to see Sean standing next to her. His face was frightened and drained.

'You have to answer your phone, Saoirse,' he was cross, but you could tell he was also relieved. He bent slightly and touched the top of her head, she still had the cloak pulled over her and so she understood his initial fear. She pulled down the hood and looked up at him.

'Sorry, I just needed some time to myself, time to work things out, or zone out to be honest.'

'And did it help? Did you work anything out?'

'To be honest, no. I just spaced out for an hour and thought about nothing. It was heavenly.' She beamed down at her silver comb, and ran her fingers gently along its spine. Thank God for it. But she was right back in the real world again, and she had worried Sean. She hadn't meant to, but she had. 'I'm sorry I should have answered, but to be completely honest I don't know what happens now. The instructions just send us off to Dunluce, to scatter her ashes. What happens then? Is it all over? Do I have to live in constant fear of Him? Does He even know I exist? I just feel like she left us with far too many questions and no real way of getting answers. For the first time in my life, I wish I could shake my grandmother.'

'But she did leave us with clues,' he sounded assured and a little more informed than she was. He saw the look in her eyes and answered her unasked questions. 'Well, the instructions are clear: we go to Dunluce and sprinkle her ashes. She left you the cloak, so I'm assuming it has some kind of powers, just like your comb. No doubt we'll find out soon enough. She's kept Father Michael out of the loop, I'm assuming that was to protect him and his faith, so I'm guessing things will get a whole lot weirder from here on in.'

Saoirse was annoyed, how he had worked all of that out from a map of Ireland and travel arrangements for the North. He knew far more than he was letting on. Her grandmother must have left him more information for sure.

'So tell me, what else did she leave you? And don't tell me "nothing", because I'll know you're lying.'

She was right. Sean explained how that when he had gotten

home, his father was sitting at the kitchen table waiting for him. They needed to have a 'chat'. Saoirse's grandmother had been to see him and had explained the whole situation to the extent that she could without endangering him. He had another letter for Sean, with more instructions. She had predicted that Saoirse would know that Sean was onto something and had given her blessing that Sean could share the contents of the letter when Saoirse worked it out and demanded he do so.

'So. . .' She was impatient and Sean was deliberately taking his time. She nudged him slightly.

'So, look out the window.'

Saoirse looked out over the ever-quieting and darkening harbour, the buoy bobbed gently and blinked crimson at her, but she was lost to know what it was she was supposed to be looking at. She scanned back and forth. . .

'Look down!'

There it was, just outside the garden fence and as she caught sight of it, it turned its head and its amber eyes gazed up at her, they'd become familiar in last number of weeks. She felt she knew the fox at this stage, it was a friend. Majestic and aloof standing guard at the gate. . . standing guard.

'He's protecting me!' It was a realisation that came suddenly. Foxes don't hang around houses without tearing at rubbish and making a nuisance of themselves. This fox had cried in what seemed like genuine pain with Saoirse the night her grandmother died. It was protecting her: a guard dog, or rather, guard fox. She could have sworn it was now smiling up at her, as she pressed against the window peering down at it.

'Rua is an old friend of your grandmother's from before your grandfather's time. He's a shape shifter, but this is his preferred form. He promised your grandmother he'd protect you until we are sure you are out of danger. His contacts in the fairy world will keep an eye out to see if we can figure out if He knows you exist and what He plans to do about it if He does.'

'Have you heard yourself? Fairy world, shape shifter. . . this is getting more and more ridiculous by the minute.'

'Saoirse, it is what it is. Remember I'm not the freak here, you are!' He dug her softly, but playfully, in the ribs. 'I'm just from a long line of great and noble men.' He stood back and beat his chest like Tarzan. 'You, however, are the mysterious, dark creature of folklore that has brought all this fantasy, fiction and excitement into my life.'

'Don't forget the death, despair and sorrow.' There was no comeback for that; she had most certainly brought that too. They looked at each other. There was that pull again, that magnetism between them and it was becoming increasingly difficult to resist it. Saoirse longed to put out her hand and stroke his chest, to pull him into the cloak with her, wrap his arms around her, pull him against her and feel his lips on hers. It was an animalistic desire, uncontrollable, almost, and deep within her. It was a feeling she had never felt before, but one that was intensifying with every unfulfilled encounter with him. Her breath quickened, as did his. They were lost in each other's eyes and only a shrill howl from Rua below brought them back to their senses.

'He's off. Needs to do a thing or two before tomorrow, I'm guessing. So I'm going to stay.'

It was said so matter of factly, that Saoirse burst into laughter. The fox outside the window had a thing or two to do. It was insane. She turned to look at him again, but he was already half way across the lawn and heading towards the library steps, still watching as he disappeared down the steps. 'How do you know he has a thing or two to do?'

'Because he told me. He's not always a fox, Saoirse. He was waiting for me when I got home.'

Saoirse pictured the red fox sitting at Sean's table sipping tea. Her world was becoming more and more bizarre as the days passed. Perhaps she had fallen down a rabbit hole at some point and lost her mind. Sean looked at her.

'I know what you're thinking, but remember: he's a shape shifter. He's quite a big man in reality. The only thing that gives him away are his shocking red hair and grizzly beard. It's exactly the same colour as his fur.'

'So you're on puca watch, while the fox is away?' Her voice didn't muster the sarcasm she was hoping for: the ridiculous was no longer so strange to admit.

'I most certainly am, but your dad says I can't stay in your room all night. He's made up a bed downstairs on the couch.'

They both blushed: even Saoirse's dad had noticed the attraction. It reared its tempting head and tugged at them both once more. They looked at each other intently; this was going to be a long night. Sean squeezed her shoulder and gently, but quickly kissed the top of her head and then turned and headed towards the door. Saoirse looked back at him, through the dark, and saw him silhouetted by the light of the hallway, he seemed to have grown in the past day or two. He looked taller and stronger and his knee had been forgotten about. She felt safe and relaxed back into the window seat.

28

aoirse woke refreshed. Stretching her long limbs and drawing her robe around her, she went to the window to check the weather. It was dry and crisp, a slight breeze rustled the last few surviving leaves on the trees below and a watery, pale sun crept over the horizon in the distance. She took a deep breath and was saddened by the absence of the warm smell of cinnamon porridge, a resounding reminder that her grandmother was no longer there.

She checked the cathedral clock and it was just before seven. The cathedral looked cold and hard in the morning light and she was glad her grandmother's funeral was not taking place there. Her grandmother was warm and loving, it was grey and clinical. She needed warmth – and in that moment she decided it would be a good and fitting tribute to make them all her grandmother's porridge.

She pulled her slippers on and bounded down the stairs. The kitchen was dark and a little unsettling. She had never been first up before. Even at Christmas her grandmother had something cooking on the stove when she bounded in all excitement and noise. It was quiet, too quiet, so she went and put the radio on: some anonymous company. She busied herself with pots and pans, cinnamon and sugar, happily distracted by the work.

The porridge was bubbling lightly, the warm, welcoming smell of cinnamon filling the kitchen, when something grabbed her shoulder. Ladle in hand she turned to face her attacker, only to be met by Sean in absolute hysterics.

'That's really not going to do much for you, if it was Him that grabbed you.'

'It's not funny, Sean. You frightened the life out of me.' She was cross. She wasn't sure what annoyed her most: the fact that he had just scared her or that she had forgotten he was here and she was standing in front of him in a big fluffy robe and mouse slippers. Mortification all around, she decided.

'Well, you made enough noise with those pots and pans to wake the dead. I thought you'd hear me coming. Sorry I frightened you. How are you feeling?'

'Let's not jump into the heavy stuff just yet. Gran always said: "breakfast first". So let's eat first and chat after.'

Saoirse served them both steaming bowls of porridge with a drizzle of honey. They both ate silently, grabbing quick glances at each other now and then. When she was done, she poured two large mugs of coffee and popped two slices of bread into the toaster. She settled herself back at the island and readied herself for the questioning. Today was going to be a hard day, no doubt, and Sean was going to be there every step of the way. She needed him, so she had to let him in.

'I'm surprisingly okay. I keep expecting a tsunami of grief to hit me, but I'm still waiting. Yes, I'm sad she's gone, but gone is all I think she is. I don't feel she's dead. Yes, of course I know we're taking her body for cremation today, which means she is actually dead, but I don't know what it is. . . I just feel I'll meet her again someday. I'm crazy, aren't I?'

The toast popped and she went to the counter, smeared them both with butter and honey and put each piece on a plate. She poured more coffee and settled herself back on the stool. It was very domesticated, very comfortable: she liked it. She liked it a lot.

'I don't think you're crazy, Saoirse. I think it's all part of the grieving process. I still feel like I'm going to see my mum again. Death is a strange thing and it does strange things to the people left behind.'

Saoirse wanted to interrupt him and tell him that it wasn't just a feeling, that she knew, she was almost certain, that she was going to see her grandmother soon. But she didn't have the heart. His mum was gone and had been for some time. Who was she to say her case was different, that she would get what she wanted? He had opened up, his face was genuine and caring, she couldn't fight that. She leant across the table and squeezed his left hand, letting her fingers linger softly, caressing his skin as she drew it back.

'Thank you, thank you for everything; I don't think I could be going through all this without you.'

He grabbed her hand softly, but firmly, just as she was about to put it back on her coffee mug. He looked intently at her and was about to say something when Saoirse's father sauntered into the kitchen. His whole demeanour told them he wasn't doing as well as Saoirse was. His face was pale, old stubble starting to form a beard and his shoulders slumped. He was a mess. His face brightened slightly when he saw them both, but it wasn't until Saoirse plonked a large bowl of porridge in front of him that a genuine smile appeared.

'You are so like her, you always have been. I suppose I'll always have a part of her with you around, honey.' He pressed his lips firmly into the top of her head and pulled her tightly towards him and then let out the smallest saddest sigh. He shook his head and settled himself on the stool next to Saoirse, in front of the bowl she had just put down. Without looking at Sean, he began to shovel the porridge into his mouth. Saoirse delighted in the awkward chit chat that followed, as her father sternly asked Sean how the couch had been. The two men in her life were sizing each other up and both seemed to be up for the challenge. It was entertaining and a welcome distraction from the day ahead.

Her mother broke up the masculine banter with her appearance at the kitchen door. She was breathtaking in a figure-hugging black dress, her hair pulled back off her porcelain face and a simple pearl necklace with matching earrings. She became slightly embarrassed by the stares from her unwanted audience and quickly headed towards the stove, but Saoirse's father grabbed her and swept her into his arms. She flushed with embarrassment at Saoirse and Sean seeing this display of affection.

'If only this dress wasn't just for funerals,' her father said, kissing her playfully. She wriggled helplessly in his arms, slapping him softly until he released her. She smoothed herself down and looked sternly at him and scolded.

'It's the day of your mother's funeral, have a bit of respect.'

Saoirse caught the sneaky wink and fleeting smile her mother gave her father and smiled inwardly. She loved how in love her parents still were and secretly hoped she'd have that too one day. . . and with Sean if she was lucky.

Her mother settled into breakfast with them, around the island, built for four. It was strange to have it full, without her grandmother there. Sean was an outsider, but not a stranger. It felt different, but right all the same.

The day was mapped out over coffee and honeyed toast and before she knew it Saoirse was standing in front of the full length mirror in her mum's room, dressed in her own figure-hugging black dress and black tights. Her mother was fixing the silver comb into her hair, which she had put up for her in a low bun. She had brushed the slightest bit of bronzer on her cheeks and licked her eyelashes with mascara. Saoirse smiled in delighted, she looked different, more womanly and grown up. The geeky teenager was lost. Her mother grasped her shoulders softly and smiled at her in the mirror.

'I'm proud of you, baby. You're being very strong. I love you and I'm here for you if you need me.' She kissed her softly and admired her once more in the mirror. Saoirse was about to tell her she loved her too, but before she could, her dad beeped the horn outside and it was time to go.

29

Saoirse had never been in a crematorium before and didn't know what to expect. They had left the house and taken the ferry across the river following the hearse. Saoirse rested her head against the window and watched the landscape whizz past her in the rain, finding it hard to believe this was all happening, it was all real and her Gran was gone. Sean sat beside her, holding her hand. Finally, as the sun broke weakly through the clouds, they turned left and onto a bridge that took them to a little island. The crematorium was nowhere to be seen, but large oak wooden doors built into the rock face opened as they pulled into a small car park and an elderly man with dark rimmed glasses walked towards them. Frank, the manager, was a very welcoming man and explained that her grandmother had wanted no fuss or fanfare and had requested that the coffin be in place before the crowd arrived.

Two men appeared behind Frank and helped the undertaker to lift the coffin from the back of the hearse. They placed it on a small silver trolley, then, turning it towards the entrance with almost military precision, the three men slowly wheeled the coffin into the darkness beyond the doors. Frank ushered them all after it.

A hand carved tunnel in the rock led them towards a bright light and Saoirse followed the cobbled path towards it, her hand still in Sean's. The short tunnel opened out into a dazzling bright courtyard, which, like the tunnel, was carved from the rock. To her left there was a sheer rock face, in front of her a lone tree and bubbling water feature and to her right a low, limestone building built into the rock. Large sliding oak doors and glass windows lined the entire wall of this side. The overall effect was one of calming solitude, beautiful but strong. Saoirse saw why her grandmother had chosen this place. It had an otherworldly quality to it and Frank had a glint in his eye that Saoirse read instantly as the look of a man who knew, and was, far more than his appearance showed.

She hadn't realised that she was still and staring until Sean's hand jerked her forward, towards the second last oak door, into which the coffin had just disappeared. The small group moved sombrely along, following Frank inside. Father Michael was waiting in the room beyond and greeted them warmly, shaking hands and kissing Saoirse and her mother softly on the cheek.

Saoirse was distracted: inside was as beautiful as outside. It was small, with simple chairs, laid out in uniform rows, but the ceiling was magnificently vaulted in old red brick, not something she had seen before, not in reality at least. It fell and rose in one perfectly formed dome. It was complimented by the muted colours of the large flagstones on the floor. Its only competition were the stained glass doors that were just opening to reveal the display shelf where they were about to place the coffin. The deep greens and vivid blues were captivating, an homage to the sea surrounding them outside. The room was breathtaking, the whole island was. It was so close to home: Saoirse couldn't believe she had never known it existed until now. It was a very fitting place to say goodbye to her wonderful grandmother. Saoirse let go of Sean's hand and slowly spun around, taking in every square inch of the place. Tranquil music played in the background and she caught snippets of whispered conversations going on around her, but she was mesmerised. It was just so beautiful and she felt as if her grandmother was there with her.

'You okay?' His question was a whisper, brushing her ear softly.

'I am. It's beautiful isn't it? I just can't get over it. It's her, it's so her. She loved old things, maybe because she was one.'

They both smiled. Father Michael joined them, having just spoken to Frank and Saoirse's parents. He had his black suit on today but no white collar, which Saoirse found a little strange, considering it was a funeral. He looked so much younger without it. She must have been staring because he chuckled softly and answered her.

'I'm here as a friend today, to say goodbye, not as a priest. Your grandmother asked specifically that there be no prayers or religious pomposity so I reckoned the collar was part of that. I had to wear the suit though, because I don't own another one. Well, at least I don't own another coloured one. Frank is about to let everyone in. You both okay? Is there anything I can do for you before we start?'

There wasn't, and Saoirse and Sean took their seats in the front row next to Saoirse's parents. Kate's funeral had been a traumatic affair, hordes of people, rivers of tears, echoes of sobs and wailing. This was far more upbeat. Frank opened the doors, and one by one people filed in to pay their respects. Locals and strangers alike were quick to share anecdotes and say how wonderful it had been to know her. There was no wailing or sobbing, a few giggles and chuckles were more the style.

Twenty minutes after the doors opened Saoirse spotted a very tall and well-built man with a shock of red hair and a grizzly beard: Rua – it had to be. His amber eyes were so familiar. He slouched into the room, bending his head as a mark of respect. Out of sync with the other mourners, he went to Saoirse's mum and dad first and then to her. Sean winked at him and Rua nodded. When he put out his hand to shake Saoirse's, she took his in both of hers and stood to hug him. He was clearly embarrassed by the gesture, and Saoirse's dad looked a little shocked, but it felt right.

'I feel like I know you, even though we're complete strangers. Thank you for being there for my grandmother and now for me.' She whispered it softly in his ear and as she did his grip tightened. She heard him swallow a lump in his throat and felt one form in her own. He bent towards her ear and replied softly.

'Keep your wits about you today, love, I've a feeling He might pay a visit.'

He squeezed her softly and then released her, shuffling off to stand at the back of the congregation. Saoirse scanned the crowd and saw lots of faces she recognised. . . and lots she didn't. These faces had new meaning now: hidden mysteries. How many were just her grandmother's acquaintances that she had never met. . . and how many of them were like Rua, amazing mythical creatures she had never thought existed? And was one of them Him?

Sean touched her shoulder softly. They were about to begin.

Father Michael welcomed everyone, introducing himself as Michael, a dear friend of Beibhinn. He explained that when she had found out this day was coming she asked him to do the service, but not to lose the run of himself, like he was known to at mass. He was to make it short and sweet. He was a man of his word, he explained, so it would be just that: short and hopefully, sweet. A small man with strangely elfish features joined Michael at the small podium and was introduced as another old friend, Fionn. Saoirse thought it was funny that a few months ago her initial reaction to Fionn's appearance would have been one of disbelief and perhaps even pity. But strange and alien as his appearance was, she was beginning to accept her new world: one where everything and everyone is possible.

From the pocket of his tweed jacket Fionn pulled a wooden flute, a delicate dark wooden instrument. Without introduction or comment he placed it to his lips, closed his eyes and took a breath. The air filled with the most haunting, moving music Saoirse had ever heard. She knew the song all too well, 'The Lonesome Boatman', one of her grandmother's favourite pieces. She had told Saoirse the story of the lonesome boatman and his ship Silent Annie so many times. She had always been fascinated by it and loved to drift off into the music imagining the boat and the adventures they had had.

The music was captivating and as the flurries were building, Saoirse shivered violently. The hair stood on the back of her neck and an uneasy feeling settled at the pit of her stomach. She reached for Sean's hand and as she did so, a figure appeared in the doorway: a tall dark man with a full beard and heavy overcoat. She couldn't make out his features as he was silhouetted against the bright courtyard outside, but the feeling at the pit of her stomach told her she knew exactly who he was: it was Him. She just hoped He didn't know who she was.

He moved in from the doorway, head bowed and moved towards the back. Saoirse heard a soft gasp, badly disguised as a cough as someone further back recognised Him too. Saoirse squeezed Sean's hand and gave him a knowing glare. She could tell he was lost in the music, so as subtly as she could she leant forward and whispered: 'He's here!'

Sean glared back at her in disbelief and his grip tightened. She sensed his body moving closer to her, to protect her, but she also saw a fear creep across his face. Neither of them knew who they were facing.

'Where?'

'Back corner, I think. I just know it's Him. Don't look, it'll be too obvious. He can't do anything right now in front of all these people.' She could see him fighting the instinct and to help combat it he gripped her hand even tighter and stared ahead.

The music stopped playing and Michael invited Saoirse's dad to the podium. He joked how his mother had always been too quick for him, even in her old age, particularly at cards and how she was always outwitting him, even in death. He thanked her for being a wonderful mother and grandmother, and then read the words she had left for him to read, joking that she was always putting words in his mouth. The piece was short, but had a massive emotional impact: she thanked the world for the wonderful life she had been given, the experiences she had and the joy she had felt being a wife, a mother and grandmother. Saoirse's mother was in bits and her dad left the podium to comfort her. Michael resumed his place at the podium, and continued with the service, but Saoirse didn't hear a word of it. She was too distracted. Why was He here? What did He know? Was she in danger? What could He really do to her?

She was brought back to her senses as the stained glass doors in front of her began to close and the coffin retreated. Michael was finishing up, and inviting the congregation back to the Titanic Bar for refreshments. Then her grandmother's favourite song was played: an old tune that Saoirse had never been able to name. The electronic hum of the gates added to the melody and the whole thing was over before she knew it. People began to file out and others who had been late queued up to pay their condolences. Sean shot up at the first opportunity and, through an over-exaggerated stretch, she saw him scan the crowd. Rua was quick to join him and they left the hall together, getting lost in the departing crowd.

Saoirse was left sitting directly in front of the closed stained glass gates. She could see the coffin still on its shelf inside them. The crowd dwindled, and in the end it was just Saoirse and her parents. None of them were sure what to do next. Saoirse's mother decided to go off in search of Frank, and her dad moved up a seat into the one her mother had just vacated.

'Hard to believe this is it, and that's her. It just all seems so sudden. But I suppose we just have to get on with it'

Saoirse felt he was trying to convince himself more than he was trying to convince her. She took his hand and held it tightly. God she loved her dad.

'Who was the red-headed guy?'

The confusion, sadness and uncertainty were gone, there was conviction in the question and she knew she had to answer him.

'Rua. He's one of Gran's friends.'

'Friends or *friends*?'

'*Friends*. She's arranged that he keep an eye on me until we know I'm safe.'

She wasn't sure whether she should explain that he was usually a fox that kept watch over her at night. Or that he and Sean had just taken off after the guy they thought may be trying to harm her. There were far too many ifs and maybes, but knowing someone was looking out for her might just be enough.

'He is the fox, right?' Saoirse looked at him in shock. 'That hair, those eyes, I'd know them anywhere.'

Perhaps she wasn't giving her father half enough credit, after all he was his mother's offspring, there must be a little of the fairy in him too. He squeezed her hand and pulled her close to him.

Frank appeared through a small door in front of them. Saoirse hadn't noticed it before as the gates had covered it. He had removed his glasses and Saoirse confirmed her earlier suspicions, seeing the twinkle in his eye. He winked at her recognition and beckoned for them to follow him. Saoirse's mother joined them on the other side of the wall and she took her hand as Frank busied himself with several buttons on the wall. The coffin that sat on the shelf outside was also visible from here and Frank manoeuvred it so it slid effortlessly from the shelf onto a trolley. It clunked down onto the metal and echoed as if it was empty. Saoirse's eyes widened in surprise. She looked to Frank for answers.

'Oh, it doesn't always sound like that, but she was such a slip of a thing. Nothing left when you take away the soul.'

He continued to push buttons and pull levers, explaining what each one was doing as he did so. Finally the coffin was loaded into the single furnace and the hatch closed.

'She asked that you were here when I started it up. She wanted you to see it was all over, that she was actually gone.' He was looking directly at Saoirse as he said it; it was a message especially for her. He pressed the button and they heard the furnace roar into action.

Frank led them back through the now empty service area and into his small office beyond it. It had the same vaulted ceiling and red bricked walls and flagstones with a large writing desk and a comfortable couch. The walls were lined with specimen urns, all proudly displayed in glass cabinets. He motioned for Saoirse and her mum to take a seat and then courteously and professionally went through the paperwork with her dad. It didn't take long. Her grandmother had been very organised and in no time at all Frank was shaking their hands and telling them he would see them on Monday for the collection. He was showing them out through the courtyard, when he took Saoirse's hand gently and slipped a small cream envelope into it. Her name was written beautifully in her grandmother's handwriting across the front of it. 'Some more instructions!' He winked and was gone.

Sean was waiting alone in the empty car park, casually draped across the boot, looking strong and handsome. It was only now Saoirse spotted that he was wearing the same black suit he had worn to Kate's funeral, but he looked far more relaxed and handsome in it today. When he saw them coming, he jumped up and came towards them.

'Rua followed our guy, to see what he's up to or where he's off to, and to make sure he's not planning on joining the wake. Just got a text there to say he's headed up the Dublin road. Maybe he's seen enough and you're in the clear.'

Strangely Saoirse was disappointed: all that fuss, the sacrifice, heartache, it was all for nothing. Where was the danger her grandmother had feared? Where was the adventure? She felt a little cheated, but at least they were all safe now. The road trip was the next step and because He had come and gone, Saoirse rested easy in the knowledge that the only danger she had to worry about now was her desire to kiss Sean. But perhaps that was the worst danger of all. She didn't know if she could contain herself much longer. Especially when they were finally alone.

30

The days after the funeral had passed in a haze. The wake had been a wild party that dragged on well into the small hours and had been suffered by many for a day or two after. Rua, it turned out, had quite a voice and while most of the crowd hadn't known the words to his songs, the melodies had been upbeat and infectious. Sean had kept his distance, spending time with Rua and his dad, and Saoirse had been glad. She hadn't had the strength physically or emotionally to fight the urge to kiss him.

The Tuesday after, Frank appeared at the door with a beautifully hand-painted cardboard urn. Her grandmother's request, as she wouldn't be staying in it very long. Saoirse knew what had to be done. Frank's envelope had given 'burial' instructions. Saoirse was to take the urn to her grandfather's grave on Sunday the 16th, dig a small hole and place a fistful of her ashes into it. The rest were to be scattered in the wind on the cliff overlooking Dunluce on the 1st November. Frank looked at her knowingly and nodded. He handed over the urn and hugged Saoirse tightly.

'Your grandmother was a marvellous woman. Such a help to us lost souls. I hope she's found her peace. Good luck and safe travels.'

He was gone before she could ask him anything. Saoirse wondered what he was: a fairy, a shape shifter, perhaps something else. There were so many things he could be. Saoirse sat in the hallway clutching the urn, overwhelmed by the enormity of it all. Days before she had chatted, laughed and sung with over a hundred people. How many of them had been human, and how many were from the world she now belonged to?

On the Sunday morning, the 16th, she had eaten breakfast with her parents and then set off to fulfil her grandmother's requests. Opening the heavy front door, a cold breeze hit her stiffly. She shivered ever so slightly and hugged the urn closely. Climbing the steps, she left the Crescent and made her way to the local cemetery.

The walk was a short one, but uphill all the way, and by the time she stood in front of her grandfather's headstone, she was warm and clammy. She loosened the scarf and sat herself on the curb stone. Only then did she realise that she hadn't really thought this through. She had left the house without digging equipment, no gloves or anything. She looked down at the gravelled grave and laughed. All the instructions and letters from her grandmother had been so she could be prepared and now she realised she could have been, but wasn't. Her grandmother would not have been impressed.

Saoirse bent down and placed the urn on the graveside, took off her scarf, folded it and put it on the ground to cushion her knees. The grave was immaculately kept: weeds pulled, flowers fresh, all her grandmother's work. Saoirse knelt and carefully gathered back a section of the green and grey-flecked stones. Underneath the ground was hard and dry and she really had to dig her nails in to break the earth. She clawed awkwardly at it and eventually she had a nice rough hole made. She wiped her hands on her coat and took the urn in her hands, lifted the lid and stared in. She had half expected the ashes to fly up to meet her in the breeze, but they were tightly secured in a plastic ziplock bag inside. It was weird: this was her grandmother, and she stared at it in amazement and wonder. This was the woman she had loved, cherished, hugged, smelt, laughed with. This grey, lifeless dust was all that remained. It seemed ridiculous that someone so full of life could be reduced to this.

The breeze gusted ever so slightly and Saoirse got the scent of her grandmother's perfume. She looked around to see if there was a flower, or if someone was there. No, the graveyard was empty, although she didn't feel alone. The smell hung in the air and she smiled softly, she was there. She took the bag, carefully opening the top and taking a fistful, she dropped it into the hole, only releasing her grip when she was sure the ashes would not blow away. She quickly scrabbled the soil back in on top of them, settled the gravel and returned the remaining ashes to the urn. It had taken no more than ten minutes, but Saoirse was exhausted. She dropped her bum to her heels and rested her head in her hands.

'I thought ye weren't religious.'

Her fright sent the urn flying and they both scrambled to catch it. The lid flew off and Saoirse was grateful for the ziplock bag inside. The look of horror on Sean's face confirmed that he, like Saoirse, had assumed the ashes would be loose inside. She giggled softly and dug him playfully. They must have looked a sight, both face down on hands and knees in the centre of her grandfather's grave, the urn open in front of them.

'You frightened the life out of me!'

'Well, at least you're in the right place!' he joked, 'I'm sorry, I just spotted you here in deep prayer. I came to say goodbye to Mum, before we head off. So were you praying?'

'No, Gran left further instructions that a little piece of her be left here with Granddad. I had to dig a hole and put some of her ashes here. Didn't realise it would be so difficult. I was knackered and taking a little break.'

She looked down at her hands and spotted the dirt wedged beneath her finger nails. She sat up and, as gracefully as she could, got to her feet, collecting the ashes and the urn as she did. She turned and watched as Sean struggled to his feet and remembered his knee. It seemed like an age ago, but it was only a couple of weeks. She held out her free, and quite dirty, hand to help him and as he caught it electricity shot through her. He felt it too and as soon as he was balanced he quickly let go, embarrassed to look her in the face. They had to sort this out, they were about to head off on a three-day journey together alone. They couldn't ignore the elephant in the room; although they were convincing themselves they were doing a good enough job.

'Can we talk?' she was surprised it was her speaking, but she couldn't go on this trip without having everything out in the open and knowing where she stood. She took his hand and led them both off the gravel and onto the solid path. He looked as nervous as she felt, but she knew it had to be done. 'I know we've been through this already, I know we agreed that the timing is all wrong and it's not the time or place to be starting something, but I don't think I'll cope if we have to spend so much time together, alone. . . do you know what I mean?'

She felt awkward, ridiculous almost, trying to explain herself, trying to voice the growing desire within her. He had had his head bowed and when she gently called his name, pleading for a response, he looked up and into her eyes. He took her chin in his hands ever so gently and pulled her towards him. Their eyes never blinked and she gazed deep into his soul. She saw her desire mirrored in his eyes. Their stare was only broken when he shut his eyes and pressed his lips firmly against hers. Saoirse's eyes shut tight and a warm tingling sensation spread across her body from their point of contact to the pit of her stomach and lingered there.

The kiss was passionate, but gentle, his tongue slowly teasing hers, his arm holding her firmly against him, both their hearts pounding. Saoirse was overwhelmed, but comfortable, she wanted this feeling to last forever. It was better than anything she could ever have imagined, but before she knew it Sean had pulled away and was apologising. He still had her in his arms, but had let go of her chin.

'I'm sorry, I just had to do it. I've wanted to do it since the first day I met you. I'm sorry your first real kiss is here in a graveyard, for God's sake you're holding your grandmother's ashes. Oh my God, I'm so sorry. . .'

Saoirse looked at him, his shoulders dropped in deflation. How could he feel so bad when she felt so great? It was the perfect place, in the presence of two true soul mates; they were having their first kiss in front of the only two people that could have ever really understood what they were and what they were going through. Her grandparents had sacrificed everything to be together. It was the perfect time and the place; although it must have seemed particularly odd to the people passing the graveyard. She kissed him again, surprised yet again at her forwardness, but thriving in the sensation.

'Can we say nothing until after we come back? It'll buy us a little time, both on the Kate front and so my father won't kill you before we leave?'

Sean looked sad and ashamed and Saoirse's heart dropped. She was confused: surely this was a good thing, she had made the move.

'I did love her, you know? I haven't just forgotten about her and moved on, but the connection with you has been so strong from the very beginning, even Kate noticed before she died. . .' He trailed off and she saw the guilt and sadness in his face again. That was what the argument had been about, the one Saoirse had seen in the dream. They had argued over her and she saw that he was blaming himself. She took his hand and squeezed it tightly.

'Her death was not your fault, Sean. I saw it happening and wanted to warn her, but Gran explained that death is death: it will come one way or another. Your time is your time. This can just be between us for now; I just didn't think I had the strength any more to resist it. I want to be with you and if that means keeping it a secret, so be it.'

He pulled her close and hugged her tightly, releasing her, he bent his head towards hers and she shut her eyes in anticipation, but his lips brushed past hers and up to her ear, 'Cuddling and kissing in the graveyard isn't going to keep us a secret now, Ms O'Donnell, so I will love you and leave you. Text you later.'

And with that he was gone, leaving Saoirse standing at her grandfather's grave alone, her grandmother's urn under her left arm, her coat and hands covered in dirt and her face wearing the biggest smile it was capable of. Life had been turned upside down, but she was beginning to think it might just be worth it. She was beginning to believe.

31

The next couple of weeks were strange. She and Sean saw each other at school, but kept their distance, knowing how impossible it was to resist the magnetic pull they both felt. The evenings were full of text messages about their upcoming adventure and long talks over coffee in the kitchen. It felt as though they were inhabiting a strange limbo: real life was carrying on all around them, they were in it, and yet they were part of a very different reality too. One that would really take off once mid-term break arrived.

On the morning of the trip, Saoirse woke ready for anything. Her bag stood at the end of the bed, packed and ready to go. The grey cloak, her grandmother's urn and the silver comb all safely tucked away in the top. Her clothes lay neatly folded on the window seat, ready for her to put on. She had spent far too much time mulling over what she should wear. For the first time in her life she was really trying to impress and it was hard work. She settled on comfort and warmth, but made sure it looked good too.

She met Sean at the train station at nine-thirty. His dad was so busy fussing over Sean's license and asking him to be careful that he barely noticed when they arrived. Sean's sister, Niamh, hugged him tightly, squashing her baby boy Liam between them as she did. Sean drew back and took Liam in his arms, cuddling and kissing him.

'Take care of him, Saoirse, he's our only brother and we're quite fond of him.' She ruffled his hair and nudged him softly. Sean blushed. He snuggled Liam once more and handed him back to Niamh. His dad now took him by the shoulders, held him at arm's length and then pulled him into a great bear hug. Sean collapsed willingly into it. All the while Saoirse and her mum and dad stood on and watched. Niamh was like her mother, but Sean, his dad and Liam were carved from the same rock, each one just a smaller and younger version of the other. She realised they were staring and turned to her own mum and dad.

'Right so, I guess this is it. I feel like I'm heading off for an eternity, not three days. I'll ring when we get to Dublin and again when we reach Belfast.'

Her mother had tears in her eyes and her father looked terribly nervous. It was only three days, but it was the first time she had been away from them on her own, and there was the threat of bumping into Him. She felt her mother's emotions and her father's nerves invade her and she rushed at them both and pulled both of them into a group hug. She loved them so deeply. Tears filled her eyes and they were mirrored in her parents'.

'Be careful, love. Don't do anything stupid.' Her father's words were loaded with meaning; not just the obvious take care, but behave as well. Her mother squeezed her hand and motioned at the train pulling into the station. Saoirse turned and saw her father take Sean's hand.

'She's our only daughter, Sean, take very good care of her, or you'll have me to deal with.' Again, his words were loaded, and he made no attempt to hide the threat behind them. Saoirse saw Sean swallow hard and nod in agreement. He glanced at her and she saw the desperation in his eyes: they needed to be on that train now, away from both sets of parents. Saoirse grabbed her bag, kissed her mother and declared her love for them both, and hopped on the train, Sean gratefully followed suit and they waved from the closing doors, before turning and finding a seat on the row furthest from the platform.

'Thank God for that. Are they still there?'

Saoirse glanced over her shoulder and saw all of them still on the platform, waving frantically.

'Yeah, they're still there.'

Sean checked his watch and sighed heavily, the train wasn't due to leave for another three minutes. Saoirse giggled.

'Does my father really frighten you that much?'

'He thinks I'm stealing his baby, to do untold things to you. On top of that is the added pressure of having to protect you. He feels helpless to a certain extent and he's taking it out on me. Yeah, damn right, he frightens me.'

'What untold things?' She feigned innocence, but her cheeky grin gave everything away. She squeezed his thigh softly and winked. She liked the sound of 'untold things'.

'You're not helping. He'll kill me.'

The train began to pull away and they both turned and waved at their families on the platform. As they disappeared from sight, Sean turned and sank into the seat and sighed with relief, resting his head against the window. He took a deep breath and then righted himself in the seat.

'Right so, let's get this adventure underway.' He pulled his large brown weekender bag onto his lap and from the side pocket he pulled a flask and two plastic cups. He poured hot milky tea into both and handed one to Saoirse. She smiled.

'Niamh is real old school,' he winked, 'I propose a toast: to this great adventure, kindly financed and organised by your dear gran. Let us travel safely and please God avoid encounters with Himself. To safe travels!'

They clinked cups in a mock grand gesture and Saoirse slyly snuck in a 'To us!' as they did. It made Sean smile and he kissed her softly in reply. The tea was warm and milky with just the right amount of sugar.

'All we're short now is a few biscuits.'

Sean handed her his cup and rummaged in the side

pocket, pulling out a small package, wrapped in tin foil. He held them out like a magician producing a rabbit from a hat, but the best part of the trick was when he opened the foil to reveal homemade ginger snaps with a chocolate coating. The smell of ginger filled her nostrils. Resting the biscuits on the bag Sean took his cup from Saoirse, freeing her hand and allowing her to take a biscuit. It snapped deliciously in her mouth and melted away, washed down perfectly by the sweetened tea.

'She's good, isn't she?'

Saoirse couldn't answer, her mouth full of the crumbling goodness. She nodded agreeing and half smiled, crumbs spilling onto her lap. Sean laughed and joined her in the feast. They were barely fifteen minutes into the journey and already the tea and biscuits were gone.

They changed trains in Cork city and Sean texted Rua, who was meeting them in Dublin, to let him know that they were on their way. It all felt so strange but exciting. Once settled on the train, Saoirse opened her bag and gently stroked the urn. What wild adventure was she sending them on? Why herself and Sean and not her mum and dad? Why so many unanswered questions? She closed the bag back up and Sean put it overhead and sat across from her, the table separating them. She raised an eyebrow questioningly and a little disappointed that he hadn't sat next to her.

'We have work to do, madam.' His answer had, as always, read her mind and he pulled out the five books from his bag. Saoirse had completely forgotten about them in recent days and really didn't see the point of lugging them all the way to Dunluce. Again he answered her unvoiced thoughts.

'If I'm heading out into the unknown with the fear of meeting Himself I want to know as much about him as possible. We got side-tracked before; a nice long train journey should keep us focused.'

Saoirse had had visions of holding hands, cuddling, listening to music from the same set of earphones... She had to admit she was disappointed and it must have shown on her face, because he leant forward and brushed her cheek, winking cheekily, 'There'll be plenty of time for that later.'

They had been through the books before and had found little. This time was no different. He was a puca, not a very menacing character, but once crossed or provoked could be mischievous and potentially malicious. There was nothing to suggest He need be feared in the manner Saoirse's grandmother had feared Him and more than an hour into the train journey they were still frustrated.

'I need a break, you fancy a tea? I'll get one from the dining cart.' He nodded in response, enthralled in what he was reading and she headed off in pursuit of tea.

Absent-mindedly wandering between carriages, the world whizzing by outside, she questioned herself. There must be something they were missing, something glaringly obvious that they just hadn't seen yet. Maybe Rua could throw some light on it when they saw him in Dublin.

When she reached the dining cart, she joined the back of the queue. She stood patiently, rocking to and fro with the motion of the train. Her attention was grabbed by the arrogant and hot-headed man in front of her. He was barking ignorantly at the poor attendant behind the counter. She turned away from him trying to mind her own business and bumped into an elderly man, who was in the queue behind her, knocking his coins and scattering them all over the floor. She heard the first man tut at her as she dropped to her knees and scrambled to collect the escaping coins. Eventually, flustered and a little out of breath, she returned the last of the coins to the old man and apologised.

'I'm terribly sorry, I didn't mean to. I hope I've found them all.'

'Don't worry love, tis only a cuppa I'm after anyways and I have more than enough here.' He held her hand softly and a little longer than necessary, but it wasn't uncomfortable and Saoirse realised this wasn't just an ordinary old man. He winked devilishly at her recognition and let go of her hand.

'So where are you and your young friend off to?' She looked puzzled. How did he know she was travelling with a friend? 'I saw you in the carriage back there. Myself and the wife are off to Dublin to see the kids. Not that they're kids any more – three grandchildren we have now: ten, six and four.'

His tone was chatty and friendly, almost familiar, and Saoirse didn't have the heart not to answer him.

'Heading to Belfast and then onto Dunluce for a visit.' She didn't feel it was right or even appropriate to explain exactly what they were doing; she didn't know this man or for that matter she didn't know what he was. Better to be honest, but not too honest. He nodded and shuffled forward to the counter. Saoirse ordered three teas, insisting she pay for his.

'I've never been to Dunluce before. Hear it's a beautiful place. Legend has it that all things queer and wonderful happened up there a long time ago.'

He caught her off guard and she turned and gaped at him, waiting for him to go on, but he didn't. She felt he was teasing her and she pushed him to go on as subtly as she could.

'What's queer and wonderful these days?' It sounded so lame the minute she said it, but she couldn't just ask him straight out. The dining cart was crowded and noisy, and he dramatically looked around and then leaned in and whispered.

'Oh, legend has it that there was a serious love story went terribly wrong or terribly right up there centuries ago – depending on who is telling the story of course. Back then the world as we know it was very different. The world of humans existed quite peacefully with the world of fairies. They accepted each other's existence and got on with life. From time to time they crossed paths, but not too often. Some humans and fairies chose to be friends, but for most they were happy to stay out of each other's ways and each other's business. Unfortunately for certain creatures of the fairy world, humans are their business, particularly the poor banshees.' He eyed her ever so suspiciously and then continued. 'The poor banshees' basic existence was to inform the humans of coming death. It was what they were created to do and they had no choice but to have dealings with the humans and at such a traumatic and awful time. It is no wonder they got such a bad name and had such a hard time. The fairies looked after them, though, and created tools to help them deal with their hardship.'

He took her by the hand and they sat at a nearby table that had become vacant. She was enthralled and he was loving the audience. Perhaps Saoirse could get some new information from him. She urged him to go on and he checked over his shoulder again and leant in towards her, before he continued.

'Anyway the legend says that the poor, unfortunate banshee of Dunluce was a beautiful sensitive creature, loved by all, from both worlds. Her human family the O'Donnells accepted and understood her ties to them, and the fairy world warmed to her personality. She was an amazing sight to see, so they say: long auburn hair, porcelain white skin and grey-green eyes. The world and his mother were in love with her and that is where the issue lay. A banshee is a solitary creature, alone and supposedly without friends. The Dunluce banshee had too many. The tale tells how two men, one from the fairy world and one from the human world, fell madly in love with her. She was caught, unsure of what was happening, and not knowing what to do next. Banshees could not love, or at least it had never been heard of before. She cared deeply for both men, but she felt she was in love with one. She confided in the local cailleach and asked what she should do. The cailleach was an ancient and wise woman and said she had read of such things happening in ancient times. Her advice was to go with her heart, the ways and the means would be found if it was true love.

'The cailleach consulted ancient writings and found that the banshee could be transformed, but only by someone with enough power and a true love for her. Her heart was broken. She loved her human, but her only way of being with him was through the power of her fairy love, the puca. How could she break his heart and then ask him to change her to be with the other man? She knew she could not exist without her true love, but didn't have it in her to break the puca's heart. She went half-mad for months wailing uncontrollably on the cliff beside the castle, pining for her love and putting the fear of God into half the village.

'The puca got wind of her unusual behaviour and went to comfort her, only to find the human there before him. It broke his heart and crushed what soul he had. He was enraged, but beneath it all, he did truly love her and granted her wish that she be human. Overwhelmed with anger and sadness, he made her agree to never return to Dunluce until her bones had turned to ash and she agreed.

'That night, during an unearthly meteor shower, the immortal banshee became a mortal woman. She left Dunluce as she promised and they never returned. Legend has it she lived to a ripe old age, surrounded by dozens of children and grandchildren. A testament to true love and happiness.'

He leant back into the seat and took a breath and then a long sip of his now very cold tea. Saoirse was disappointed:

she knew all this before, well, most of it anyway. She hadn't known the puca was in love with her grandmother, but that still didn't explain everything. She sipped her own cold tea, contemplating how all this may help her, but finding no answers. She looked at the little old man in front of her, sitting back, content to have told his story and had an eager ear to hear it.

'What happened to him?'

'Who?'

'The puca?'

He pulled himself forward towards the table and checked over his shoulder again. Saoirse really had no idea who he thought would be listening to them, but his concern seemed genuine.

'Legend has it that his broken heart drove him insane. He had been a powerful creature before, now he was even more powerful, adamant that no one around him would be happy. He plotted his revenge, in case his love and her new husband ever set foot in Dunluce again. They say he still guards the cliffs of Dunluce, waiting for her to return.'

The train ground to a halt and the tea sloshed in the cups. She checked her watch, she'd been gone over an hour, Sean would be freaking out. The old man stood to his feet as soon as the train was completely stationary.

'It's been a pleasure to meet you...?' He held out his feeble hand to shake hers, and Saoirse rose to meet him.

'Saoirse, Saoirse O'Donnell. A pleasure to meet you too...?'

She smiled and waited for him to give his name, but instead he eyed her suspiciously and took off down the carriage, back towards his seat. Saoirse thought it was odd, but then again wasn't everything lately? She ordered two fresh teas and made her way slowly back the train, which was now moving again towards Dublin.

She had worried that Sean would be anxious that she had been gone so long, but she need not have been; he was engrossed in the third book, the others scattered around it on the table, opened and marked with little Post-it notes. She remembered back to the day in the library, the new book smell, the English project. So much had happened since then. She sat in next to him and handed him the tea.

'So did you find anything?' she was dying to tell him what she knew, but was being polite as he looked as if he had been very busy.

'Some stuff, but nothing that really answers any of our questions. That is. . . until the little old man you bought tea for rushed back here and asked me were you really Saoirse O'Donnell. When I told him you were, he told me to be very careful, that Dunluce was not the place for us. Then he and his wife took their bags and high-tailed it out of here. So what did you say to him?'

'I didn't say anything really. I just told him we were on our way to Dunluce for a visit and that my name was Saoirse O'Donnell.'

'Well, whatever you said you frightened the life out of him. He left here looking like he'd seen a ghost. Did he say anything?'

'Oh, he said a lot! Turns out Gran is a legend – an actual legend! He told me all about how she had two suitors, one human – my grandfather – and one from the fairy world: the puca or Him. Turns out he loved Gran, and though she cared for him, she truly loved my grandfather. The poor puca, in a cruel twist, was the only one with the power to make her human, and he did, but swore he would kill them both if she ever set foot in Dunluce again. Legend has it his broken heart turned him completely evil and intensified his power. The only way Gran could return to Dunluce was as ash. Apparently he patrols the cliff, plotting his revenge, expecting her to return.'

'So that's why we couldn't work out why she feared him so much, he was a crossed lover. This legend isn't in any of the books, but at least we know he is a puca. They can only take certain forms. You've seen his human form and I have marked all the other forms in the book that are associated with them. At least we know what to look out for.'

Saoirse was a little confused, 'But it's over isn't it? Gran is returning to Dunluce as ash, it's what he wanted, surely that will be the end of it?'

Sean didn't look convinced, 'Perhaps. Maybe Rua can enlighten us when we get to Dublin. Fancy a sandwich?'

He pulled another package from the side pocket of his bag, which was resting at his feet under the table. He closed and cleared the books away and opened the tin foil to reveal four scrumptious looking sandwiches, cut into triangles, each with a different filling. The tea was bland, but the sandwiches were gorgeous. They ate in silence as they both contemplated what they had just heard. Maybe they were getting to the end of it; maybe they were no longer in any serious danger. They would be in Dublin in twenty minutes, perhaps Rua could help them decide.

32

They pulled into Heuston Station where Rua and his wife Sally were waiting on the platform, waving frantically like parents welcoming home long-lost children. Sally was a motherly looking woman, with rosy cheeks, a cheerful smile and an oversized cardigan. She hugged Saoirse tightly and took her bag. Rua slapped Sean on the back and grabbed his too.

'Sall will drop us to Connolly. Pain in the arse we can't go from here. Always wondered what idiot came up with that idea – two railway stations in one city.'

'Now, now love, not in front of the kids,' she scolded him lovingly and Saoirse, for some strange reason, noted the smallest tinge of sadness in her eyes. She wondered what it was, that made such a cheerful looking woman so sad within. Rua caught her staring and totally misread her look, thankfully.

'Nope Saoirse, she's not one of us. Myself and your grandmother had lots in common, fell for the wrong folk: humans.'

He nudged his wife playfully and with his free hand pulled her close and kissed the top of her head. Sally gazed up into his eyes, the sadness vanishing momentarily.

'We had our price to pay too,' he continued but faltered, 'But sure, as I always tell her, what's meant to be is meant to be.'

Saoirse could hear the pain that she had seen in Sally's eyes echoed in Rua's voice. What price had they paid? Whatever it was, Rua was putting a brave face on it. The price you pay for true love, it was cruel, she thought. She glanced at Sean and he smiled limply, they both felt the sadness, and it made them feel a little awkward.

Outside the train station was madness: taxis, cars, buses and the Luas trams all moving at once. Sall drove like a mad woman, weaving in and out of traffic, busy chatting and watching mirrors. Before they knew it they were on the opposite side of the city and Sall was dumping them all out at the entrance to the station. She was nattering away about parking and an appointment. She kissed all three of them warmly, lingering in Rua's arms, then whispered in his ear and was gone.

'She's something else, isn't she?' There was an overwhelming pride in his voice as he stood and waved her off. Saoirse thought it was the sweetest thing she had seen in a long time.

A quick confirmation of departure and arrival times and they were headed for Platform Three and the Belfast train. They were just going through the turnstiles when Saoirse heard a familiar voice calling her name. She turned and scanned the crowd, the platform was busy, but towards the back she could see movement, gesturing and a ripple of chaos moving with the sound.

Suddenly Father Michael came into full view, no black suit, no collar, looking very casual in a pair of denims and a hoody and beaming from ear to ear. He was out of breath when he joined them and they stood impatiently waiting for an explanation. He kept waving his ticket and bending, hands on knees, trying to catch his breath. The loud speaker crackled slightly and announced the last boarding for the train to Belfast. They looked at each other annoyed but intrigued and grabbed Michael and bundled him onto the train. He would have to explain later.

Settled in their seats Michael finally had his breath back.

Saoirse, Sean and Rua all sat staring at him, still a little dazed and confused by his appearance. No one had spoken one word to him since he had appeared on the platform; they weren't sure what to say or why in fact he was even there. He saw their bewilderment and held up his hands in defence.

'I know, I know, I shouldn't be here. I know she didn't want me to be in danger, but I couldn't help myself, I couldn't miss out.'

He sounded like a child pleading forgiveness for having stowed away on a pirate ship. But while he wanted forgiveness, he had no intentions of heading home: he was along for the adventure. He dropped his hands and eyed them all like an over-excited puppy.

'So what have I missed?'

Saoirse laughed and it broke the tension. 'You know you sound like a four-year-old?'

'I know, I know. I'm sorry, but I just couldn't stay at home. I was worried about ye.' He tried to act concerned, but it was a thin veil and they all easily saw through it. Michael loved the idea of danger and adventure, priest or no priest, he wanted in on this trip. 'So! What did I miss?'

'Quite a bit actually.'

Saoirse filled Rua and Michael in on the train journey from Cork and what they had learned from the old man. Sean informed them of all the forms the puca could take and what they needed to be vigilant for. From Belfast on they were in more danger as Sean saw it, out of the protection of the hustle and bustle of the populated city and towns. They could be open to attack on the quiet rural roads. The old man had said the legend told of how the puca guarded the cliffs of Dunluce. He hoped this was true as it would mean their journey to that point would be safe. But Sean feared he had already broken his pattern. Saoirse had seen him at the funeral, he had left the cliffs, he knew Saoirse's gran was dead. Who knew what he was up to now or what he planned to do next? The uncertainties made Sean weary and he begged that they all stay vigilant.

Saoirse was surprised at his seriousness, but watching him go through the map and stories from the books, Saoirse realised she had been far too flippant in her notions about this trip. It was far from the romantic getaway with her new love that she had concocted in her head. That was glaringly obvious now. Sean was here on a mission: to protect her. The puca was a real threat, in his eyes, and he was intent on keeping her safe. She liked this serious, protective side, but she also felt guilty: these three men, Sean in particular, were all in some sort of danger and it was all because of her. They were here for her. She hoped she was right and they were reading far too much into this. But if she was wrong?

'I need to stretch my legs, visit the ladies room. Be back in a minute.'

She left them huddled over the books and maps on the table and headed back along the carriages. What had she gotten them all into? Correction, what had her grandmother gotten them all into? Saoirse couldn't understand why her grandmother hadn't told her the full story. Why couldn't she have been honest? The truth hadn't been so bad. Maybe she was embarrassed. She would never know.

She pushed the button for the automatic door to the toilet and it closed behind her. It stank, like all public facilities, that strange mixture of stale urine, vomit and artificial citrus scent: a failed attempt at hygiene. She contemplated not going at all, but all the tea had her over the comfortable limit and she wasn't sure she could last until Belfast. She spread toilet paper across the seat in two layers and settled herself uncomfortably on top. She needed to be quick.

A strange cold feeling ran through her mid-flow and the

hair on her neck stood. It was the same uneasy feeling she had felt that day at the crematorium and she held her breath. She heard footsteps and then loud aggressive voices; she couldn't make out who they were or what they were saying with the noise of the train. Her heart began to pound and she stood up, fixing her clothes and placed her ear against the door, straining to hear what was going on outside. There was a bit of a scuffle and then silence, an eerie silence. All Saoirse could hear was the clickity-clack of the train and the slowing pounding of her heart. It was Him, that she was sure of, but was he still out there? She sat back on the toilet, trying to figure out what to do next.

It took her thirty minutes or so to move, and even then it wasn't her own decision, but a gentle tapping on the door that made her move. She stared at the door not knowing what to do, should she open it?

'Are you okay in there? You've been in there quite some time now. Is everything okay?'

It was a female voice. Saoirse pressed the button and released the door. It pulled back to reveal a pretty young, blonde lady about twenty-five dressed in the railway company uniform. The look of concern on her face was genuine and Saoirse knew she had nothing to be afraid of.

'Your companions sent me on a wild goose chase for you. They seemed a little worried, so I said I'd try the toilets for them.'

She smiled warmly and Saoirse saw the intrigue in her eyes. Three men on a train journey to Belfast frantically looking for a tall, willowy sixteen-year-old red head they had lost. What must she have thought? Saoirse smirked, imagining if Michael had been wearing his collar and suit, what would she have thought then?

'God, I'm very sorry, they shouldn't have been so worried. I just needed a little peace and quiet for a few minutes, and figured the toilet was the best place. I must have lost track of time.'

Saoirse scanned the carriage and the aisles beyond, no sign of Him. She thanked the lady for her help and hurried back to the others, dying to tell them about what she had thought she had felt and who she thought she heard.

Michael and Rua were debating a route on the map when she got back to their seat, but Sean was nowhere to be seen. Rua looked annoyed.

'Where have you been? You were gone for ages.'

'The loo, like I said. Where's Sean?'

She wanted him to be there too, when she told them about her suspicions.

'He went to find you about a half hour ago. I assumed he had found you!'

Rua was definitely annoyed, but not just at Saoirse, at Sean too. He must have thought they were off together, up to no good. But they weren't. So where was he? Saoirse scanned the aisles again and spotted Sean the carriage up, running in their direction. It didn't take him long to reach them. He fell into the seat, cradling his knee.

'So I'm guessing you know He's been here?'

Saoirse knew by the look on his face he had seen him and she now knew it was his raised voice she heard outside the toilet. The other two looked up from their maps, shocked and surprised.

'I had a strange and uneasy feeling after you'd left and went looking for you, only to spot this suspicious looking character, checking the toilets from carriage to carriage. He was a tall, dark guy in dark clothing, pretty much fitting the description you and Rua had given me. So I followed him. Turns out he was looking for you. When we got to the last carriage I knew you had to be in that toilet, so I confronted him before he had a chance to find you. He is angry,

Saoirse, very angry. To say he hated your grandmother and grandfather is an understatement. He says they robbed him of his happiness and damned him to an eternity of loneliness and unhappiness. He wants his revenge. He's reneging on his promise: your grandmother is never allowed to return to Dunluce, ashes or not.'

'He can't do that; it was her dying wish.'

'That's the reason he's doing it: a last chance to get back at her when there is nothing she can do about it.'

'What about me?'

'What about *us*, you mean. He knew all about us: my family history, our connection, your powers. Michael, he knows you're a priest and is baffled as to why you would be dabbling in these things. He has cursed us, or at least he says he will, if we continue on this trip. He thinks we're young and foolish, coaxed on by an evil old woman; we didn't bring this on ourselves. If we turn back now and go home, he will leave us alone. If we don't, he said to be prepared to feel his wrath.'

They all sat in silence, dumbfounded at Sean's words which seemed to hang thick in the air between them. Sean had met Him, spoken with Him and was still standing. But things had changed. This wasn't a childish adventure any longer, it was far more serious. They were in real danger if they continued.

No one said anything for a long time, each one contemplating what had just been said and deciding what to do next. Saoirse was furious: how dare He go back on his promise? She was going to Dunluce to scatter her grandmother's ashes, whether He liked it or not. She wasn't afraid of Him and she was willing to do it alone. Her grandmother had asked her to do this and she was going to keep her word. Her mind was made up, she spoke first.

'It might not be the answer you were all hoping for, but

I've made my decision. No one, not even the puca, is going to tell me what I can or cannot do. And He's certainly not going to stop me fulfilling my grandmother's last request. I'm continuing on from Belfast, but I don't expect any of you to come with me. I couldn't put you in that kind of danger. I can do this alone.'

She hadn't thought the plan through fully enough, because she couldn't do it alone: she couldn't drive the camper van and she didn't have the money for public transport. She hoped one of them would join her, but she couldn't ask them to. She had no need to fear, Michael spoke next.

'How dare He say that I was dabbling and would know nothing about these things or His powers? Shame on Him and His arrogance. I believe in good triumphing over evil and the good Lord will protect me, I'm in!'

Saoirse's hand was resting on the table in front of her and in an overly grand gesture, fit for cinema, Michael added his to it, palm down. Rua joined him.

'He robbed us of the joy of children. We've paid for long enough and been afraid for far too long. I'm in.'

All three of them looked at Sean in anticipation, was he going to be the only one to pull out?

'Well, isn't it a good thing ye all have balls. I've already told Him we'd be continuing on, that we had a dying wish to fulfil and nothing, not even He would stop us. So I guess that means I'm in too.'

He slapped his hand down on top of the other three and a pact was sealed. The adventure was far from over.

33

An old friend of Rua's handed over the keys to a small campervan in the train station's car park. It was small, very small, and old, very old. With Michael now along for the ride, it was going to be a very cramped and unpleasant journey. They all piled in and hit the road, eager to get started. About twenty minutes outside Belfast, Sean pulled into a lay-by and they all hopped out again, spreading maps across the bonnet and hatching a plan.

The tone and seriousness of the situation had deepened since Sean's encounter. There was a real and immediate danger and they were about to face into it. Daylight was their best protection, as far as they could make out. He couldn't operate in broad daylight, not when there would be bystanders to see. There were only a few hours of daylight left today so it was decided to drive as far as Ballycastle, taking the coastal road as far as was possible, park up and stay in a hotel. The more people around them the better. They could head off then as soon as it was light and hopefully be back to the hotel, mission complete, before nightfall the following day.

Michael was to drive, and Rua and Sean would keep an eye out for anything suspicious. . . whatever that might be. How would the puca attack? The books were ancient and gave them few useful clues. The threat of poisoning their cattle wasn't really a worry to them. Saoirse felt redundant, what was she supposed to do in all this? She stared at the road ahead of them. She knew there was danger ahead, but she was strangely unafraid. The men were anxious and spoke in stern serious voices but something deep within her told her they had nothing to fear.

'I think we should get on the road.' She was in a daze, staring off into the distance, lost in the idea of getting this over and done with. The sooner they were there and back, the better.

'She's right; you know, no point in wasting time here, not knowing what we're facing into. Best to just get into it and see.' Enthusiastic as always, Michael clapped her on the back and hopped into the driver's seat. His eternal optimism was infectious and Rua and Sean followed suit, tidying the maps away and piling into the campervan. Rua sat up front with Michael while Sean settled himself at the table opposite Saoirse.

'You okay?' His voice was low and loaded with concern.

'I'm fine,' he looked at her quizzically, but she was being completely truthful. 'I'm really ready to get this done. To be honest, I'm not afraid of Him. Don't ask me why. Everything suggests I should be, but I don't know. I guess I feel my grandmother would never have asked me to do something I couldn't do or something that would put me in any real danger. I know He's changed the goal posts, but still I'm not afraid of Him. Is that stupid?'

Sean stood and leant across the table and kissed her firmly, holding her head in place with his hands. He looked at her admiringly. She blushed slightly.

'You're amazing, you know that? Absolutely amazing. You're so strong and together. I'm petrified of what's lying ahead. I'm afraid of whatever he wants to do to you, to us. I'm afraid it's all going to go horribly wrong.' He dropped his head into his hands and sighed heavily, he was carrying all of them on his shoulders. He was trying to be the leader, and doing a great job of it, but under the brave face was a frightened seventeen-year-old. At that moment Saoirse saw a little boy in front of her, in need of support and reassurance. She had gotten them all into this, and she was sure as hell going to get them all out of it in one piece.

'I think we'll be safe till we get to Dunluce,' she said, squeezing his hands. 'He'll be afraid we'll outwit Him and have the ashes spread before He gets there, so He'll be protecting the cliffs. I reckon we'll have a safe enough passage till then. And then. . . I think I have a plan.'

Saoirse went through her plan with Sean, step by step. They would still follow the same route as before, but her ending was slightly different. Sean didn't like it, it left her open, isolated and vulnerable, but he agreed that in theory it would probably work. He smiled unconvincingly, taking her hand in his and drawing her around the table towards him, he tucked her under his arm.

'Just be careful, I don't know what I would do without you.'

She leant back into his arms and allowed her head to be cradled in his arm. She could smell his deodorant and feel his heart beating. The closeness was intoxicating; she gazed up into his eyes, longing for his lips to meet hers. He looked down and shook his head scolding her, but his heart beat quickened and while she knew he would not give in to her here in front of Michael and Rua, his heart told her he would soon.

The van screeched to a stop. Saoirse shot forward, out of Sean's arms banging her head, full force on the table in front of her. Dazed and a little confused, she sat upright as quickly as she had been thrown forward. Michael was swearing profusely in the front and Rua was rubbing his head, a large purplish bump already growing on his forehead. Saoirse looked at Sean. His face was deathly pale. Blood gushed down her forehead gathering in her left eyebrow and then dripped through her eyelashes and onto her cheek. Saoirse felt the warm dampness and went to put her hand to her head. Sean grabbed it before she could.

'You've a nasty gash over your left eyebrow, nasty but I don't think it's too deep. Let's hope Rua's friend has a first aid kit in here. You feel okay, you're not dizzy or anything?'

'I'm fine, really! I was actually wondering what the hell just happened?'

Sean stood and moved forward, helping Saoirse to her feet. It was pointless to ask her to stay in the campervan, it was easier to just help her up and let her see what had just happened. He handed her a small tea towel from the kitchenette and she held it to the wound. Then they both joined Rua at the front of the vehicle, gazing at the windscreen. A large crack ran down the centre of it, but it hadn't shattered. They had a clear view of the massive rock slide up ahead, completely blocking the road in front of them. They looked at each other in disbelief and then back at the rubble. It had been a very close call, and if this was Him, which of course it had to be, He meant business. He was not to be messed with.

Saoirse swallowed hard and moved between Rua and Sean to get a better view.

'Please tell me there wasn't anyone in front of you. Please say we haven't inadvertently killed some innocent bystander.'

'No, Saoirse, there's been nothing on the road for miles, absolutely nothing. It was beginning to freak us out. We couldn't figure out how one of the most travelled roads in the country had no one on it. At least now we know why.'

The bump on Rua's head was beginning to darken in colour and was increasing in size, but other than that he was calm and relaxed. Michael was still swearing and banging the steering wheel, physically uninjured but obviously in shock. Rua tried to calm him unsuccessfully.

Saoirse turned to see why Sean wasn't interjecting, but he was nowhere to be seen. She took the tea-towel from her head, which was now soaked through with blood, and went outside. She found him standing in the middle of the road, a few hundred metres from the campervan looking up at the steep cliff face. She followed his gaze and when she reached the top, she just caught sight of the black swishing of the tail of a stallion.

'Well He means business, doesn't He?' She knew it sounded too flippant and the look that greeted her confirmed it.

'We could have all been killed, Saoirse!'

'But we weren't!'

She was about to apologise and try to defuse the situation when a large JCB rounded the corner behind them. Saoirse had to laugh: of all the times and the places! Rua and Michael had come to join them on the road and they began to fight over who had sent the JCB. Michael was claiming it for God and Rua for the fairies. Sean totally disagreed with the pair of them and thought it was just luck.

John was a local builder, heading home for a sneaky cuppa from a building site a few miles up the road. It was pure coincidence really. He was in the right place at the right time. He was surprised by the rock fall: there hadn't been one for years, since the council had spent millions securing the cliffs overhead. After a quick call to a buddy at the council, he made light work of the clearing, dumping the waste over the small stone wall and into the ocean below.

When John was finished he hopped down from the cab and invited them back to his house. 'The wife will have sugary tea ready for ye in an instant, great for the shock.' The offer was extremely tempting, but all four knew now that they could not drag more people into this: going to John's house could put him in danger. They were better off sticking to the plan.

It was Michael who made their excuses and thanked him for all his help. The JCB disappeared around the next corner in the fading light and they were left standing in the middle of the road.

'Cushendall is ten miles away, there's a hotel in the centre of the town. We'll talk about all this over dinner. We'll have to get that windscreen fixed, I'm not too sure it'll hold for much longer and Michael looks like he could do with a stiff drink.' Rua grabbed him playfully around the shoulders and turned him in the direction of the campervan.

'Will they have a doctor?'

It was Sean. They all looked at him in surprise. 'Are ye serious? You're just going to ignore the volcano about to erupt on Rua's forehead and the gaping hole in Saoirse's head?'

'I thought it was a gash.' She was poking fun at him and he didn't like it. His face dropped and anger flashed across his face. He was serious.

'I'm sorry Sean, I know this is serious, but I feel fine. I promise if it's still bleeding by the time we get to Cushendall I'll go and see the doctor.'

She squeezed his hand softly, trying to reassure him and pulled him towards the campervan: they needed to get going.

It was a short and silent journey to Cushendall and thankfully uneventful. Michael pulled up outside a pub on the main street and Saoirse asked where the hotel was. Everyone laughed, except for her. This was the hotel. It took in four of the buildings on the short main street and was painted in bright colours with empty flower boxes on the windows. Off-season meant that they were quiet, but a roaring fire and a friendly middle-aged woman greeted them at reception. Her accent was musical and a welcome reminder of her grandmother. She looked delighted to see them – four paying guests.

'I've been expecting you all day, O' Donnell, right, party of four?'

The four of them nodded, a little dumbfounded. This stop had not been planned; they were supposed to be staying closer to Dunluce.

'Mrs O'Donnell said there would be four of you, and true enough there are. But she did say there'd be a priest.'

Michael stood forward raising his hand, almost like a school boy declaring his presence and then realised how foolish he must look and resumed his place within the group. Margaret smiled at him warmly and led them upstairs and to their rooms: Saoirse with Michael, Rua with Sean. Saoirse couldn't hide her disappointment and Michael feigned insult. Dinner would be available in the bar when they were ready.

The rooms were surprisingly modern, but homely: neutral colours with accents of turquoise to be found in the pictures on the walls and the throw cushions on the beds. The beds looked comfortable and Saoirse threw herself down on the one nearest the window, letting out a sigh. Michael followed suit on his own bed and they both stared up at the ceiling. The silence was comfortable, neither felt the need to make idle chit-chat: they were like old friends, except for the fact that they only knew each other a few short weeks.

'She was phenomenal, you know that. I still can't get my head around her.'

'She had you well sussed anyway. Clear instructions not to come and she still booked you in.'

Saoirse sat up and laughed softly at him. She really had him all figured out. He sat up to face her and chuckled heartedly.

'I guess she knew the adventurer in me would never have been able to resist. I wonder how she knew we were going to stop here.'

'Well she'd guessed you were coming, so she knew we wouldn't all fit in the campervan.'

'True, true. She'd spotted the spark between you and Sean too, putting you in here with me.'

'It was inevitable, or so she told me. Destiny brought us together.'

Saoirse over-dramatised the destiny bit and they both burst out laughing and fell back onto their beds. A knock on the door stopped them and in walked Sean and Rua, Rua holding an ice pack to his forehead.

Saoirse looked at Rua and he shrugged his shoulders, taking down the pack, he revealed the nasty bump. She looked back at Sean.

'He won't see a doctor, which I can understand, but the ice pack is a compromise. Now it's your turn Miss, let me have a look at that gash.'

She had forgotten completely about it and as she stood to show him, her feet were a little unsteady beneath her and she felt woozy. They all saw it, there was no disguising it and Sean sat her back on the bed. The three men gathered around her, concern etched on all their faces, as Sean eased back her hair to reveal the wound. It had scabbed over already and looked much better. The weakness must be hunger. Dinner was called for and the sooner the better.

Sean sent Rua and Michael to enquire about the windscreen to give Saoirse some time to freshen up, and, once they were gone, he settled himself on the bed next to her and took her hand in his. The touch sent shockwaves through her body. She turned her head towards his. Their lips met in a passionate embrace, releasing all the tension and fear that had built up during the day. They both relaxed and relished the moment: it felt so right. Pulling away softly, he nestled his head between her neck and shoulder, softly kissing the delicate skin. Saoirse was in heaven.

'We need to eat!'

He was right. These stolen moments were short but

magical. She could wait; she knew it would be worth waiting for.

Four stools stood at the bar counter. Rua and Michael occupied two and the other two had dinner settings waiting for them. The menu was short. Saoirse could have eaten everything on it, but decided on a vegetable soup to start and a carbonara for main. The service was quick and friendly and the food homely and delicious. It was devoured in silence and after desserts of warm apple pie were ordered, they all retired to the couches at the fire place to plan for tomorrow.

The pub was quiet, only one or two other tables were occupied and they had privacy to a certain extent. The desserts arrived with two more pints of Guinness and two freshly brewed coffees. Saoirse inhaled the rich aroma, the caffeine igniting her nostrils; it had been a long twelve hours since her last cup.

'So, what happens tomorrow?'

Michael's voice, as always, could not hide his enthusiasm and despite the seriousness of the day that lay ahead of them they all laughed. Saoirse explained her plan in every detail and then they relaxed. Saoirse left the three men chatting at the fireside; Michael slightly intoxicated from one too many pints, and headed outside: she needed some time to clear her head.

34

She pushed the main door and went out into the cool night air. It was busy, much busier than she had expected. People were moving past her quickly towards the end of the street. She couldn't see any faces, the crowd were dressed in black and many wore masks or had ghoulish faces. She felt like she had stepped into another world, a horror movie. The crowd was pulsating and chanting, all moving in the one direction and she was swept along with them. Bodies swarmed around her and she felt uncomfortable, but she feared if she stopped she'd be knocked over and trampled. Ahead of her she could see a bonfire blazing and the crowd gathering around it. As she was carried towards it she could feel the heat and the atmosphere intensify, images of one her nightmares flashed in her head. The heat was something she knew and it turned her stomach. All around her she saw strange faces, images of death. She felt boxed in and suffocated, her head began to spin.

She turned to leave but was pushed even closer to the fire by the boisterous movements of a group of young skeletons behind her. She lost her footing and felt herself falling until she caught the back of the person in front of her. They turned angrily and Saoirse was greeted by a grotesque half-eaten face, who swiped at her hand, glared and walked on. Saoirse's breath caught. She needed to get back to the hotel. Looking anxiously around her, she tried to get her bearings.

Her gaze fell on a face she recognized and she froze. He was here. At the other side of the bonfire.

He stared back intently, the flames distorting his dark face. Her heartbeat quickened, fear grew inside her, but she was stuck, and couldn't seem to break His stare. He smirked back, knowingly. His glare grew more intense and Saoirse began to panic. Over the roar of the flames and the shouting of the crowd Saoirse heard His deep voice shout at her: 'You! You don't belong here!'

She felt His words inside her head. They bounced around inside her skull and made her feel dizzy. His stare penetrated her and made her skin crawl. He stood holding her in his gaze and she felt herself moving closer to the flames.

Suddenly she was falling towards the bonfire, rushing towards the unbearable heat. She heard Him laugh and then just as quickly she felt a hand on her, tugging her back away from the flames and she was standing on her feet again. Margaret was standing next to her, still clutching the back of her jacket firmly in her hand.

'Right, let's get you back to the hotel, honey,'

Margaret brought her straight back to the hotel. She opened the door and checked the room before ushering Saoirse inside.

'Saoirse, my darling, I'm terribly sorry, I should have perhaps warned you. Tonight is Halloween night. Here in Cushendall we celebrate with a bonfire. The children love it, but it does bring out some undesirables. He is very powerful at this time of year, but you're safe here. That's why your grandmother chose it. She also left clear instructions that I was to leave this package for you and make sure you got it before you left in the morning. I came in to turn down your sheets and leave it here for you, but I saw you weren't here so I went looking for you, I just had this feeling. Lucky I did.' At this she winked playfully at Saoirse and a small smile crept into the corners of her lips. As it did the youth returned to her face. 'He's been here most of the day you know. He stood around outside for a while, but He won't come near you in here, He can't. But be careful, my love, He is not someone to be crossing. Your grandmother did once and we all have been paying the price since. . . Oh how we loved her. What a creature she was. You're very like her, you know. But there's something different about you, too. Your mother is human, and a looker I'm guessing.'

Saoirse blushed, and wasn't sure why: her mother was beautiful and her grandmother also, there was nothing to be embarrassed about. But her shyness and awkwardness had returned. She hadn't felt like this in a long while. She shook it off, thanking Margaret for the compliment. Margaret smiled back at her, grinning knowingly.

'Your grandmother was a very humble woman too, never realised how beautiful she was, or the enchanting effect she had on everyone who met her.' She hugged Saoirse and placed a beautifully wrapped package into her hands. 'She insisted I make sure you read the letter and do as you're told. Good luck, my love. He's gone for the night and Dunluce calls. But He's not gone for good. So take care.' With that she slipped past her and out the door.

Saoirse sat down on her bed, in the spot that Margaret had just vacated, and gazed out the window. She visualised the spot the puca had been standing in, and wondered why she was safe here, why he hadn't come in. Margaret must be someone he feared, or at least could not harm. Obviously that's why her grandmother had hoped they would end up here. But what had just happened? It had all happened so quickly. One minute she was looking straight into the puca's eyes, the next she was hurtling towards the bonfire and now she was back settled on her bed. She shivered at the thought of those dark eyes. The hatred in them. Her head was heavy and her eyes cried out for sleep. She kicked off her shoes and crawled in under the duvet, too tired to brush her teeth.

She pulled the package up next to her on the pillow and mustered up the strength to open it. As always the package and the note inside were beautifully wrapped and written. Her grandmother had such a way with words. Out of the little parcel came a locket: old filigree silver, exquisite, quite similar to the workmanship of her comb. Her comb! Saoirse scrambled out of bed and pulled her comb from the top of her bag. Running it through her hair, she felt the calmness overcome her and found the energy to focus on the locket and the note with it.

The locket was yet another fairy gift. According to the note, she was to take a small amount of the ashes and place them in the sealed side of the locket. Her grandmother's picture was in the other. Saoirse pulled the urn out of the bag, and took the ziplock bag into her lap. She carefully took a tiny amount of the ash and placed it in the open compartment, sealing it tightly with the clasp when she was done. She gazed at her grandmother's beautiful face and asked herself again what she had gotten her into. A chill ran through her and she took the grey cloak from the top of the bag and wrapped herself in it and then in the duvet. Sleep overcame her.

A soft tapping on the door woke her with a start. She was unsure how long she had been asleep, but she was already feeling refreshed. Sean appeared around the door, awkward and embarrassed, his eyes averted to the wall.

'You decent?'

'Yeah, I think I'm a decent enough type of person, but if you want to know am I fully clothed, I am.'

'Don't be mean, Saoirse. I was just checking in on you, making sure you're okay before I head to bed. Michael is going to crash with us tonight, not sure he's in much of a fit state to be sharing with a lady.'

'Poor Michael, I think the whole situation has gotten a little too much for him. He's like a kid at Christmas with the excitement. It's nice to see though, so often the church is seen as group of fuddy-duddies. I wonder what his bishop would make of all of this?'

'Not sure he'd approve. And you can be sure that Michael won't be giving him the details of the adventure. How are you? You okay with everything? You look a bit better than when you left us.'

'How long ago was that?'

'About an hour? Michael was telling us stories about his days in the seminary and even gave us a rendition of "O Holy Night"!'

Sean laughed at the memory, and his face lit up. Saoirse smiled back at him, admiring the masculinity of his face. He was everything she had never wished for but was sure she would have if she had been looking. She played absentmindedly with the locket, now secured firmly around her neck.

'What's that?'

'Oh, I had a visitor when I got back: Margaret had a message from my grandmother, another gift with, of course, more instructions. It's nice though isn't it?'

Sean crossed the room and sat on the bed next to her; he took the locket in his hand and examined it. It glinted in the half light.

'It's beautiful.' He stared longingly into her eyes. Still holding the locket in his hand, he leant forward and kissed her deeply on the lips. Pulling back and letting the locket fall from his hand, he said, 'I'll let you rest, we've a big day tomorrow. . . and I'd better go before I do something your dad wouldn't like!'

He kissed her softly again and was gone. Saoirse flopped back onto the bed, letting out a deep sigh full of frustration, passion and contentment. How could she be feeling all these things at once?

Her grandmother had sent her on this amazing adventure, and while it frightened the life out of her and frustrated the hell out of her, she was glad she was on it. Yes, they were in danger but ultimately she was the one who had to do this. It was her responsibility and it should be her sacrifice. She had to do it alone. She couldn't endanger the others any more than was completely necessary.

She settled back in the bed wrapping the cloak tightly around her and going through the details in her head. She could do this; she just hoped He'd fall for it. It was very risky and maybe she was underestimating him, but she had a feeling and she hoped, for all their sakes, she was right. If she wasn't they were all in danger. She didn't even want to think about what that could mean. She hoped this time tomorrow they would be heading back to Belfast and heading back to reality.

35

It was a crisp clear morning. Saoirse could see the dew gathered in little cobwebs hanging between the bushes outside the window. It looked cold, not a cloud in the clear blue sky: hopefully it was a good sign. Saoirse showered and stood looking at herself in the bathroom mirror. She had changed. Not physically, but mentally. Her body wasn't the awkward, hideous thing she had thought it was. She felt she had grown into it and she was beginning to like it. Yes, she was tall and slim, but feminine none the less. She was what she was, and she liked it.

A tap on the door brought her back to her senses. She wrapped the warm fluffy robe on the back of the door around her and opened the door expecting to see Sean, but Michael's sorry, hung-over face greeted her apologetically.

'Oh Saoirse, I'm mortified. I'm so sorry about last night. I had one too many. I think I've let the whole situation overcome me. It's been a long time since I've let myself go so much. Are you ready for breakfast?

The plan was rehashed over a late breakfast and several cups of coffee. Margaret busied herself with refilling their cups and Saoirse; sure she was trying to eavesdrop on their conversations, felt a little uneasy. By midday she was getting very unsettled and was eager to get on the road. The arrival of the guy who had fixed the windscreen was the perfect excuse to get going. They were all nervous but there was an excitement too. Saoirse wasn't sure what exactly lay in front of them, but she knew they had to do this. Her grandmother had been the most powerful influence in her life, this was her dying wish and she was going to do it, puca or no puca!

Sean had been quiet all morning, no playful nudges, no lingering gazes, he looked tired and worried. He packed the van and, as the other two settled in the front, chatting with Margaret, he took her to the side with a firm grip on her elbow.

'This is going to work, isn't it?' His eyes pleaded with her.

She swallowed hard and tried her best to put on her most reassuring face, 'Of course it will, the plan is simple, all smoke and mirrors.' She felt she was trying to reassure herself too, the plan was extremely simple, but maybe it was too simple. Maybe they were being completely foolish to think it would work, but she had to believe it would. She squeezed his arm and looked into his eyes, 'Of course it will.'

He said nothing, just held her close, she could feel his heart thumping in his chest and she did her best to remain calm for him. This could go wrong, horribly wrong, but she couldn't think about that. She had to dare to believe that it was going to work and this time tomorrow they would be back to normality, or at least their normality.

Margaret coughed gently and broke their embrace. 'Those two are over-eager to get started; I think ye better hit the road.' She shook Sean's hand and then pulled him close and whispered in his ear. He nodded and got in the van. Saoirse wondered what she had said, but had little time to think, because Margaret locked her in an embrace. 'Take care of yourself darling, I'll see you tonight.' She didn't give Saoirse the time to answer or question, she just pushed her into the van and closed the door. Rua started the engine and they were off, Margaret waving frantically on the road behind them as they drove away.

The van was quiet for the first ten miles or so and then Michael woke from his hangover and the questions and planning started again. Rua and Michael had clear instructions, Sean was to stay in the van and Saoirse had her job to do. None of the men were pleased that Saoirse was leaving herself so exposed, but she explained that it was necessary. It was, after all, her burden to bear and while she was delighted they had come along with her, she felt that in this final part the danger should lie with her.

The clear crisp morning had vanished the minute they had set out. A thick heavy fog covered the road in front of them and it was difficult to see anything. Saoirse felt uneasy: the fog had a foreboding air to it, and she didn't like it. Rua was frustrated and argued with Michael about directions and eventually they pulled in and had to get out to see if they could find their bearings. To Saoirse's delight they had pulled into the car park of the Giant's Causeway. Her fear disappeared and was replaced by a childlike giddiness. She had always been mesmerised by the stories of Fionn and the Fianna and had delighted in the fact that there was clear evidence that they existed still in the world. As a child she had dreamt of walking the causeway to Scotland and meeting the traumatised Giant on the other side. The others could have a coffee and argue over maps, she was seeing the Causeway.

Sean held her hand and they braced the cold and fog together. She told him excitedly about how she had always wanted to see the Giant's Causeway and how her grandmother had always been slightly saddened by her excitement and love of the place, because she knew she could never take her. When they reached the end of the hill Saoirse was disappointed: the fog robbed her of the view she had been expecting. Sean saw the disappointment in her eyes and pulled her on towards the columns; maybe further up they might be able to see more. He started to climb, Saoirse's hand tightly in his, the rocks were slippery in the damp fog.

Suddenly she heard a gruff voice behind them. She turned. A man stood about five feet behind them, his bearded face stern and cross-looking. Where had he appeared from? The fog was heavy, but surely they would have seen him. 'I'd get down if I were you. You don't want to fall.'

Saoirse pulled Sean gently back, and they returned to the road below. As they did a rumble from the cliff above sent a shower of rocks onto the place where Saoirse and Sean had just been. Saoirse looked at Sean and then back to the man who had spoken to them, but he had disappeared into the fog.

They looked at each other, realising what could have just happened.

'I'm going to be just fine, you know, she would never have sent me if she thought I was in any real danger, of that I'm certain.'

'I'm not certain of anything anymore Saoirse. Sometimes I think I have it all worked out, and then something like that happens. You're a banshee for God's sake, the puca is out hunting for you and we are on a mission to scatter your grandmother's ashes with a priest and a fox! How much more ridiculous can it get?' His voice waivered and she could sense the fear in his words. He was frightened and overwhelmed, why wouldn't he be? It was hard to believe, even for her.

'I know I'm struggling with it myself, but I keep telling myself, after tonight, we can go back to normal. He'll want nothing more to do with us and we can go home and move on.' She squeezed him tightly; he looked unconvinced, but said nothing.

They met Rua and Michael in the coffee shop. The two men were surrounded by empty coffee cups and tucking into steaming bowls of vegetable soup and doorstep sandwiches. Saoirse and Sean joined them after ordering at the counter from a very pretty lady. Saoirse was taken by her beauty and the depth of her eyes, they looked far older than her youthful appearance. When she winked at Saoirse, her suspicions were in some way confirmed. Sean looked annoyed, left out of yet another thing. As they walked away from the counter the girl caught Saoirse's arm and pulled her towards her.

'You just had a lucky escape; He is out to harm you. Be careful. Tonight is a new moon. That might work in your favour, it'll be dark. And remember, it's the 1st of November today, the feast of All Saints! That's important!' She let go and smiled warmly as if she had been talking about the weather and Saoirse joined the others at the table.

They all ate quietly. Saoirse's mind was exhausted and anxious; she just wanted it to be over now. Why did the moon and the date mean anything? All she wanted was to have the ashes scattered and be back on the train to Dublin and onwards to home. She couldn't let them know she was faltering; she had to muster some enthusiasm and keep her head up. These three men had chosen to take this journey and stay with her, regardless of the danger, she had to stay positive for the last few hours.

Saoirse cornered Rua on the way to the camper van and asked him about what the waitress had said.

'The new moon is very important in the fairy world, Saoirse, it signifies new beginnings. But it also means that His power will be slightly weakened. He would prefer a full moon, no doubt, when He is at full power. And All Saints Day, it means that all the good spirits in the world are at large tonight. He will have lots to contend with, other than us. God, why hadn't I thought of this? I was so caught up in the whole thing that I never checked those small details. Of all nights to do this, tonight is our best chance.'

Saoirse relaxed ever so slightly. Her grandmother really had thought of everything.

36

The trip from The Giant's Causeway had been uneventful but difficult. The fog had thickened even more and they had had to stop several times to find their bearings. Eerily it lifted as they pulled into the car park facing the castle and the ocean beyond, but it cleared to reveal not clear skies but ominous storm clouds gathering on the horizon. Michael and Rua got out to take a look. When they were alone, Sean pulled Saoirse towards him and held her tightly. She could feel the fear in him, his shoulders tense and his breathing deliberate. He pulled away and smiled at her lovingly, 'I'm here, I'll always be here.' His voice was weak and she could tell he was trying his best to hold it all together.

They joined the others in the small car park and followed the grassy path down towards the castle. Saoirse's heart began to race and her breath caught in her throat. She was finally here. It felt so surreal, not at all what she had been anticipating. She had expected there to be some kind of connection with the place, but instead she was a little disappointed. Dunluce was certainly beautiful. The stone ruins hung tightly to the cliff edge and the waves crashed below. But in her head Saoirse had almost expected it to be like it had been the day her grandparents left: the beautiful home that had been part of her family for hundreds of years, not the wounded, derelict shell that remained. The puca had had his way, destroying any reminders of her grandmother and half the castle had fallen into the ocean during one of his fits of rage. Saoirse sighed heavily; he wasn't going to take this easily.

They wandered around the ruins and Sean watched the building storm clouds worryingly gathering on the horizon. Saoirse knew there was nothing she could do to dispel his anxiety and fear, other than forgetting all about this and returning home. But that was not an option and Sean knew that. They had come this far to scatter her grandmother's ashes and they were going to do that no matter what. She clasped the locket around her neck and held it tightly. She was afraid too, it could go terribly wrong, awfully wrong, but she had to try. A knot began to grow in her stomach and the fear she had been fighting invaded her body. Worries spiralled around her head and for the first time in over a month that horrible dizziness overcame her – she needed the comb, she needed to compose herself, she needed to be alone.

'I'm just going to have a rest,' she smiled as best she could and turned to go back up the grassy embankment to the car park. Michael caught her arm and looked into her eyes.

'You okay?'

'I'm fine, honestly, just a little tired and overwhelmed, that's all.'

The castle ruins weren't empty, there were two or three small groups of tourists mulling around, taking snaps and trying to get as close to the edge as possible. Saoirse checked her watch as she made her way back to the camper van. The site closed shortly and it was getting dark already. There was a clap of thunder in the distance and the startled shouts of the American tourists below carried up the hill to her on the wind. Saoirse hoped the storm would hold off long enough.

She climbed into the campervan and pulled her cloak and comb from the bag. It was chilly, but she held off putting on the cloak, she would need its warmth later. She pulled the comb from its box, let down her hair and started to comb; with each stroke calmness washed over her.

Sean startled her, brushing her cheek softly, he was smiling. Outside the clouds were coming in fast and the light was fading, Saoirse saw Michael and Rua drinking from camping cups and eating sandwiches on the bonnet of the van. They had their jackets pulled up around their chins. You could see they were cold, but they were chatting animatedly, biding their time. Saoirse looked to the cliff, then the castle. She picked up the urn that sat at her feet and cradled it in her arms.

'I guess this is nearly it! Are all the tourists gone?'

'Yeah, and the guy from the visitors' centre. Michael spun him a line about meeting a friend and that we'd stay here a little while, we'd be gone before the morning and he was happy to head off. You ready? You have everything you need?'

'I think so.'

Saoirse knocked on the window to call Michael and Rua. They bounded in, like two young boys ready for an adventure.

'So, Michael, I'll give these to you and you know what to do. Rua, you sure about the plan? You'll be able, right? I know it's not really a fox's thing.'

She handed Michael the bag and looked to Rua for reassurance. Both nodded certainly and then Saoirse looked at Sean. He was very much on the outside; there was no part for him to play except wait. She had deliberately planned it that way. She couldn't risk him being involved: he was the perfect target if the puca decided to play dirty, and she knew that if he was in danger or hurt, she would never forgive herself. She knew he didn't like it, that he felt helpless and that he would have done anything if she had asked. She had asked him to do nothing, and he had unwillingly agreed. His face was ashen, the worry evident. Saoirse's heart broke for him, but this was how it had to be done and she took comfort in knowing through it all he would be out of danger.

Michael held the bag tightly, did up his jacket and checked his watch. Night was rolling in quickly and they had planned that they would do it as soon as darkness fell in order to be back on the road and out of Dunluce as soon as possible. Michael coughed awkwardly and looked around at the other three. He leant in towards Saoirse, squeezed her arm and whispered softly, 'Good luck and take care.'

He opened the van door and disappeared into the dark. Rua did the same, holding Saoirse just a little longer and smelling her hair: the fox in him couldn't resist. He left them and ran into the wind outside, a howl signalling his change, just feet from the van. They were left alone to say goodbye, both unsure of what to say or what was going to happen next. Saoirse didn't want to say goodbye, she didn't want to hold or kiss him for fear that she would break down and chicken out, but she couldn't leave him like that. She held out her hand for him to hold and she looked him straight in the eye.

'You've changed me; you've made me feel things that I never thought I could. I feel our connection, I know it's something special, and whatever happens, it does not end tonight. Real love triumphs, my grandmother and grandfather proved that. I will be back.'

With that she kissed him softly and pulled the grey cloak around her tightly, tying the string around her neck and tucking her locket under it. Without looking back at Sean she opened the van door and stepped into the wind. She heard the door close behind her and as she walked the short distance to the gate leading to the field next to the car park she heard the engine start and the van pull away. She could only imagine what Sean was feeling driving away, but she hoped it wouldn't be long before she would be back in his arms and all this would be over.

The gate was locked and in the swirling wind she found it difficult to climb, swaying awkwardly at the top and stumbling on her descent onto the soft uneven ground below her. The clouds raced in the sky and Saoirse caught the odd glimpse of the cliff she was heading towards in the half light. The wind and the uneven ground made it a difficult walk to the cliff top. When she finally got there she was out of breath and a little disorientated. She looked back towards the castle below her and searched for Michael's torch, she caught a glimpse of it bobbing towards the foot bridge and then she peered over the edge wondering if Rua had taken up his spot also. A howl rolled up the cliff face towards her. All were in place. It was time.

37

She stood at the cliff edge, her grandmother's grey cloak wrapped tightly around her. Her hair had escaped from beneath the hood and danced like a sprite in the wind. She hadn't really thought through what exactly she would do now, how she would get Him to come. She had hoped He would just come to her.

Peering over the edge and down at the angry sea below, she pulled her locket from beneath the cloak and held it tightly in her hand. She closed her eyes and thought of her grandmother. Without knowing why, she began to sing. Her voice was unlike anything she had ever heard before. It sounded unhuman and magical, high pitched and ethereal. It echoed and swirled around in the wind and she sang louder, delighting in the sensation in her lungs and ears. The wind picked up more and swirled dangerously around her. In the distance a fork of lightning hit the water and the clouds clapped echoing up the cliff. She felt free and alive and relished the sound of her own voice.

Suddenly the thunder cracked violently again and more lightning lit up the sky. The waves swelled and the wind caught her and she lost her footing. He appeared, grabbing her from behind and slapping His hand over her mouth silencing her. His hand was claw-like in its grip and the bones of his fingers dug into her skin. He turned her to face Him and she saw His black eyes raging with anger. Her breath caught in her throat and she doubted her strength. He saw the doubt and sneered.

'HOW DARE YOU! Do you not know who I am? Do you not

realise I could wipe you and your stupid friends out in one sweep of my hands? You fool, to think you could take me on! You are as crazy as your grandmother. Stupid creatures.'

His voice was unlike anything she had ever heard. Partly human but at the same time it had an animal growl within it. It echoed in her ears, hanging ominously above the noise of the storm brewing around them. Saoirse saw the anger grow in His eyes when He mentioned her grandmother. His grip on her face tightened, piercing her skin. His facial features morphed with the strength of his anger and He spat in her face as He spoke. She tried to whimper, but His hand muffled the sound. The wind howled around them, swaying them violently and threatening to push them over the edge. The pain was becoming unbearable and Saoirse tried desperately to free her face from his hands. He delighted in her struggle and closed his grip further, laughing at her discomfort and fear. Tears streamed down her face and she began to panic, gulping for breath and thrashing at His hands. In the struggle her cloak gaped open and He caught sight of her locket. The puca roared like an animal wounded and dropped His hands. Saoirse was free, but only for a second. He came back at her, grabbing and clawing at her neck.

'How dare she? How dare she use this gift in such a way?'

His rage was uncontrollable. A heat radiated from His tight grip as He grasped her neck and squeezed viciously. Saoirse felt her feet lift from the ground. The panic heightened as her airway closed and she regretted the plan she had devised, the bravery she had felt before. She had been naive to think she could outwit Him: there was no way she could defeat the puca. Her grandmother's ashes would be spread in Dunluce by now, but it looked like she would be paying the ultimate price.

She felt her lungs screaming for air, her head pounding

with pressure, her hands frantically grasping at her throat, and she felt her life drain from her. Everything became dark, as the world closed in around her and she gave in to its numbness. He looked into her eyes as she was about to close them and Saoirse saw not anger, but pain. His grip loosened a little and He looked down once more at the locket around her neck. A single tear formed in His black eye and hung to His eyelid. He turned his face into the wind and it was swept away. Saoirse gasped for breath and forced her fingers between His grip and her neck. His grip had loosened but He began to shake her violently.

'How dare she use a gift of love to protect you in her wrong doing. Well, let's see if her gifts protect you now.'

Suddenly He became very calm and the shaking stopped. It was unnerving. The chaos of the past few moments replaced by stillness. Saoirse heard Him take a deep breath as she felt herself being lifted. He took several steps towards the edge of the cliff, turned and held her out over the water below. He said nothing, but Saoirse saw evil in His eyes. He looked deep into her eyes and then calmly let go.

She lost sense of everything. The wind rushed at her as the water got closer and closer. It must have only taken a few seconds, but Saoirse felt as though she hadn't fallen as quickly as she should have. There was no great impact with the sea either, perhaps the wind had held her up. She fell into the stormy sea and was immediately engulfed. The howling of the wind and the darkness above was gone, replaced by the muffled calmness of water. The sea was choppy, the current strong, but she was calm.

This was the plan, strange and all as it seemed. She had hoped to enter the water herself, rather than being thrown in, but it had always been her escape route. The ocean was always a refuge for her, at home from the comfort of her window seat staring out at her beloved harbour. She had decided that it was the best way to go. She was a strong swimmer; she knew she could do this.

She tried to get her orientation, without surfacing, but the cloak was weighing her down, dragging her deeper and catching her neck. She fumbled with the clasp and couldn't open it. She couldn't stay down much longer. The further she sank, the more difficult it would be to get back to the surface. She whirled in circles, frantically trying to open the clasp. Her lungs were screaming for oxygen. The panic was fading and her mind was dimming. Suddenly an icy hand caught hers and released the clasp. Saoirse gasped and swallowed a mouthful of salt water. A silver misty figure hovered in the water in front of her; illuminated and smiling. Her grandmother looked young and beautiful, not the old lady she had been, but Saoirse knew it was her, she could see it in her smile. She stroked Saoirse's cheek, her touch icier than the water they were immersed in. Saoirse was exhausted; she hadn't the strength to fight. She wanted to sleep, here seemed like the perfect place to do it. She closed her eyes and let the ocean take her back to her grandmother.

Rua tugged on her hair and dragged her forcefully to the shore. She had been under too long and the stormy sea had meant he had spent too long trying to find her. Her pale skin was almost luminous in the dark water. Why had it taken so long to find her?

The waves at the cliffs were heavy and Rua knew he would have to try and catch a wave in from here and avoid the cliff. The waves came in sets, it seemed, and the last one was just a little weaker than the others. He watched and waited as two rolled in, Saoirse remained still, her eyes closed and he became impatient. Finally he took a wave; it dragged them under and sent them tumbling upside down. He knew he had to hold on to her. Around and around they went and just when he thought they couldn't take any more, he felt the hard thud of the beach slamming into them and the drag of the wave back out to sea. He scurried to his feet and dragged Saoirse up the beach, out of its grasp. He rolled her onto her back and scanned the beach for Michael, but there was no sign of him. Just as he was beginning to panic, he appeared with the flashlight. Rua sighed heavily and collapsed back onto the beach. His strength gone, he had failed her.

Michael took her mouth and quickly blew into her lungs, her chest rising and falling with each continued breath. Panic grew between them. They knew they had to get her back to the warm campervan – and fast. They carried her together up the beach and the steep cliff path, to the fields above. No one thought of the puca, they all assumed he had done his best and was finished with them.

Getting Saoirse to Sean was the priority now. They moved quickly and undisturbed across the field and along the narrow country road, Michael all the time flashing the torch, signalling to Sean where they had come up. They were out of breath and beginning to slow when the van rounded a corner and came straight at them.

Sean stopped the van immediately and left it running, jumped down from the driver's seat and ran towards them. He took Saoirse in his arms and huddled her lifeless body into the van. He undressed her carefully, wrapping her in the crocheted blanket, keeping her close, hoping the warmth of his body would heat her up. She was deathly pale and unresponsive. He took the silver comb from its box, pulled her long tangled and matted hair to the side and began to comb. The comb's teeth flowed through the maze of curls and seaweed with ease and with each stroke Sean saw colour return to Saoirse's face and life to her body. Suddenly she took a massive breath and opened her eyes and looked straight at Sean. She had made it. They both broke down in tears; Sean pulled her towards him and held her. Rua and Michael collapsed into a heap at the campervan door, that had been too close, far too close.

EPILOGUE

The van hurtled through the night and back towards Cushendall. Rua driving at speed, Michael grasping the sodden cloak he'd rescued from the beach. The roads were quiet, the storm about to break, but their job was done and they were all alive. Sean pulled Saoirse up in his lap and sat her upright leaning against him. He stroked her hair with his hand.

'We made it.'

'We did. Your grandmother is home. It's over.'

At that moment an unearthly scream rang out across the coast, thunder rumbled and the skies burst open. They had survived, but the puca wouldn't let this go. They would have to watch their backs. Saoirse's grandmother had returned home against His will and He would get His revenge. Sean cradled Saoirse's broken body and held her hand in his. Her face and neck were badly marked from the puca's grip. The wounds deep and bleeding, but they would heal. She nestled into his warm body and sighed with relief. Love had conquered the puca once more, it could do it again. She was sure that whatever else was to come, whoever and whatever else was out there, they could defeat it together. The world had become a wondrous place, full of danger, mystery and intrigue. Saoirse accepted what that meant for her and finally had the courage to believe.

ABOUT THE AUTHOR

Trish grew up in the island town of Cobh, Co. Cork. A lover of the sea and books, her passion for English led her to UCC and having graduated she became a teacher. She spent her summers wandering the world, reading books and dreaming of becoming a writer. Settling down to motherhood, married life and a diagnosis of being a BRCA1 carrier, Trish decided it was time to make dreams a reality. Inspired by her local town and love of Irish folklore, Saoirse O'Donnell became the main character of her first novel. It may have taken four years to write, but it is only the beginning.

COMING SOON

DARE TO BELIEVE
— BOOK TWO —

HUMAN CHILD

Saoirse's relationship with Sean is as new as her knowledge of her true identity... but that relationship is put under extreme pressure when one of Sean's family becomes gravely and mysteriously ill. Sean wants answers that modern medicine and Saoirse can't give him. The quest to find those answers opens up the new world of fairies and mythological creatures even more to Saoirse, but can she find the cure before it's too late?

Ingram Content Group UK Ltd.
Milton Keynes UK
UKHW010619130423
420098UK00006B/515

9 780995 646407